"*Faking It* has it all. Sexual tens[...] characters all wrapped up wit[...] humor."

—Colleen Hoover, #1 *New York Times* bestselling author

"A stellar follow-up to my favorite novel of 2012. A must-read!" —Jennifer L. Armentrout,
New York Times and *USA Today* bestselling author

"*Faking It* is everything I want in a book—sexy romance with mind-blowing chemistry, funny, smart, and deeply poignant. It's slice-of-life and every woman's fantasy all rolled into one. I need more Cora Carmack!"

—Sophie Jordan, *New York Times* bestselling author

"I dare you to read *Faking It* without laughing out loud, falling crazy in love, and crying at the end of this heartfelt journey." —Wendy Higgins, author of *Sweet Evil*

"The perfect blend of heat, humor, love, and heartache."
—K.A. Tucker, author of *Ten Tiny Breaths*

ALSO BY CORA CARMACK

Losing It

FAKING IT

CORA CARMACK

EBURY
PRESS

3 5 7 9 10 8 6 4

First published in the United States of America in 2013 by William Morrow
Paperbacks, an imprint of HarperCollins Publishers
Published in the UK in 2013 by Ebury Press, an imprint of Ebury Publishing
A Random House Group Company

The Random House Group Limited Reg. No. 954009

Addresses for companies within the Random House Group can be found at:
www.randomhouse.co.uk

A CIP catalogue record for this book is
available from the British Library
ISBN 9780091953393

To buy books by your favourite authors and register for offers visit:
www.randomhouse.co.uk

The Random House Group Limited supports The Forest Stewardship
Council® (FSC®), the leading international forest-certification organisation.
Our books carrying the FSC label are printed on FSC®-certified paper.
FSC is the only forest-certification scheme supported by the leading
environmental organisations, including Greenpeace. Our
paper procurement policy can be found at
www.randomhouse.co.uk/environment

Printed and bound in Great Britain by Clays Ltd, St Ives plc

To my mother.

Thank you for being my best friend, my teacher, my coach,
and nothing like the horrendous moms in my book.
You loved me and loved words, and taught me how to love both as well.

Thank you. A thousand times, thank you.

1

Cade

You would think I'd be used to it by now. That it wouldn't feel like a rusty eggbeater to the heart every time I saw them together.

You would think I would stop subjecting myself to the torture of seeing the girl I loved with another guy.

You would be wrong on all counts.

A nor'easter had just blown through, so the Philadelphia air was crisp. Day-old snow still crunched beneath my boots. The sound seemed unusually loud, like I walked toward the gallows instead of coffee with friends.

Friends.

I gave one of those funny-it's-not-actually-funny laughs, and my breath came out like smoke. I could see them standing on the corner up ahead. Bliss's arms were wound around Garrick's neck, and the two of them stood wrapped together on the sidewalk. Bundled in coats and scarves, they could have been a magazine ad or one of those perfect pictures that come in the frame when you buy it.

I hated those pictures.

I tried not to be jealous. I was getting over it.

I was.

I wanted Bliss to be happy, and as she slipped her hands in Garrick's coat pockets and their breath fogged between them, she definitely looked happy. But that was part of the problem. Even if I managed to let go of my feelings for Bliss completely, it was their happiness that inspired my jealousy.

Because I was fucking miserable. I tried to keep myself busy, made some friends, and settled into life all right here, but it just wasn't the same.

Starting over sucked.

On a scale of one to ghetto, my apartment was a solid eight. Things were still awkward with my best friend. I had student loans piling so high I might asphyxiate beneath them at any time. I thought by pursuing my master's degree, I would get at least one part of my life right . . . WRONG.

I was the youngest one in the program, and everyone else had years of working in the real world under his or her belt. They all had their lives together, and my life was about as clean and well kept as the community bathrooms had been in my freshman dorm. I'd been here nearly three months, and the only acting I'd done had been a cameo appearance as a homeless person in a Good Samaritan commercial.

Yeah, I was living the good life.

I knew the minute Bliss caught sight of me because she pulled her hands out of Garrick's pockets, and placed them safely at her sides. She stepped out of his arms and called, "Cade!"

I smiled. Maybe I was doing *some* acting after all.

I met them on the sidewalk, and Bliss gave me a hug. Short. Obligatory. Garrick shook my hand. As much as it irked me, I still really liked the guy. He'd never tried to keep Bliss from seeing me, and he'd apparently given me a pretty stellar reference when I applied to Temple. He didn't go around marking his territory or telling me to back off. He shook my hand and smiled, and sounded genuine when he said, "It's good to see you, Cade."

"Good to see you guys, too."

There was a moment of awkward silence, and then Bliss gave an exaggerated shiver. "I don't know about you guys, but I'm freezing. Let's head inside."

Together we filed through the door. Mugshots was a coffee place during the day and served alcohol at night. I'd not been there yet, as it was kind of a long trek from my apartment up by the Temple campus and because I didn't drink coffee, but I'd heard good things. Bliss loved coffee, and I still loved making Bliss happy, so I agreed to meet there when she called. I thought of asking if they'd serve me alcohol now, even though it was morning. Instead I settled on a smoothie and found us a table big enough that we'd have plenty of personal space.

Bliss sat first while Garrick waited for their drinks. Her cheeks were pink from the cold, but the winter weather agreed with her. The blue scarf knotted around her neck brought out her eyes, and her curls were scattered across her shoulders, windswept and wonderful.

Damn it. I had to stop doing this.

She pulled off her gloves, and rubbed her hands together. "How are you?" she asked.

I balled my fists under the table and lied. "I'm great. Classes are good. I'm loving Temple. And the city is great. I'm great."

"You are?" I could tell by the look on her face that she knew I was lying. She was my best friend, which made her pretty hard to fool. She'd always been good at reading me . . . except for when it came to how I felt about her. She could pick up on just about all my other fears and insecurities, but never that. Sometimes I wondered if it was wishful thinking. Maybe she never picked up on my feelings because she hadn't wanted to.

"I am," I assured her. She still didn't believe me, but she knew me well enough to know that I needed to hold on to my lie. I couldn't vent to her about my problems, not right now. We didn't have that kind of relationship anymore.

Garrick sat down. He'd brought all three of our drinks. I didn't even hear them call out my order.

"Thanks," I said.

"No problem. What are we talking about?"

Here we go again.

I took a long slurp of my smoothie so that I didn't have to answer immediately.

Bliss said, "Cade just finished telling me all about his classes. He's kicking higher education's ass." At least some things hadn't changed. She still knew me well enough to know when I needed an out.

Garrick nudged Bliss's drink toward her and smiled when she took a long, grateful drink. He turned to me and said, "That's good to hear, Cade. I'm glad it's going well. I'm still on good terms with the professors at Temple, so if you ever need anything, you know you just have to ask."

God, why couldn't he have been an asshole? If he were, one good punch would have gone a long way to easing the tightness in my chest. And it would be much cheaper than punching out a wall in my apartment.

I said, "Thanks. I'll keep that in mind."

We chattered about unimportant things. Bliss talked about their production of *Pride and Prejudice,* and I realized that Garrick really had been good for her. I never would have guessed that out of all of us, she'd be the one doing theatre professionally so quickly after we graduated. It's not that she wasn't talented, but she was never confident. I thought she would have gone the safer route and been a stage manager. I liked to think I could have brought that out of her, too, but I wasn't so sure.

She talked about their apartment on the edge of the Gayborhood. So far, I'd managed to wriggle out of all her invitations to visit, but sooner or later I was going to run out of excuses and would have to see the place they lived. Together.

Apparently their neighborhood was a pretty big party area. They lived right across from a really popular bar. Garrick said, "Bliss is such a light sleeper that it has become a regular event to wake up and listen to the drama that inevitably occurs outside our window at closing time."

She was a light sleeper? I hated that he knew that and I didn't. I hated feeling this way. They started relaying a story of one of those nighttime events, but they were barely looking at me. They stared at each other, laughing, reliving the memory. I was a spectator to their perfect harmony, and it was a show I was tired of watching.

I made a promise to myself then that I wouldn't do this again. Not until I had figured all my shit out. This had to be the last time. I smiled and nodded through the rest of the story, and was relieved when Bliss's phone rang.

She looked at the screen, and didn't even explain before she accepted the call and pressed the phone to her ear. "Kelsey? Oh my God! I haven't heard from you in weeks!"

Kelsey had done exactly what she said she would. At the end of the summer, everyone was moving to new cities or new universities, and Kelsey went overseas for the trip of a lifetime. Every time I looked at Facebook, she had added a new country to her list.

Bliss held up a finger and mouthed, "Be right back." She stood and said into the phone, "Kelsey, hold on one sec. I can barely hear you. I'm going to go outside."

I watched her go, remembering when her face used to light up like that talking to me. It was depressing the way life branched off in different directions. Trees only grew up and out. There was no going back to the roots, to the way things had been. I'd spent four years with my college friends, and they felt like family. But now we were scattered across the country and would probably never be all together again.

Garrick said, "Cade, there's something I'd like to talk to you about while Bliss is gone."

This was going to suck. I could tell. Last time we'd had a chat alone, he'd told me that I had to get over Bliss, that I couldn't live my life based on my feelings for her. Damn it if he wasn't still right.

"I'm all ears," I said.

"I don't really know the best way to say—"

"Just say it." That was the worst part of all of this. I'd gotten my heart broken by my best friend, and now everyone tiptoed around me like I was on the verge of meltdown, like a girl with PMS. Apparently having emotions equated to having a vagina.

Garrick took a deep breath. He looked unsure, but in the moments before he spoke, a smile pulled at his face, like he just couldn't help himself.

"I'm proposing to Bliss," he said.

The world went silent, and I heard the *tick-tick* of the clock on the wall beside us. It sounded like the ticking of a bomb, which was ironic, considering all the pieces of me that I had been holding together by sheer force of will had just been blown to bits.

I schooled my features as best as I could even though I felt like I might suffocate at any moment. I took a beat, which is just a fancy acting word for a pause, but it felt easier if I approached this like a scene, like fiction. Beats are reserved for those moments when something in the scene or your character shifts. They are moments of change.

Man, was this one hell of a beat.

"Cade—"

Before Garrick could say something nice or consoling, I pushed my character, pushed myself back into action. I smiled and made a face that I hoped look congratulatory.

"That's great, man! She couldn't have found a better guy."

It really was just like acting, bad acting anyway. Like when the words didn't feel natural in my mouth and my mind stayed separate from what I was saying no matter how hard I tried to stay in character. My thoughts raced ahead, trying to judge whether or not my audience was buying my performance, whether Garrick was buying it.

"So, you're okay with this?"

It was imperative that I didn't allow myself to pause before I answered, "Of course! Bliss is my best friend, and I've never seen her so happy, which means I couldn't be happier for her. The past is the past."

He reached across the table and patted me on the shoulder, like I was his son or little brother or his dog.

"You're a good man, Cade."

That was me . . . the perpetual good guy, which meant I perpetually came in second. My smoothie tasted bitter on my tongue.

"You had auditions last week, right?" Garrick asked. "How did they turn out?"

Oh please no. I just had to hear about his proposal plans. If I had to follow that up by relaying my complete and utter failure as a grad student, I'd impale myself on a stirring straw.

Luckily I was saved by Bliss's return. She was tucking her phone back into her pocket, and had a wide smile on her face. She stood behind Garrick's chair and placed a hand on his shoulder. I was struck suddenly by the thought that she was going to say yes.

Somewhere deep in my gut, I could feel the certainty of it. And it killed me.

Beat.

Beat.

Beat.

I should say something, anything, but I was stalled. Because this wasn't fiction. This wasn't a play, and we weren't characters. This was my life, and change had a way of creeping up and stabbing me in the back.

Oblivious, Bliss turned to Garrick and said, "We have to go, babe. We have call across town in like thirty minutes." She turned to me, "I'm sorry, Cade. I meant for us to have more time to chat, but Kelsey's been MIA for weeks. I couldn't *not* answer, and we've got a matinee for a group of students today. I swear I'll make it up to you. Are you going to be able to make it to our Orphan Thanksgiving tomorrow?"

I'd been dodging that invitation for weeks. I was fairly certain that it had been the entire purpose of this coffee meeting. I'd been on the verge of giving in, but now I couldn't. I didn't know when Garrick planned to propose, but I couldn't be around when it happened or after it happened. I needed a break from them, from Bliss, from being a secondary character in their story.

"Actually, I forgot to tell you. I'm going to go home

for Thanksgiving after all." I hated lying to her, but I just couldn't do it anymore. "Grams hasn't been feeling well, so I thought it was a good idea to go."

Her face pulled into an expression of concern, and her hand reached out toward my arm. I pretended like I didn't see it and stepped away to throw my empty smoothie cup in the trash. "Is she okay?" Bliss asked.

"Oh yeah, I think so. Just a bug probably, but at her age, you never know."

I just used my seventy-year-old grandma, the woman who'd raised me, as an excuse. Talk about a douche move.

"Oh, well, tell her I said hi and that I hope she feels better. And you have a safe flight." Bliss leaned in to hug me, and I didn't move away. In fact, I hugged her back. Because I didn't plan on seeing her again for a while, not until I could say (without lying) that I was over her. And based on the way my whole body seemed to sing at her touch, it might take a while.

The two of them packed up to leave, and I sat back down, saying I was going to stay and work on homework for a while. I pulled out a play to read, but in reality, I just wasn't ready for the walk home. I couldn't spend any more alone time locked in my thoughts. The coffee shop was just busy enough that my mind was filled with the buzzing of other people's lives and conversations. Bliss waved through the glass as they left, and I waved back, wondering if she could feel the finality of this good-bye.

2

Max

Mace's hand slid into my back pocket at the same time the phone in my front pocket buzzed. I let him have the three seconds it took for me to grab my phone, then I elbowed him, and he removed his hand.

I'd had to elbow him three times on the way to the coffee shop. He was like that cartoon fish with memory problems.

I looked at the screen, and it showed a picture of my mom that I'd snapped while she wasn't looking. She had been chopping vegetables and looked like a knife-wielding maniac, which she pretty much was all the time, minus the knife.

I jogged the last few steps to Mugshots and slipped inside before answering.

"Hello, Mom."

There was Christmas music on in the background. We hadn't even got Thanksgiving over with, and she was playing Christmas music.

Maniac.

"Hi, sweetie!" She stretched out the end of *sweetie* so long I thought she was a robot who had just malfunctioned. Then finally she continued, "What are you up to?"

"Nothing, Mom. I just popped into Mugshots for a coffee. You remember, it was that place I took you when you and Dad helped me move here."

"I do remember! It was a cute place, pity they serve alcohol."

And there was my mom in a nutshell.

Mace chose that moment (an unfortunately silent moment) to say, "Max, babe, you want your usual?"

I waved him off, and stepped a few feet away.

Mom must have had me on speakerphone because my dad cut in, "And who is that, Mackenzie?"

Mackenzie.

I shuddered. I hated my parents' absolute refusal to call me Max. And if they didn't approve of Max for their baby girl, they sure wouldn't like that I was dating a guy named Mace.

My dad would have an aneurysm.

"Just a guy," I said.

Mace nudged me and rubbed his thumb and fingers together. That's right. He'd been fired from his job. I handed him my purse to pay.

"Is this a guy you're dating?" Mom asked.

I sighed. There wasn't any harm in giving her this, as long as I fudged some of the details. Or you know, all of them.

"Yes, Mom. We've been dating for a few weeks." Try three months, but whatever.

"Is that so? How come we don't know anything about this guy then?" Dad, again.

"Because it's still new. But he's a really nice guy, smart." I don't think Mace actually finished high school, but he was gorgeous and a killer drum player. I wasn't cut out for the type of guy my mother wanted for me. My brain would melt from boredom in a week. That was if I didn't send him running before that.

"Where did you meet?" Mom asked.

Oh, you know, he hit on me at the go-go bar where I dance, that extra job that you have no idea I work.

Instead, I said, "The library."

Mace at the library. That was laughable. The tattoo curving across his collarbone would have been spelled *villian* instead of *villain* if I hadn't been there to stop him.

"Really?" Mom sounded skeptical. I didn't blame her. Meeting nice guys at the library wasn't really my thing. Every meet-the-parents thing I'd ever gone through had ended disastrously, with my parents certain their daughter had been brainwashed by a godless individual and my boyfriend kicking me to the curb because I had too much baggage.

My baggage was named Betty and Mick and came wearing polka dots and sweater vests on the way home from bridge club. Sometimes it was hard to believe that I came from them.

The first time I dyed my hair bright pink, my mom burst into tears, like I told her I was sixteen and pregnant. And that was only temporary dye.

It was easier these days just to humor them, especially since they were still helping me out financially so I could spend more time working on my music. And it wasn't that I didn't love them . . . I did. I just didn't love the person they wanted me to be.

So, I made small sacrifices. I didn't introduce them to my boyfriends. I dyed my hair a relatively normal color before any trips home. I took out or covered my piercings and wore long-sleeved, high-neck shirts to cover my tattoos. I told them I worked the front desk at an accounting firm instead of a tattoo parlor, and never mentioned my other job working in a bar.

When I went home, I played at normal for a few days, and then got the hell outta Dodge before my parents could try to set me up with a crusty accountant.

"Yes, Mom. The library."

When I went home for Christmas, I'd just tell her it didn't work out with the library boy. Or that he was a serial killer. Use that as my excuse to never date nice guys.

"Well, that sounds lovely. We'd love to meet him."

Mace returned to me then with my purse and our coffees. He snuck a flask out of his pocket and added a little something special to his drink. I waved him off when he offered it to me. The caffeine was enough. Funny how he couldn't afford coffee, but he could afford alcohol.

"Sure, Mom." Mace snuck a hand into my coat and wrapped it around my waist. His hand was large and warm, and his touch through my thin tee made me shiver. "I think you would actually really like him." I finished the sentence on a breathy sigh as Mace's lips found the skin of my neck, and my eyes rolled back in bliss. I'd never met an accountant who could do *that*. "He's very, ah, talented."

"I guess we'll see for ourselves soon." Dad's reply was gruff.

Hah. If they thought there was any chance I was bringing a guy home for Christmas, they were delusional.

"Sure, Dad."

Mace's lips were making a pretty great case for skipping this morning's band practice, but it was our last time to practice all together before our gig next week.

"Great," Dad said. "We'll be at that coffee place in about five minutes."

My coffee hit the floor before I even got a chance to taste it.

"You WHAT? You're not at home in Oklahoma?"

Mace jumped back when the coffee splattered all over our feet. "Jesus, Max!" I didn't have time to worry about him. I had much bigger issues.

"Don't be mad, honey," Mom said. "We were so sad when you said you couldn't come home for Thanksgiving, then Michael and Bethany decided to visit her family for the holiday, too. So we decided to come visit you. I even special ordered a turkey! Oh, you should invite your new boyfriend. The one from the library."

SHIT. SHIT. ALL OF THE SHITS.

"Sorry, Mom. But I'm pretty sure my boyfriend is busy on Thanksgiving."

Mace said, "No, I'm not." And I don't know if it was all

the years of being in a band and the loud music damaging his hearing, or too many lost brain cells, but the guy could just not master a freaking whisper!

"Oh, great! We'll be there in a few minutes, sweetie. Love you, boo boo bear."

If she called me boo boo bear in front of Mace, my brain would liquefy from mortification. "Wait, Mom—"

The line went dead.

I kind of wanted to follow its lead.

Think fast, Max. Parentals in T-minus two minutes. Time for damage control.

Mace had maneuvered us around the spilled coffee while I was talking, and he was moving to put his arms back around my waist. I pushed him back.

I took a good look at him—his black, shaggy hair, gorgeous dark eyes, the gauges that stretched his earlobes, and the mechanical skull tattooed on the side of his neck. I loved the way he wore his personality on his skin.

My parents would hate it.

My parents hated anything that couldn't be organized and labeled and penned safely into a cage. They weren't always that way. They used to listen and judge people on the things that mattered, but that time was long gone, and they'd be here any minute.

"You have to leave," I said.

"What?" He hooked his fingers into my belt loops and tugged me forward until our hips met. "We just got here."

A small part of me thought maybe Mace could handle my parents. He'd charmed me, and for most people that was akin to charming a python. He may not have been smart or put together or any of those things, but he was passionate about music and about life. And he was passionate about me. There was fire between us. Fire I didn't want extinguished because my parents were still living in the past, and couldn't get over how things had happened with Alex.

"I'm sorry, babe. My parents have made an impromptu visit, and they're going to be here any minute. So, I need you to leave or pretend like you don't know me or something."

I was going to apologize, say that I wasn't ashamed of him, that I just wasn't ready for that. I didn't get a chance before he held his hands up and backed away. "Fuck. No argument here. I'm out." He turned for the door. "Call me when you lose the folks."

Then he bailed. No questions asked. No valiant offer to brave meeting the parents. He walked out the door, lit up a cigarette, and took off. For a second, I thought about following him. Whether to flee or kick his ass, I wasn't sure.

But I couldn't.

Now, I just had to figure out what to tell my parents about my suddenly absent library-going-nice-guy-boyfriend. I'd just have to tell them he had to work or go to class or heal the sick or something. I scanned the room for an open table. They'd probably see right through the lie and know there was no nice guy, but there was no way around it.

Damn. The coffee shop was packed, and there weren't any open tables.

There was a four-top with only one guy sitting at it, and it looked like he was almost done. He had short, brown curls that had been tamed into something neat and clean. He was gorgeous, in that all-American model kind of way. He wore a sweater and a scarf and had a book sitting on his table. News-flash! This was the kind of guy libraries should use in advertising if they wanted more people to read.

Normally I wouldn't have looked twice at him because guys like that don't go for girls like me. But he was looking back at me. Staring, actually. He had the same dark, penetrating eyes as Mace, but they were softer somehow. Kinder.

And it was like the universe was giving me a gift. All that was missing was a flashing neon sign above his head that said ANSWER TO ALL YOUR PROBLEMS.

3

Cade

was people watching, filling in imaginary lives to keep my mind off my own life when she looked at me.

I'd been watching her with her boyfriend for the last few minutes, puzzling them out. They both exuded confidence and looked effortlessly cool. The guy was all dark—dark hair, dark eyes, dark tattoos. All his ink that I could see was depressing or violent—skulls and guns and brass knuckles. She on the other hand was bright—from her vividly red hair to her painted lips that naturally turned upward to her tattoos. She had a few small birds flying up her neck, and what looked like the top of a tree poking out from the heart-shaped neck of her 1950s-style dress.

As often as he touched and kissed her, I saw no real connection between them. She didn't glance over at him once as she talked on the phone. And when she wasn't paying attention to him, he didn't bother even looking at her. Like they were part of two different solar systems, neither revolving with or around the other, and both were just with each other for the passing moment.

He hadn't even bothered to pick up the cup of coffee when she'd dropped it. He just moved her out of the way, and a barista came around and took care of it.

Now, he was gone and she was looking at me like I had something she wanted. It made my mouth go dry and stirred something in my chest. Stirred up other things, too.

She walked up to my table, her hips swinging her wide skirt, and I got my first really good look at her face. She was beautiful—full lips, high cheekbones, and a straight nose. A white flower was tucked into her riotous red curls. She looked like the edgy version of a 1950s pinup girl. She was the complete opposite of any girl I had ever dated or thought about dating. She was the complete opposite of Bliss. Maybe that was part of the reason I couldn't take my eyes off of her.

I could see now that the tattoo on her chest was definitely a tree. Bare branches stretched up toward her collarbone, and when she leaned over and rested her hands on my table I got a good look at the trunk of the tree disappearing down between the valley of her breasts.

I swallowed, and it took me longer than it should have to avert my gaze to her face. She said, "I'm going to ask you something, and it's going to seem crazy."

It would match with the rest of my thoughts then.

"Okay," I said.

She slid into the seat beside me, and I could smell her . . . something feminine and sweet and completely at odds with her inked skin. I was still thinking about that damn tree, imagining what the rest of the tattoo looked like, wondering how soft her skin was.

"My parents showed up in town uninvited, and they want to meet my boyfriend."

She slid a little closer and tapped red-painted nails against the table.

"And how can I help?"

"Well, I'm supposed to introduce them to a nice, sweet boyfriend who I met at the library, which is not actually the boyfriend I have." Her hand curled around my forearm that rested on the table, and I cursed all my winter layers because I wanted to feel her skin.

"And you think I'm nice and sweet?"

She shrugged. "You look it. I know this is crazy, but I would really appreciate it if you'd pretend to be my boyfriend until I manage to get rid of them." I looked back at her cherry red lips. They brought to mind several things that were neither nice nor sweet.

What she wanted *was* crazy, but I'd be acting, the very thing I'd been missing for the last few weeks. And part of me was all for duct taping Nice-Guy-Cade and throwing him in the trunk. That part of me thought spending time with this girl was a very good idea.

She said, "Please? I'll do all the talking, and I'll end it

as fast as I can. I can pay you!" I raised an eyebrow, and she continued, "Okay, I can't pay you, but I'll make it up to you. Anything you want."

Somehow I had a feeling that she wouldn't have said that last part to someone who didn't look "nice and sweet." Since that part of my brain was currently indisposed, I had a good idea of what I wanted.

"I'll do it." Her whole body relaxed. She smiled, and it was gorgeous. Then I added, "In exchange for a date."

She pulled back, and those full red lips puckered in confusion.

"You want to go on a date with me?"

"Yes. Do we have a deal?"

She looked at the clock on the wall, cursed under her breath, and said, "Fine. Deal. Now give me your scarf." She didn't even give me a chance to move before she started tugging it off my neck.

I grinned. "Taking off my clothes already?"

One side of her mouth quirked upward, and she looked at me in surprise. Then she shook her head and wrapped my scarf around her own neck. It covered up her delicate birds and the smooth, porcelain skin of her chest, broken only by the thin black lines of her tattooed tree. She grabbed a napkin off the table and wiped off some of her bright red lipstick.

"All my parents know is we met in the library. You're nice and sweet and wholesome. My parents are crazy conservative, so no jokes about me taking your clothes off. We've been dating for a few weeks. Nothing complicated. I haven't told them anything else, so it should be pretty easy to sell."

With practiced hands, she started smudging off some of

the dark that lined her eyes. She pulled her hair forward so that it covered the array of piercings in her ears.

"What about you? What do you do?"

"I'm an actor."

She rolled her eyes. "They'll hate that as much as they hate me being a musician, but it will have to do."

She kept fussing with her makeup and smoothing down her hair, looking around like she wished she had a hat or something to cover it.

I placed a hand on her shoulder and said, "You look beautiful. Don't worry."

Her expression froze, and she looked up at me like I was speaking Swahili. Then her lips pressed together in something that was almost a smile. I was still touching her shoulder when a woman at the front of the store called out, "Mackenzie! Oh, Mackenzie, honey!"

Mackenzie.

She didn't look like a Mackenzie.

She took a shuddering breath, and then stood to face the woman I supposed was her mother. I rose with her, and let my arm stretch across her shoulder. She seemed frazzled, which was funny, because up until now confidence was practically running out of her pores like honey.

I mean, she'd asked a complete stranger to pretend to be her boyfriend. She had seemed fearless. Parents were apparently her Kryptonite.

I looked at the middle-aged couple approaching us. The man was balding with wire-rimmed glasses, and the woman's hair was graying at her temples. The hands between them were intertwined, and their outer arms were reaching forward like they expected their daughter to run up for a group hug. She looked like she'd rather run off a cliff.

I smiled.

This . . . I could do.

I gave her shoulder a squeeze, and said, "Everything is going to be okay."

"Boo boo bear! Oh, honey, what atrocious thing have you done to your hair? I told you to stop using those dyes out of the box."

Mackenzie was biting down on her lip so hard as her mother pulled her forward into a hug that I was surprised she didn't draw blood. Her father took over, and she had to let go of my hand. I stepped to the side, and reached a hand out to her mother.

"It's so nice to meet you, Mrs.—"

The words were already out of my mouth before I realized I had no idea what Mackenzie's last name was. Hell, I hadn't even known her name was Mackenzie.

Her mother took my hand and was looking at me with her head cocked sideways, waiting for me to finish my sentence. I saw Mackenzie wiggle out of her father's hug next to me, her face full of slowly dawning horror.

Damn it.

I put on my best smile and said, "You know, I've heard so much about you from Mackenzie that I feel I should just call you *Mom*." Then I moved in for a hug.

4

Max

HE WAS HUGGING MY MOTHER.

A total stranger. I could only handle a few hugs a year from her without feeling smothered, and he was wrapped up in her boa constrictor arms for three, four, five seconds.

It was still going.

And it was a full-on hug, not one of those awkward side ones that I gave my dad.

Jesus Christ, her head was tucked under his chin. His chin!

The seconds seemed to expand into lifetimes, and his

wide eyes caught mine over my mother's head. From the way my mother was latched on, he was never going to get free. It was like one of those sad stories where a little kid smothers a cat because he hugs it too hard.

He laughed and patted her on the back. Unlike my laughs around my parents, he managed to pull it off without sounding like he was being held at gunpoint.

Finally after a nearly TEN-second hug, she released him.

At ten seconds I would have been hyperventilating. Then again, she probably wouldn't have let go of me after ten seconds. I'm convinced she thinks if she could just hug me long enough, she'd squeeze all the devil's influence out of me.

He stayed there, still in hugging-range, and said, "It's so wonderful of you both to make this impromptu trip. Mackenzie won't say it, but she misses you both terribly."

I cringed when he called me Mackenzie, and my mother beamed. I didn't know if her aversion to Max was just because she thought it was a boy's name or if calling me by a nickname reminded her of Alexandria . . . of Alex.

She looked at me over his shoulder, and there were tears in her eyes. Fifteen seconds and he had her crying fucking tears of joy. Were my ex-boyfriends really all that bad in comparison to him?

Okay, so I had made the mistake of introducing them to Jake. He'd insisted on them calling him by his nickname . . . Scissors.

But that was a low point! And it had mostly been to piss them off. Not all of them had been that bad. My pretend boyfriend turned to my father and said, "Sir, I'm Cade Winston. You've raised an amazing daughter."

My father shook his hand and said, "Really?"

REALLY. He said *really.*

No, "Thank you" or "I know." It took him a full five seconds before he smiled . . . like me being amazing was his doing. He said, "It's nice to meet you, son."

They'd already married me off.

I needed to sit down.

I didn't even say anything as I moved toward the table, but my pretend boyfriend, Cade, must have some kind of weird sixth sense. He was at my side in seconds, pulling out my chair for me. My parents stayed standing a few feet away, staring, like they wanted to preserve this picture of us in their memories forever.

Cade grabbed my hand and laced our fingers together. His skin on mine caused a jolt of electricity to run up my arm. It shocked all of the exasperated thoughts out of my head, and I sat staring at him as my parents stood staring at us. Mom pulled out a handkerchief. Maybe someday I'd be able to look back and laugh at the ridiculousness of this moment. Maybe someday I'd also get on a subway car that didn't smell like urine. The future had much to look forward to.

Finally Dad turned to Mom and said, "Let's get some coffee, Betty. Cade, Mackenzie, we'll join you in a moment."

I waited until my parents were in line, and then I turned on him, barely containing the urge to do physical harm.

"What the hell was that?"

His brows furrowed, his head turned to the side, and our hands were still laced together. Why hadn't I pulled my hand away yet?

"I was meeting your parents."

I tried to hold on to my anger, but really boys should not have such gorgeous eyes and long lashes. An unfamiliar heat crept up my neck, and I knew I was blushing.

I was *not* a blushing kind of girl.

I ripped gaze away from his face, and then my hand out of his. My voice was shaky and all my anger had fled when I said, "More like ruining my chances of them ever liking one of my actual boyfriends." It was easier when I wasn't looking at him. My thoughts became clearer. "I mean, you *hugged* my mom. Hugs are like crack to that woman."

"I'm sorry. You didn't tell me your last name, so I improvised."

I crossed my arms over my chest. He had done a pretty good job, and my parents seemed convinced and happy. He was clearly good at this kind of thing. That should have made me less nervous. It didn't. I still felt like I was going to go into cardiac arrest at any second. "Just . . . don't hug her again." Heaven forbid she start expecting me to follow his lead. "I just need to survive this without them getting suspicious. No need to go for the Oscar. And the last name is Miller."

"Of course, I'm sorry, Mackenzie."

The name grated against my ears. It had been years since someone besides my family called me that, and somehow I hated it even more now. I was almost snarling as I said, "*Don't call me Mackenzie.* It's Max."

My anger didn't faze him at all. He paused for a second, and then smiled. "Max. That fits you much better."

Damn him. He had this way of extinguishing my anger that was so beyond frustrating. He put his arm around my chair and turned toward me. My personal bubble popped like a frat boy's collar. Between the arm on my chair and the one resting on the table in front of me, I felt surrounded by him. His caramel-colored eyes were right there, and the scent of cologne, spicy and sweet, wafted up to my nose. I should have pulled away. I should not have been looking at his eyelashes again. He leaned in, and the stubble on his jaw brushed my cheek. Warning sirens blared in my mind, even as I closed my eyes. He whispered, "Your mom is coming back. I'm sorry. No more hugging, I promise."

His lips were still by my ear when my mother returned. He was pretending. He wasn't putting the moves on me. He was just trying to keep my mom from hearing. That's all. The warning sirens quieted, but I still felt ill at ease.

Cade stood and pulled out my mother's chair for her while my father waited on their drinks. I closed my eyes and tried to sort out the mess of my thoughts.

Mom asked, "So, Cade, Mackenzie tells me the two of you met at the library."

I opened my mouth to answer, but Cade spoke first.

"Oh, yes. That's right. *Max*"—he shot a quick smile at me—"actually helped me find the book I was looking for. I was looking in the entirely wrong section."

Mom's perfectly plucked eyebrows arched. "Is that so? I wasn't aware she knew her way around a library. When she was younger, we could barely convince her to read anything unless it was one of those lyric sheets that came with a CD. Normal children you can bribe with candy to do their homework. Not our Mackenzie."

I ground my teeth to keep from popping off about just who the *normal* one in our family was. Cade didn't miss a beat.

"Well, it was a book on music composition I needed for my paper, so I got lucky in finding an expert. She was exactly what I needed." He looked sideways at me, and the arm around my chair moved to my shoulder. "She still is." This guy had the strangest affect on me. A really small part of me wanted to swoon at that cheesy declaration. Most of me wanted to vomit. Not that it mattered, since this was all pretend.

It did the trick for Mom though. She aww'ed loudly and forgot about how much she hated my interest in music.

"Paper?" she asked. "Are you in school?"

"Yes, ma'am. I'm getting my master's from Temple University."

Jiminy fucking crickets. What happened to not overdoing it?

"Master's degree?" Mother's face lit up for a moment, and then dimmed. "In music?"

"No, ma'am. Acting, actually. I was writing a paper on the use of original music in theatre."

"Acting? Isn't that nice." Mother's smile stiffened. Finally, something my mother didn't love about this guy.

"Yes, ma'am. It's what I love. Though I'm also interested in teaching on the collegiate level."

"A professor, how wonderful!"

I give up. In the war for my parents' approval, I'd lost to a complete stranger.

Dad returned with two mugs of coffee, and asked, "What are we chatting about?"

Mom didn't give either of us a chance to answer before she exclaimed, "Cade is getting his master's degree to become a college professor. Isn't that just fantastic?"

Mom could qualify for the Olympics in selective hearing. "That does sound nice."

Cade said, "Thank you, Mr. Miller."

Dad paused in blowing on his coffee to say, "Oh please, call me Mick."

MICK?

I had a nightmare like this once. Though, in that one I was naked. I wish I could say knowing it could be worse made things better, but it didn't. Cade grinned easily, and relaxed back into his chair. He looked so calm, almost like he was enjoying this.

"Of course, Mick, thank you. So how was your trip?"

Dad huffed. "Terrible. Airports are the armpits of the universe. They treated your mother and I like we were terrorists, making us take those X-ray things. Probably gave us cancer. I say we get rid of them and go back to train travel. It takes longer, but it sure would be simpler."

And so began the crazy.

Cade said, "You know, I've only taken a train once, but I thought it was a really enjoyable experience. I'll have to try it again sometime."

Trains. I kept reminding myself that it could have been worse. If my father had tried to talk trains with Mace he probably would have assumed my dad meant the perverted kind of train. That would have been disastrous.

"Enough about us. I want to hear more about you. Why has our baby girl been keeping such a nice boy a secret from us?"

Cade looked at me, and I glared at him. *Now I get to talk?*

He laughed, and squeezed my shoulder. His fingers stayed there, distracting me as he spoke. "I can't speak for

Max, but I think we just wanted to keep it between us for a while. Take it slow."

And there were the magic words. I didn't do long relationships, and I'd take things slow when I was dead. Life was too short. I think my three months with Mace was one of my longest relationships, and we were already talking about moving in together. Good thing we hadn't done that yet.

My parents *hated* my tendency to move too fast. By the time they finished their cups of coffee, my parents would probably be begging to trade and have Cade as their child.

"What about hobbies?" my dad asked. Probably looking for someone to go golfing or play tennis with him. Lord knows none of my previous boyfriends had.

Cade shrugged. "School takes up most of my time. I also volunteer once a week at ASAP, it's an after-school program for at-risk youth."

Unfuckingbelievable. Mace didn't know the meaning of "Hey, I don't want your hand on my ass in public," and this guy didn't know the meaning of "Lay off!"

I leaned over, placed my hand on his thigh, and pinched. His thigh was strapped with muscle, and he didn't even jump at my pinch. He put his hand over mine, and flattened my palm against his leg. I tried to pull away, but he held it there, his large, warm hand pressed mine into his hard thigh. Now it was me who needed to be pinched because I was looking at my hand on his leg, and thinking too much about the skin that lay beneath the material of his jeans. I'd forgotten why I was upset in the first place.

I shook my head and smiled at my parents; splitting my

lips to show teeth felt like cracking open concrete. "Listen, Mom and Dad, Cade and I really have to get going. I didn't know you guys were coming or I would have rearranged my schedule."

Dad hefted himself up from the table, and tugged his pants up higher. "Oh, no worries, Pumpkin. We're staying at a hotel not too far from you in the nicer part of town."

Meaning my place was a dump. Which it wasn't, it was just in Chinatown, and Dad felt uncomfortable when all the signs weren't in English.

Mom joined him, "Besides, we'll see both of you tomorrow for Thanksgiving!"

"Oh, Mom, I really don't think Cade can—"

"Nonsense. I heard him say over the phone that he was free, and I won't take no for an answer. No more hiding this nice, young man from us. You clearly adore each other, and sooner or later *slow* becomes an excuse like any other."

We *did not* adore each other.

My eyes caught on the line of his jaw, but I forced my gaze away.

We didn't.

I didn't care how handsome this guy was or how warm his hand was on mine.

"Mom—"

"Mackenzie Kathleen Miller, don't you argue with me. Now, Cade." She fixed her eyes on him, and it was her maniac stare, the one like the picture on my cell phone. "Tell me you'll see me tomorrow, and then go talk some sense into my daughter."

Cade looked at me. I knew what he was going to say, and had no way to stop him, short of tackling him (which was either a very good or a very bad idea).

"Sure, Mrs. Miller. I'll see you tomorrow."

"Excellent." She leaned down and placed a kiss on his cheek. "What happened to calling me Mom?"

5

Cade

There was a moment of silence after Max's parents left that reminded me of those few shocked seconds right before a car crash. Your brain screams at you to step on the breaks, but it takes too long for your body to follow through. It was in those quiet seconds that Max smiled a slow, sinful smile.

Then slapped me.

It didn't hurt. Not really.

But it felt surreal, like the car had crashed, and I was flying through the windshield. I'd never been slapped by a girl before. I think I was definitely the only guy in the world to ever get slapped for impressing a girl's parents.

I couldn't help it. I laughed.

Max's cheeks turned pink, and she raised her hand to do it again.

"Easy, babe." I caught her hand as it started to swing, and pushed it down onto the table. That meant I had one hand pressed to my leg and the other to the table. The violent little thing was tied up in knots. She tilted her chin and met my gaze like she was going into battle. Fire sparked in her eyes, and she looked dangerously sexy.

"Why are you trying to hurt me?" I asked.

"Because it will make me feel better!"

Having her hand on my thigh was not helping me take her anger seriously. And her skin had flushed from her cheeks, down her neck, and I wished she wasn't wearing my scarf. "It's not like I wanted to say yes. Your mother isn't exactly easy to say no to."

She huffed and squirmed in her seat, trying to pull her hands free. It only brought her closer to me. The red in her cheeks matched the vibrancy of her hair, which smelled divine.

"You could have at least not made up such a ridiculous backstory. I mean, volunteering at an after-school program? I told you to take it easy!" She growled the words through gritted teeth.

"Max, I didn't make that up. I just told the truth. And stop struggling, people are starting to stare."

She stopped and a lock of scarlet hair hung down in front of her face. She blew it back and said, "You told the truth?"

After a few moments, I released her hands, and held my right out between us. "My name is Cade Winston—MFA student, volunteer, mom-hugger, and your boyfriend for the next twenty-four hours. It's nice to meet you."

She hesitated, and her lips puckered. I knew she was only thinking, but the pucker sent my mind running in an entirely different direction.

"You really do volunteer to help kids after school?" She made it sound like I was aiming for the Nobel Peace Prize or something. They were just kids who needed a place to hang out.

I said, "I really do."

After a few moments of hesitation, she slipped her hand into mine and shook. She frowned and said, "Max Miller—musician and raging bitch. I'm sorry for slapping you."

"And pinching me," I added, even though I wasn't sorry. It had given me an excuse to touch her.

"And pinching you. And thank you, I guess, for today. And for tomorrow. And sorry number two that you have to spend your Thanksgiving with my crazy parents."

I smiled. She had this scrunched look on her face, and I could just tell that an apology from this girl was a rare occurrence. I shrugged. "Hey, don't feel bad. I was planning to spend tomorrow home alone with some Chinese food. I'm sure your mother's turkey is much better."

She smiled begrudgingly. "It is. She's a crazy good cook. Emphasis on the crazy."

"But the slapping . . . that you can feel bad for."

She rolled her eyes, and moved away. "I said I was sorry!"

"What? No offer to kiss it better?" She raised an eyebrow, but I swear her eyes dropped to my lips for just a second. I thought of kissing her, just doing it, without thinking about the fact that we didn't know each other or about her real boyfriend. But she stood, and the moment passed.

She said, "Well, Cade Winston, I really have to get going. I'm already late for my band practice, but can you come over early tomorrow before my parents arrive? We can map out the rest of our story then, so there's no more need to *improvise* with hugs." She grabbed a pen from her purse and wrote her address and her number on a napkin.

I pocketed it, threw my empty cup in the trash, and followed her to the door. I knew she said she had to go, but I wanted just a little bit longer with her. "You never got to drink your coffee," I said, thinking back to when she'd dropped it earlier during the phone call from her parents. "Let me get you another cup."

She shook her head. "I should be the one buying you coffee."

"You're having a stressful morning. You deserve a break." She looked at me like I'd just made some grand gesture. Her boyfriend must have been a real dick if she was impressed by a cup of coffee. I added, "Besides, I don't actually drink coffee, so it's a moot point."

She laughed. "I think that's the first time I've ever actually heard someone say 'moot point.' And if you don't like coffee, what are you doing in a coffee shop?"

"I was supposed to pretend to be a girl's long-lost brother, but she canceled at the last minute. It's cool, pretend boyfriend gigs are so much more fun."

We stepped up to the cashier, and she said, "Medium coffee."

I watched her mix in a cream and two packets of sugar. As she stirred the drink, she eyed me like I was a puzzle to piece together.

"You're kind of funny, Winston."

She took a sip of her coffee, and what was left of her lipstick left a red smudge on the rim of the cup. It drove me crazy.

I said, "I'm more than kind of funny. You'll see."

"And cocky." She smiled up at me. "You're a little hard to puzzle out, you know."

"I'm willing to spend as much time with you as you'd like while you try to figure me out."

She laughed. "Let's just stick with tomorrow for now. See you later, boyfriend."

"Until tomorrow, Mackenzie."

She made a noise halfway between a scoff and a laugh, and shook her head. As she pushed open the glass door at the front, she called over her shoulder, "You do not want to play that game, honey."

She looked back just for a second as she crossed the street, and her eyes met mine through the window. A thrill bubbled up in my chest that reminded me of a race, of auditioning and fighting for a role that I knew should be mine.

I stood there like an idiot watching her leave until the cashier said, "Hey man, did you need something else?"

"No, I'm good, sorry."

I stepped out into the crisp winter air thinking about how good I really felt. She didn't know how right she was. This whole thing *was* a game. She wasn't my girlfriend, even if her parents did love me. *Especially because her parents loved me.* I'd never dated a girl like her, and she'd probably never dated a guy like me. But sometimes you don't know what you're looking for until it's already knocked you flat on your back. And what was the point in living if I was only going to travel the same roads again and again?

I replayed the last twenty minutes or so in my mind—our conversation, the meeting with her parents, seeing the way her face went red when she was mad. Maybe I was broken, but even the slap had felt kind of good.

Despite the absolute absurdity of everything, it was the most normal I'd felt in months. Like the clouds had finally parted. Like I'd pulled my foot free from being stuck in the past and had stepped into the now.

It felt better. And I was determined for it to stay that way.

It was time to start living, to actually enjoy my life. And I just so happened to know someone who was *really* good at enjoying life.

I dropped my stuff off in my apartment, and then went across the hall. I rapped my knuckles against my neighbor's door and called, "Milo! You home?"

The sound of some kind of Latin music, salsa maybe, was leaking out from underneath the door, so I knew he was home.

"Milo!" I pounded against the door a few more times.

The door flew open, and Milo lowered a pretty brunette into a dip so fast that her head nearly hit me in the crotch. I jumped back.

Milo grinned up at me, his teeth white against his dark skin. He pulled the girl up against him fast, and her curls went flying.

I glanced at my watch.

Only Milo would be doing the salsa in his living room at 10:00 A.M.

"Too loud, amigo? I'll turn it down."

I held up a hand, "No. No, it's cool. I was actually wondering if you wanted to hang out tonight?"

He quirked an eyebrow at me. I'd been bailing on plans all week due to holiday dread and depression, but it was time to shake that off.

"I have plans already, man, but you should come with. This is my friend, Sasha." The brunette stayed tucked into Milo's side but waved her fingers at me. I didn't recognize her, but Milo spent time with a new girl every week, so that was unsurprising. "She's dancing tonight. A new job."

"Oh, like a show?" I asked.

Milo laughed raucously. So did Sasha.

"A little like a show, mostly like a bar."

I blinked. She was dancing in a bar. Was she a stripper?

Milo must have known me well enough by now to interpret the look on my face. He said, "Easy, *hermano*, it's not like that."

Then what was it like?

"I'll knock on your door at nine, okay? We'll have a good time."

Then Sasha tugged on his arm, and they went back to their dance. The dance was all swaying hips and skimming hands, and it looked much more interesting than anything I'd ever done at 10:00 A.M. I'd intruded enough on his early morning seduction, so I closed the door and retreated back to my apartment.

Something told me I was going to be in for an interesting night.

6

Max

When I walked into Trestle, the bar where I worked and the band practiced, I was nearly twenty minutes late. I wish I could say Mace and Spencer were pissed, but I didn't think they had even noticed. Spencer's bass was forgotten as he looked through the various kinds of alcohol behind the bar. Mace at least had his drumsticks tucked in his pocket as he played a game on his phone.

"Hey, guys! Sorry I'm late."

Spencer poured himself a bit of Maker's Mark, and said, "It's cool, Max."

"Good. You know what else is cool? *Not* stealing from the place where we get to practice for free."

I recapped the bottle of booze and returned it to the shelf. Spencer shrugged, adjusted his black-rimmed glasses, and downed the liquor in one gulp. I grabbed him by his black, skull-print bow tie, and pulled him toward the area where our instruments were set up. I pushed him toward his bass.

I slid a hand underneath Mace's chin and tilted his head up toward me. He let me, but he just raised the phone higher to keep his eyes on the game.

"Come on babe, I know I'm late, but we only have until noon before Sam kicks us out."

"Yeah, yeah, just hold on. I can't stop running. If I look away, I'm going to die."

Maybe I was still a little angry about how easily he bailed on me earlier or maybe I was just a bitch, but I snatched his phone out of his hand and held it behind me.

"MAX! Come on!" He reached for the phone, but we both heard the sound of the game ending.

"God, Max, sometimes you can be a real bitch."

For a split second, Cade's face popped into my head, but I pushed it away.

I said, "Yeah, well, you're a dick most of the time. Deal with it."

There was only a little heat in my words. I tucked his phone into his front pant pocket, and used that pocket to pull him toward me. His mouth was set in a thin line like he was angry, but that didn't stop him from sliding his hands down my back to my ass. I didn't elbow him this time. I kissed the underside of his jaw, and he stopped clenching his teeth so tightly. He kissed me, nipping my bottom lip a little too hard for it to be comfortable.

Spencer said, "I liked it better when you guys weren't molesting each other constantly." Spencer and I had been making music together since I moved to Philly a few years ago. Besides me, he was the only member of Under the Bell Jar that hadn't changed frequently.

What could I say? I had a thing for drummers.

"Can we get to playing now?" Spencer asked, shooting a glare at Mace.

He couldn't stand Mace, but didn't make much of a fuss because he didn't figure the relationship would last. It would be nice if it did, though. Mace was the best drummer we'd ever had.

I pulled back and went for my guitar.

"Okay, so this is the last chance we'll get to rehearse all together before the show next week. We need to practice and nail down the order of our set list."

We started with a cover of "A Better Son/Daughter" by Rilo Kiley. I felt like I lived this song already this morning. The intro started soft and small. My lips brushed the cold metal of the microphone and I felt like I was home. It didn't matter that we were in a grungy bar with no audience, or that I'd be back here tonight working until all hours of the morning, only to have to get up and pretend for my parents. It didn't matter that this morning my love life had taken a sharp left at complicated straight into bizarre territory. It didn't even matter that I'd been carrying this band like a yoke around my neck for years with no money and no break in sight.

When I sang, none of it mattered.

I was not an emotional person. I hadn't cried since I was thirteen. Not really. I made a promise to myself then when my life had been awash in tears that I wouldn't be one of those people. The kind of person who would cry uncontrollably when something bad happened, but two days later be walking around like nothing had changed. Crying was for moments of such drastic pain that you had to let it out, had to shed the dead skin on your soul so that you could breathe. I still had my life, so I refused to cry over stupid shit like boyfriends and parents. I was good at turning off the pain. The only time I let it out was when I sang.

When the strings on my guitar vibrated and notes rose from my lungs, I felt the good and the bad, the hope and the devastation. I felt it all.

> *Sometimes in the morning, I am petrified, and can't move*
> *Awake but cannot open my eyes.*

I sang about the weight of expectation and toxic relationships and lost innocence. I sang about the way depression can curl over your head like a wave, pulling you under so far that you don't know which way is up and where to go to breathe.

The song unspooled something inside of me and deflated all the pressures of the day. *This* was what my parents didn't get. They wanted me to give this up, get a job, and a steady paycheck. Mom said she'd never be able to really relax until her baby girl was all taken care of, which to her meant a husband and a job and a bun in the oven. But then it would be me who was never relaxed.

They wanted me to be the perfect daughter Alex was supposed to have been. But I wasn't Alex. I'd tried to be that for them . . . tried to fill the void she left behind. I spent four years of high school playing the good girl, the popular girl, but it was never real. I always screwed something up, and then they would look at me like I hadn't just disappointed them, I'd somehow disgraced Alex too by failing to live up to her memory.

Just living with them had been like suffocating, like all the air had been sucked from the house leaving only grief behind.

I got so twisted and wound up and smothered by life.

Music unraveled me.

It kept me sane then, and it keeps me sane now.

After that song we moved on to one by the Smiths, another by Laura Marling, and one by Metric. We covered everything from Radiohead to the Beatles, and then moved on to our original songs. Some were Spencer's, but most were mine. The songs were all different, but they were all honest. When we finished the first run-through, we took a quick break. I headed to the bathroom because I needed a second.

I always needed a second to get the last of the emotion out, to bring the walls back up. Spencer got it. We'd known each other long enough that he gave me the space, but Mace was still learning. He followed me into the bathroom and pressed me up against the sink, his chest against my back.

His lips found my neck, and he moaned. He rocked his hips into me.

"God, you're so hot when you sing. Let's end practice early and go back to your place. Then I can make you sing on your bed, on the table, against the wall."

All my emotions were still too close to the surface. The weight of him against my back felt crushing, and his hands on my wrists were like shackles. I met my own gaze in the mirror, and my eyes were wide and panicked. More than that, they were vulnerable . . . breakable. They were everything I never wanted to be. I squeezed my eyes shut and something in me snapped. I pushed my elbow into his middle, turned, and shoved him backward. He wasn't expecting it, and he stumbled back and slammed into one of the stall doors. The noise echoed through the bathroom, and Mace yelled, "What the *fuck*, Max?"

I stood there blinking, my mouth hanging open. I knew I should be sorry, but I wasn't. I was breathing and in control and that was what mattered. Mace stood and brushed off his pants. His mouth was a thin blade, and his eyes were bullets. "Well?" he yelled, and I battled off a flinch.

I couldn't talk about it, couldn't explain why. Damn, if he knew me even half as well as Spence, he would know to stay the hell away. My breath still came strong, like I was catching up. I said, "You can't come over. My parents are still in town." I didn't say that technically they were at a hotel. I just needed space for the night.

"So you fucking push me? What's your deal today?"

The same deal as every day. Singing just opens me up, and I can't hide it as well.

"Mace, I'm sorry." Sorry that I was so fucked-up I couldn't have a simple conversation. "I just . . . I need a couple minutes to myself. Do you mind?"

He shook his head, bewildered, and said, "Sure, take the whole damn day. I'm out."

"Mace, I—"

The door to the bathroom slammed, and the sound echoed off the tile walls. I closed my eyes, and worked to close myself off, too. I should have been upset, but mostly I was relieved. I'd call and apologize to him later. We'd be fine.

And I'd tell him the set list for the gig, since it looked like we'd be deciding that without him. I splashed some water on my face and pressed the heels of my palms into my eyes until the black behind my eyes was as black as it would go.

Then I went back outside.

Spencer had already packed up our things and returned them to the storage closet that Sam let us use. I didn't have to say anything. Spencer had probably heard it all. Sound carried in this place. It was why I'd begged Sam to let us use it in the mornings before the bar opened. Great acoustics. Good for music, not so good for arguments.

"You okay?" Spencer asked.

I rolled my eyes and said, "What do you think?"

"I think you're fine."

"And you'd be right."

Boys were boys. I had enough other things tying me into knots without worrying every single time Mace blew a gasket.

Spencer said, "Because you've got balls of steel."

I hated when people said that, like it assumed strength and being a male were synonymous. There was strength in being a woman. "Spence, I don't have balls. Good thing, too, because they'd look terrible in the lingerie I'm wearing."

Spence adjusted his bow tie and put on a goofy smile. He said, "Lingerie, huh? Poor Mace is going to be sad he stormed out." He sidled closer and placed his hands on my hips. He wasn't hitting on me, not with that *Zoolander*-style Blue Steel face. We weren't like that anymore. Spence might be the only guy I'd ever slept with and managed to maintain a friendship with afterward. As such, we were a little more touchy-feely than most friends.

I slid out of his reach. "He wouldn't have gotten anywhere near it today anyway, and neither will you."

He crossed a hand over his heart, and looked pained.

"You're cruel. Vagina-of-steel."

I laughed so hard I had to steady myself on the table next to me.

"That's even worse. Let's just say my private parts are made of the usual private part bits. In fact, let's just never talk about my bits, okay Spence?"

He smirked. "Fine, but I make no promises when I'm drunk."

I sighed and started gathering my things. "Deal. You coming in tonight?"

"I think so. I've got a new song I'm working on. So I might come in and grab food and work on it, maybe run it by you on your break."

"Sounds good."

"You want to hear what I have so far? It's a work in progress, but it goes 'Your boyfriend's a dick, a prick, take your pick. But you should take his drumstick and—'"

"—Point proven, Spence."

He fit a fedora over his head. "I'll believe that when you do something about it. See you tonight."

I said, "I'll save you your usual table," but he was already out the door and on his way.

I used the spare key Sam gave me to lock up, and put Mace out of my mind. I had just enough time to make some ramen and catch a nap before coming back for work tonight. I pulled the hood of my jacket up over my head, and it helped to block some of the wind from my face and ears. I set off walking toward my apartment, quietly singing one of the songs by the Smiths from our set.

> *There is a better world*
> *Well, there must be . . .*

7

Cade

Milo's apartment was the quintessential bachelor pad, complete with two weeks' worth of takeout scattered all over the counters. He shoved aside an empty box from a Chinese restaurant and said, "You overthink things, *hermano*. So, I'm going to help you out." Milo opened his freezer and slammed a bottle of tequila on the counter space he'd just "cleaned."

I was beginning to get a clearer picture of how this night was going to go.

"You're going to help me stop thinking *completely*?"

He unscrewed the cap and said, "Exactly."

I picked up the bottle, and the glass was freezing against my fingertips.

"You could have at least gotten decent tequila. What is this? There's a freaking pony on the bottle."

He snatched the bottle out of my hand and said, "I'll buy more expensive tequila when you get over this Bliss girl."

I never should have mentioned her name to him. He had this tendency to drop her name into casual conversation as a way to numb me to it. So far, it was a bit like becoming numb to shock treatments. It got more bearable, but I wasn't going to line up and ask for more anytime soon.

He pulled a few shot glasses out of a cabinet, and I said, "So this is therapy, Milo-style?"

"Yep. If you're not wasted, it's not working."

He filled two shot glasses, and slid one over to me. The other he held back for himself. I gestured to his glass and said, "What are you drinking to get over?"

"You're not getting it, *hermano*. We drink so that we *don't* have to talk." I nodded and took my filled shot glass. I started to lift it to my lips, and he stopped me. "These aren't ordinary shots."

"Oh, are they magic shots? If I pour one out on the busted concrete outside will a beanstalk grow?"

"Oh, they're magic, all right," Milo said. "They're supposed to make you grow a pair."

In true Milo-fashion, he laughed at his joke before I could, and did a celebratory dance. I shook my head and said blandly, "You're hilarious."

"I know, I know. But seriously, these shots are special."

I eyed the tequila that I was sure to regret in the morning and said, "Especially bad."

He picked up his shot and said, "Each one you take is a commitment. If you break that commitment, the gods of alcohol will punish you with a hangover so bad you'll think Satan himself took a dump on you."

"And if I don't take them?"

"You can spend the night being a depressed white boy while I go get laid. Your choice."

It *was* pretty depressing when you put it that way. I sighed and gestured for him to continue.

"Cade Winston, by drinking this shot, you hereby swear to get a girl's phone number tonight. If you fail, may the alcohol gods curse you with the lowest alcohol tolerance known to man—so low that an anorexic baby could drink you under the table."

I laughed, but picked up my shot. "I don't think anorexic babies are a thing."

"How do you know? I'm sure they don't like being called chubby and having their fat pinched more than anyone else does."

I took the shot just to get him to shut up. It tasted like rubber mixed with lighter fluid mixed with death. When my throat no longer felt like the burning inferno of hell itself I said, "Okay. A number. I can do that."

He smiled and poured the second shot.

I eyed him. "If you say my punishment for this one is herpes, I'm out."

He handed me the glass, laughing. "Relax, Winston. I'll leave that between you and your giving tree."

And now I could never read that book to my kids at the after-school program again.

"You should never have children," I said.

"What makes you think there aren't a few little Milos running around out there already?"

"Because Armageddon hasn't happened yet."

Milo punched me in the shoulder, spilling half the shot. He topped off the glass and said, "Cade Winston, by drinking this shot, you hereby swear to do something out of character tonight. Should you fail, you'll be cursed to a lifetime filled with premature ejaculation."

"Seriously, man?"

He held up his hands and laughed, "Hey, the alcohol gods giveth and they taketh away."

I glared at him but took the shot without comment. I'd thought it might taste a little less heinous the second time around, but it was still the most offensive thing to ever assault my taste buds.

Milo finished his own shot with no issue.

"How often do you drink this stuff?" I asked.

"Pretty often. One of my uncles works at the factory in Mexico. He sends me coupons. It's not so bad once you get used to it."

"If I ever get used to it . . . shoot me."

Milo ignored me and said, "*Numero tres!* For this one, amigo, I want you to get pissed off. You've been too damn nice about this whole thing. I don't care if it's over a spilled drink or just how ugly some dude's face is—but by taking this shot, you promise to let yourself get angry tonight."

"What if I get pissed at you?"

He shrugged. "You probably will, but I guarantee it won't be because I've got an ugly face."

"Right, just that ugly shirt you're wearing."

"This shirt is awesome. You don't know what you're talking about."

I laughed and said, "Okay, I'll get angry. That shouldn't be too hard."

He clinked his shot with mine and said, "And none of that holding-it-in shit."

I took the shot. This time it didn't burn at all, which was worrisome. Maybe it had already corroded my esophagus. I watched him fill the final glasses and I said, "Last one."

"Hmm . . ." Milo paused, thinking. "You've not been with anyone since Bliss right?"

I shook my head, and didn't bother telling him I was never really with her either. He poured the last shot and said, "Cade Winston, by drinking this shot, you hereby swear to hook up with a girl at this bar."

"Hook up?"

"I'll let you be the judge of what qualifies as a hookup. As long as there is some kind of action involved, I'm sure the alcohol gods will be appeased. If you succeed, may you be blessed with extraordinary game and the best sex of your life."

A reward. That was new.

"And if I don't?"

He shrugged and said matter-of-factly, "You'll be cursed to a lifetime of getting hard-ons at the most inappropriate times."

That sounded more like Milo. I wondered if he'd spent time thinking this all up, or if it was just another day in the

depraved state of his mind. I wiped a hand over my face. I had
to give him one thing . . . he was good at getting my mind off
my troubles. Maybe he was right. I had spent months chasing after the relationship that wasn't, and then even more
time mourning it. Who said I needed to be in a relationship?
I'd done my fair share of partying and casual dating during
my first three years of college. But when graduation started
looming, I had thought I needed to take life more seriously,
start building a foundation for my future. Look at all the
good that had done me.

I was twenty-two years old. Why the hell was I in such a
hurry?

I picked up the glass, my chest still warm from the last
shot.

"A hookup it is." I put the glass to my lips and tipped it
back. Damn it . . . the stuff really did grow on you.

Milo cheered and slapped me on the back.

"And now, we party!"

Bliss barely crossed my mind as we made our way to a bar
called Trestle. Maybe enough time had finally passed.

More likely it was the tequila.

Milo had brought the bottle with us just in case I sobered
up during the journey. By the time we arrived outside Trestle, my liver was probably permanently damaged, but at least
my mind was clear.

The bar sat at the crossing of two smaller streets, almost
directly under a bridge decorated with graffiti. It was the
kind of place that just screamed mugging . . . or hepatitis.

From the outside, the bar looked like an old abandoned
brick building. The sign was even missing the r in Trestle.

The inside was a totally different story. There were old black-and-white movies projected onto the wall. Bright colored lights gave the dim bar a retro feel. Then there were the dancers. I saw Milo's friend Sasha on the far side of the room. She stood up on a platform behind one end of the bar, dancing several feet above the crowd. Her movements were hypnotic, her long hair bouncing around her as she moved. Between the run-down exterior, the projections, and Sasha's dancing, the bar felt like some kind of secret, underground venue.

If we had places like this back home in Texas, I'd certainly never been there.

Milo clapped a hand on my shoulder and said, "When I told you to hook up with a girl, I did not mean Sasha, *hermano*. She's off-limits."

I laughed and looked away from her. "Is she yours?"

He watched her for a moment, his eyes following her movements. "Nah, man. She's too good for me. I meant she's not available to be your rebound girl. She's been run over by enough guys for this lifetime."

I eyed him, knowing there was more that he wasn't saying, but I let him keep his secrets. I certainly had mine.

"Stop looking at me like that, Winston. I'm not going to be your rebound either."

I rolled my eyes. "I'm not drunk enough for those kinds of jokes."

"Well, that's something we should remedy!"

We moved toward the bar, but a blond girl stepped in my way. She was pretty—light curls, pink cheeks, and a low-cut top. She appeared to have had way too much to drink. She leaned forward to say something, but stumbled into me instead. I caught her around the waist and steadied her. One of her hands went around my bicep, and she giggled.

"I'm so sorry!"

She didn't let go of my arm even once I'd righted her. She looked up at me through long lashes.

She was attractive for sure, but I kept waiting for something more to hit me. I waited for the electric zing of attraction, the pull in my chest, the pump of blood.

Nothing. Nada.

She asked me the usual questions, and I made small talk, but I could have been talking to a wall for all the impression it made on me. I could make a move on a girl like her. I could forget about serious relationships and just spend the night with a pretty blonde, but I had a feeling it wouldn't make me feel any better. It certainly wouldn't fix anything. Plus, talking to this girl felt like work, and tonight I wanted something effortless.

I kept looking toward the bar, wishing I could take another drink. Maybe if I was drunker, I would loosen up and get out of my head.

The girl, Cammie, was saying something about how funny I was. I didn't even remember what I'd said to her.

I felt an elbow in my back and Milo said, "Here's your chance to avoid a lifetime of premature ejaculation"

I threw a glare over my shoulder. "Can you not say that in public please?"

"Don't be ashamed, *hermano*. It happens to lots of guys."

I shoved him, but we were both laughing.

When I looked back at Cammie, she seemed to know that

my attention was waning. She leaned closer and reached a bold hand into the pocket of my jeans, and came back with my cell phone. Her smoky eyes met mine before she entered her number into my phone's memory. I marked one thing off the night's checklist without even really trying. I smiled politely at the blonde and said good-bye. I turned to Milo, preparing to brag about how easily I'd gotten her number.

My eyes caught on something else entirely.

One of the colored lights illuminated the pale, bare skin of another dancer's stomach. She was wearing far less clothing than Sasha. She had on sheer, black tights and a short skirt. Her shirt was lacy and short, revealing a toned stomach inked with black lines. It took me a few moments to piece together the picture that the lines made, but when I did the electricity that had been missing with Cammie started rushing through my veins.

The lines were the roots of a tree.

And the girl was Max.

8

Max

Even though smoking was allowed only outside Trestle, there always seemed to be clouds of it inside the bar. Amber light fractured through the haze. That, combined with the drinking, laughing patrons below me made the whole night feel surreal. The music vibrated everything. I could feel the pulse of it in the platform below me, up through my heels, and into my legs.

As I danced I kept my eyes focused upward and away from the patrons. It wasn't that I was ashamed. I wasn't a stripper or anything. The dancers at Trestle were just for atmosphere.

We stayed clothed. I think I wore less clothing than anyone, but that was because I split my shift between dancing and bartending, and the less clothing, the more tip.

But there was nothing more awkward than making eye contact with someone below. Sam was careful to keep the bar as pervert-free as possible, but the way we were framed up here on pedestals with soft glowing light could turn just about any guy into a creeper.

Normally I tried to lose myself in the music and just dance for me. It made the time go by faster. But tonight, my mind was so full of the day's events that I just couldn't seem to turn my brain off. I took two shots before my shift started to try to remedy the problem, but so far nothing had changed.

I took turns staring at various places on the wall and ceiling to pass the time. I caught Spencer's eye over at his table in the corner. He smirked at me, waggled his eyebrows, and licked his lips.

I pretended to gag.

He shook his head and went back to scratching away at the lyrics in his journal.

This afternoon was forgotten . . . for now at least.

I smiled, swished my frilly skirt, and glanced at the front entrance as the door swung open. Another cloud of smoke rolled in through the door. Like he was stepping out of the fog, Cade appeared. My twenty-four-hour, pretend-we-met-in-a-library, mom-hugging, golden-boy-boyfriend.

He looked good.

Too good.

He laughed, and people stopped midconversation just to stare, like he was a celebrity. Dark hair tumbled down into his eyes, and he pushed it back. He had the kind of hair that just begged to be touched. He was with someone, a Hispanic guy, and he was smiling so big that his teeth were like little pearls in the dark room. He'd seemed like a pretty smiley guy when we met this morning, but only by seeing this smile in comparison did I realize how faked it had all been. He had these perfect dimples that softened the hard line of his jaw, and his eyes crinkled slightly. He laughed again, and I saw at least three girls maneuver closer to him.

One of the braver girls broke off from her friends, and stepped right up to him. I couldn't hear what they were saying, and it was too dark to read their lips.

Not that I even knew how to read lips.

She looked exactly how I pictured his type of girl. Blond, perky, and nauseating.

The complete opposite of me.

In less than a minute, he charmed her the same way he charmed my parents. She was giggling and touching his arm, falling into him, all while curling her hair around her finger. I waited for him to move in for the kill, but he didn't. They just kept talking and talking. She was clearly giving him the green light, and he was still chatting her up like an old lady in church.

Why wasn't he taking what she was so clearly offering?

He started talking to his friend, ignoring the blonde. She gave the kind of pout that was obnoxious on anyone above the age of five.

I smiled.

Some of the tension in my shoulders loosened, and I danced a little easier. I told myself that the relief I felt was a by-product of those earlier shots kicking in and had nothing to do with the blond girl he was blowing off.

Then the girl reached into his pocket and pulled out his phone. She was smug as she entered what I assumed was her number into his contacts, and I wanted to rip her stupid blond hair out. He looked over his shoulder and raised an eyebrow at his friend. The girl left, looking disappointed, and he didn't even give her a second glance.

He was saying something to his friend when he paused. His eyes were cast in my direction, and I could almost feel the weight of his gaze as it trailed up my body. His face was stretched wide in a smile when our eyes met. He froze, and my movement faltered. I should have looked away, but something about his expression held me. It wasn't lust. I knew that expression well. He looked at me . . . in awe.

He took a step in my direction, and my heart jumped in my chest. I was attracted to him . . . to a guy who was in a whole other playing field. And if I was honest, there was more than just desire thrumming through my chest.

There was fear.

I forced my eyes back toward the ceiling, and made myself concentrate on dancing. If I didn't look at him, maybe he wouldn't try to talk to me.

I closed my eyes, and the swing of my hips felt like I'd been set to sea. The shots had definitely kicked in. I was affected by them just enough that I felt warm and my head light. My skin tingled, and I wondered if he was looking at me. My muscles had loosened, and the more I twisted and rolled my body to the music, the better I felt. I imagined the look in his eyes, and it made my blood pump faster.

Trestle had a retro theme, so I didn't have to dance to any brain-liquefying pop music. With my eyes closed like this, the smell of smoke wafting in from outside, and the undercurrent of desire thrumming beneath my skin, I could almost pretend that it was the 1960s, and I was working here in the go-go bar's prime.

I opened my eyes and found Cade.

It felt natural, like the pull of gravity.

Normally, looking at someone from up here felt too awkward and intimate. Meeting his gaze was intimate, but it wasn't awkward. It was exhilarating.

Despite how much he scared me, I felt comfortable with him. It was complicated. Looking at him, I knew this wasn't the kind of fear that sent you running for the hills. It was the kind of fear that made people jump off cliffs and climb mountains—the kind of fear that told you something miraculous was waiting at the end of it, if you could only get there.

Getting there was the problem though. I wasn't the climbing mountains kind of girl. As appealing as the summit seemed now, I knew myself well enough to know I'd give up halfway there, and then I'd be left with only the pain of the journey, and none of the reward.

I preferred my life to be as uncomplicated as possible. There was nothing to learn about guys like Mace, and no journey needed to land him. What you saw was what you got. I understood him. And more importantly, he was the kind of guy who couldn't break my heart, because I would never let him have it and he would never care enough to want it.

But Cade . . .

For the life of me, I couldn't understand what Cade could

possibly want with me. I couldn't understand why his eyes were burning through the layers of my skin while a pretty blonde sat pouting a few tables away.

I tore my eyes away and threw myself into the music.

Music wasn't complicated. It was math. Patterns. Highs and lows.

Music made sense to me in a way that life and people didn't. It was predictable. My hips knew instinctively when to move. The riffs and changes untangled my mind. Time folded in on itself, and I lost myself.

I imagined I was singing up on this platform, too, instead of just dancing. The tension in me ebbed, and I floated away on a melody. I ran my hands across my sweat-slicked stomach, since I didn't have my guitar. My body was my only instrument. I let the music flow through me, and I danced for what could have been minutes or hours or lifetimes.

Eventually I started to feel the strain in my legs. The hair that lay against my neck was damp with sweat. My throat went dry.

The song changed, and in the few seconds of silence, the world came back to me. The bar intruded on my mind once again. I wasn't singing, and I wasn't alone.

Cade's eyes appeared black in the dim bar, and I could see the rise and fall of his chest from here. I turned and twisted my hips while he watched me. A tickle ran up my spine, the kind that made my whole body shiver in a good way. I must have really lost track of time dancing because there were half-eaten plates of food in front of him and his friend.

I made eye contact with Shelly, one of the bartenders, and asked her what time it was.

"Eleven!" she yelled up at me.

Shit. I should have taken my break fifteen minutes ago. Now it was time for my bartender shift. Katie, who I was taking over for, waved me off and said, "Don't worry about it. Go take your break!"

I blew her an exaggerated kiss, and waved at the new girl on the other side of the bar to let her know I was leaving. Then I hopped off my platform.

I pushed through the crowd of people trying to flag down the bartenders and escaped through the front door. My sweaty skin tightened under the caress of the cold air. I sighed in satisfaction.

Bouncer Benny asked if I wanted a smoke, and I just moaned in response. He understood. No words needed. I didn't smoke often, not anymore. But I think today, I deserved a little break. Benny was lighting the end of my cigarette when the door swung open, and Cade stepped out.

My heart sped up in response.

I took a deep drag on the cigarette, and took my time exhaling. Maybe it was seeing him at a place like Trestle or seeing him in a situation that didn't involve my parents or the connection I'd felt with him as I danced, but he didn't look quite like the nice guy I'd met this morning.

And that realization was dangerous.

9

Cade

Max was . . . unearthly. Ethereal. Unattainable.

Her pale skin glowed under the low amber light. I didn't know where to look as she danced. I wanted to memorize all of her. Her eyes were lined with dark kohl that made the blue of her eyes shine and pierce straight through me. I'd seen the branches of her tree tattoo and now the roots. Imagining the art that lay between was maddening. She bore other tattoos, too small for me to identify. From here they resembled runes or hieroglyphs, like she was a goddess. Exotic and forbidden.

Immortal.

That was what she looked like. She was the kind of sight that I would never, could never forget.

The few times her eyes met mine, my blood pumped furiously through my veins, I clenched my fists, and had the urge to do something crazy. I wanted to walk up to her platform and join her, or throw her over my shoulder and take her away where no one else could see her.

I'd always thought of myself as a fairly rational person, not one to be ruled by my desires and emotions. But this . . . nothing was logical about the way this girl made me feel. I'd gone crazy. All the stress of everything with Bliss and moving and this new university—I'd finally snapped.

That was the only way I could explain why I followed her outside when she went on break. I had no idea what I was going to say or do, but I couldn't let her out of my sight.

She said, "Hey, Golden Boy," on an exhale, smoke curling from between those ruby red lips.

"Hey, Max."

She walked away from the bouncer, and leaned up against the brick of the building. My eyes snagged on her leg as she propped a heel up on the wall behind her. I forced myself to look away. She was sexy as hell, but I was sure she got enough guys ogling her here.

"Are you stalking me, Golden Boy?"

I stayed where I was, careful to keep distance between us, so that I didn't do something stupid in my drunken state.

"Only a little."

She laughed. That was good. I'd made her laugh.

"What are you really doing here? I've never seen you at Trestle before, and I'm here more than I'm home."

I filed away that information for later.

"I've never been here. I came with a friend."

"The Hispanic guy?"

I nodded. "His name is Milo." I searched for something else to say, but my mind was moving too slowly. God, could I be any more boring? No wonder she called me Golden Boy.

This was a terrible idea. The silence between us stretched into awkward territory, and I was too drunk to hold a decent conversation. The longer I stayed, the harder it became to fight off the urge to touch her.

Time for a tactical retreat.

"I should probably go find him." She frowned and stared at me as I took a step back. "I only came to say hi." She looked at me for a second longer, and her eyes widened in shock. Then her lips turned downward, and I saw her disappointment seconds before she swept the emotion from her expression.

I looked behind me expecting to see a mugger or a UFO or a zombie. We were alone on the street except for the bouncer, who stayed silent and still outside the door.

"What?" I asked.

She shook her head. "Nothing. Don't worry about it."

My curiosity was too strong to turn around again.

"No, tell me. What was that look for?"

She took a deep inhale, and lowered her heel to the ground.

"It's nothing. I just realized something is all."

"And what did you realize?"

Her eyes were still wide, and she sputtered slightly. "I, well, I just realized that you're in *theatre*."

I was drunk, but I could tell that when she'd said "theatre," she meant something else. "Yeah, I told you I was an actor this morning."

Her heel scraped at the concrete sidewalk.

"You could have told me the rest, too."

The alcohol must have been preventing some of the synapses in my brain from firing because I had no idea what she was talking about.

"The rest?"

"You know, your *friend*, Milo. You could have told me about him. I wouldn't have judged."

The pieces were coming together, but I wished they weren't. This was one puzzle that I did *not* want to solve.

"I've had a lot of alcohol," I admitted. "But if you're saying what I think you're saying, you're wrong."

She pushed off from the wall and took a step closer to me.

"It's okay. I won't tell anyone, Golden Boy."

I winced. She patted me on the shoulder, and I grabbed her hand and held it between us. "No, Max, I'm not gay."

She held her other hand up and said, "Jesus, I get it. *You love boobs.*" She said this loudly, and then leaned close to me to whisper, "But really, Golden Boy, it's the twenty-first century. The world won't end if you come out of the closet."

Two thoughts crossed my mind—one involved a lot of yelling.

I chose the other, and used the hand I was holding to tug her forward into my arms. Her chest pressed into mine, and her lips were millimeters from my own. She exhaled sharply, and I could taste the sweetness of her breath on the air. I saw in her eyes the moment she knew she was wrong, but I wasn't done proving it to her.

I crushed my mouth to hers.

She gasped, and I slipped my tongue past her lips. She stayed there for a few seconds, her hands still at her sides, then I felt the tentative touch of her hand against my hip, and that was all the permission I needed to continue. I threaded a hand through her hair and wrapped the other around her waist. I walked her backward until she hit the wall. Her other hand came to my waist, and her fingers pressed deeper into my skin. Her lips were soft and full underneath mine, and I eased up enough to taste them. I tried to kiss her softly. I did, but there was something about her that made me desperate, and I kissed her harder.

Her hands slid around to my lower back. Her fingernails dug into me, and I groaned. I used my hand in her hair to turn her head to the side, so that I could kiss her deeper. Up until now she'd allowed me to kiss her, but as I pressed her harder against the wall, she came fully alive. Her tongue tangled with mine, and her mouth pushed harder against my own. My blood rushed south so fast that I felt dizzy. The only thing keeping me steady was my hand propped on the wall behind her, but even so I fell farther into her, until every part of my body was aligned with hers.

It still wasn't close enough. My winter clothes kept too much space between us. I wanted to conquer every piece of her. The way her hips pressed up into mine made me believe she felt the same way. The kiss was even better than I could have imagined. Her mouth tasted as exotic as she looked, and my every nerve ending seemed to be standing at attention. Her fingers dug harder into my lower back, and I was on the verge of losing my mind. Her teeth grazed my bottom lip, and I used the hand in her hair to tug her head back just enough that I could move my lips to her neck. Her skin was just as smooth as I'd dreamed. I could spend eternity tasting her.

What was that saying—I could die happy? This was so beyond that. I could never be satisfied. I would always want to kiss her again. She was addictive.

"Okay." Her voice was thick, raspy, and it only made me want her more. "Point proven."

I laughed into her neck and nipped the curve of her collarbone. Her back arched, and her breasts pressed deliciously against my chest. She was so responsive. Every time I did something she liked, her nails pressed deeper, and her breath caught in her throat. I wanted to make her do that again and again.

"We have to stop," she said.

Stopping was about as appealing as a bat to the kneecaps, but I did it. I lifted my head from her neck and looked into her dilated eyes. They were wide with shock or fear or something. Whatever it was . . . it wasn't what I'd hoped to see in her expression. I stepped backward to give her some space.

Then she slapped me.

The sound of it echoed through the empty street, and it took me a few seconds to feel the sting through my buzz. I'd been slapped twice in my entire life, both of them by this gorgeous, maddening girl. Unlike the last one, this one I deserved.

She was taken. When I wasn't looking at her, that thought was easier to remember.

I blinked, and turned back to her. She had her hands folded over her mouth in shock. She took a deep breath and said, "I am *so* sorry. I—I shouldn't have done that."

I swallowed and put a few more feet between us. "Don't be sorry. I deserved it." Logically, I knew that. But all my body knew was that it wanted to be connected to hers again. I could barely think straight for how badly I wanted her.

"I should go." I returned to the bar door, feeling like all the good of the day had been knocked loose by her slap.

You're not that guy, Cade. You practically forced yourself on her.

As I pulled open the door, I heard her ask the bouncer for another cigarette. I forced myself to walk inside the bar, to leave her alone. My track record with girls and alcohol was terrible. But one thought kept plaguing my mind.

She kissed me back.

10

Max

My cheeks burned from the cold, and my lips burned from something else as I lit up my next cigarette.

I hadn't meant to kiss him back.

I think I'd known before he'd ever touched me that he wasn't gay, but a small part of me wanted the easy out that that would have provided. I wanted him to walk away because I wasn't sure I would have the willpower to do it myself.

Then he'd kissed me, and I thought . . . a few seconds wouldn't hurt. Just to kill the curiosity. Just long enough to blame on the alcohol, then we could pretend like it didn't happen, and I could stop being fascinated by him.

That had been the plan.

But then his hand had tightened in my hair, and I was swept away by my weakness for kisses with a little edge.

It was why I didn't normally date nice guys. They were just too tame.

This kiss, though, was a paradox. It was sweet and soft, like I would expect a kiss from Golden Boy to be. But every time I'd thought of pushing him away, there had been something—a pull on my hair, a graze of teeth, a press of his hips—that had frayed my thoughts and kept me kissing him. I don't know how he managed to be soft and rough at the same time, but I had to hand it to him, it was kind of mind-blowing.

It was also the worst idea since Crocs.

I was *with* Mace. Or I was supposed to be.

God, I was such a screwup.

Mace made sense for me, and I for him. I just had to remember that.

The slap was an overreaction, but there had been a hurricane of emotion wreaking havoc in my chest—lust and fear and guilt—and I had just snapped.

I fumbled with the new cigarette Benny gave me. If I weren't careful, it would end up on the ground like my last one.

"Should I be going after that guy?" he asked. "I'm a little unclear on your feelings at the moment."

Join the club.

"No, Benny. But thank you. He's just a friend. We're both a little drunk. Nothing to worry about."

Except I wasn't drunk. Not really. I had no excuse other than stupidity for my own behavior. Well, that and how hot

Cade was. Yep, we should definitely lay the blame on his hotness.

I looked at my watch and balked, I only had about a minute left in my break. I must have kissed him for longer than I thought. Cade joined the very short list of things in life that had that kind of time-bending effect on me. Or more correctly, kissing Cade joined that list.

Benny said, "I'm going to hit the head. You want me to walk you in?"

I took a deep drag and shook my head. "No, I'm good Benny. I'll go inside in about a minute. Go ahead, I'll be fine."

I stayed by the door, finishing my cigarette. It was a pointless exercise. The slow inhale and exhale was doing absolutely nothing to calm me down. I used my heel to dig at a weed that had sprouted up between slabs of concrete. It was amazing how even in the middle of a city—a world of hard stone and cold metal—something living could overcome the obstacles and emerge to see the light of day.

The heavy metal door swung open again, and I was standing too close. It clipped me in the shoulder, and I dropped my second cigarette of the night as I pitched forward.

An arm caught me around the waist before I hit pavement.

"I gotcha, babe."

The guy reeked of alcohol. He pulled me up and close to his body. His head was shaved, and he had a few tattoos. He might have been my type on the surface, but his arm was tight around my waist in a way that didn't feel at all appealing or comforting.

I feigned a smile. "It's okay," I said. "I'm good."

His eyes were dark, and they left my face to look down at my body. His hand curved around my bare waist, and his thumb traced one of the lines of my tattoo. "I bet you are."

The hair on the back of my neck stood on end, and time seemed to slow down and speed up at the same time. Blood rushed beneath my skin and roared in my ears.

No matter how many times I felt this kind of panic, it managed to catch me by surprise. And each time, I associated it with the night of Alex's accident. The fear from now mixed and muddled with the fear from then, and I felt the terror building in my throat. One of my arms was pinned to my side, but I maneuvered the left one between us, and pushed at his chest.

"Let me go."

His breath was warm and cloying against my face. He jerked me in to him, and it bent my hand back, shooting pain through my wrist. I craned my head around, but the street was deserted, and there was no telling when Benny would be back from the bathroom.

"No need to get upset, dolly. We're just having a little fun."

"You're drunk. And I'm not having fun." I squirmed and bucked against him. He might have been stronger than me, but I would make it hard as hell to hold on to me. "Let me go, asshole!"

I tried to stomp down on his foot, but I couldn't get enough leverage to do any damage. I screamed again, and he brought a hand up to my throat.

"Would you stop screaming?"

His hand was big enough to wrap all the way around my

neck. His fingers tangled in my hair, and his thumb pressed against my windpipe. I tried to swallow but couldn't. I choked and slid my hand up to claw at his face. He was tall enough that he managed to stay just out of my reach, and I was left scrabbling at his chest. The door to Trestle swung open, and I tried to scream, but it just came out a garbled mess.

I blinked, and my vision went blurry. Then one black spot appeared, followed by another. My chest felt like it was caving in, crumbling.

Then his hand was ripped off of me. Black converged until I couldn't see anything, burning air rushed into my lungs, and for a few seconds, I felt like I was underwater. Then the air stopped burning, the black left my vision, and I saw Cade grappling with my attacker.

Cade's fist connected with the bald guy's face, and a rush of relief swept through me. I coughed and swallowed down gulps of air.

I dragged myself to my feet, and the world flipped upside down and inside out. The air sang, high pitched and off-key. I took a step, but the ground wasn't where it was supposed to be, and then I heard sweet-nothings from the asphalt.

"Max!"

I opened my eyes, and the world had rearranged itself. I was on my back, and Cade was kneeling over me. I relaxed. Everything was okay if he was here.

"Max, are you okay?"

I swallowed, and opened my mouth to answer, but something swung and hit him on the side of the head. I gave a strangled scream as my attacker went after a distracted Cade.

I heard a groan, and the sound sharpened my focus. I

pushed myself up to a sitting position, and this time I rose slowly. The world wavered, but stayed in place.

Cade was a pretty tall guy, but Mr. Clean had at least half a foot on him. Blood stained Cade's mouth. That's what pushed me into motion. My still-lit cigarette that I'd dropped when the door hit me was lying a foot or two away, so I grabbed it. I heard the sound of flesh hitting flesh again, and spun around. Cade was on his feet, but I watched him shake his head and wondered if the world was spinning for him now.

I took my chance and staggered forward. "Hey jackhole!"

Mr. Clean turned and snarled down at me. And I pushed the lit end of my cigarette into his neck. I heard the small sizzle, and his whole body convulsed in an attempt to get away from me. He screamed and shoved me away.

The ground rushed toward me. I knew the most important thing was to keep my head forward so it wouldn't hit the pavement. I wrapped my arms around my head, and my back took the brunt of the fall. I hit the asphalt and went skidding. Gravel gouged into my bare lower back, and I felt the skin stretch and tear.

"You bitch!"

I forgot about the pain and scrambled backward when he came at me again. I hit the curb just as Cade stepped between us, looking focused once more. The guy swung his right arm toward Cade, who saw it coming and ducked. He wasn't quite fast enough. My attacker's knuckles grazed his forehead. Cade's head rocked on his neck like the least funny bobble head doll ever. My attacker must have been drunk, too, because he swayed on his feet. Cade paused just for a second, shook his head, and then came up, ramming his shoulder into the guy's midsection.

Mr. Clean stumbled backward, and Cade got in a quick uppercut while he was off guard. I heard the smack of his teeth clacking together, but he didn't even seem fazed by it.

"Get inside, Max!" Cade yelled.

I didn't want to leave him. He was looking at me, and there was blood on his face, and my heart felt like it was going to burst wide open.

"Go!"

He was too busy looking at me to see the guy coming. I screamed, "Cade!" and he barely turned fast enough to avoid getting hit. I dragged myself up and ran for Trestle. My hands shook as I reached for the door handle. The metal door felt even heavier than normal, and it took all my strength to pry it open.

"BENNY!"

My throat felt like I'd swallowed burning coals, but I yelled Benny's name again. The drunken bar-goers looked at me like I was crazy. Some didn't even register my scream. But I saw Benny shouldering his way through the crowd.

"Benny, hurry!"

I ran for the door as soon as he was close to me.

"What is it, Max?"

I shoved open the door as hard as I could and breathed, "Fight."

The cold wind was like glass shards against my skin, but I didn't care. "Cade!"

My attacker was flat on his back, and Cade was on top of

him. Both of them were bloodied, but Cade was okay. Really okay if the punch he threw was any indication. Benny charged forward and grabbed Cade by his clothing. He jerked him to his feet, and I cried, "The other one, Benny!"

He looked at Cade for a few moments, and Golden Boy stared back, his jaw set in a grim line. Finally, Benny released him to address the guy still on the ground.

Cade breathed out harshly, and then faltered on his feet. I rushed toward him and took him by the arm. He smiled, and I winced at the blood in his teeth. His eyes searched my face, and when he didn't find any injuries, he rested his hand against my cheek. It might have been a side effect of being choked, but it was suddenly harder to breathe.

"Pretty impressive, Golden Boy."

He coughed, and then groaned. I moved closer and wrapped an arm around his waist. His hard body pressed into mine, and the heat of him seeped into my skin. His brown eyes met mine, and there were volumes written in his expression. Those volumes contained words that terrified me, but I couldn't look away for the life of me.

"I'm sorry," he said. His eyes closed, and he teetered toward me. His forehead pressed into my temple in a gesture that felt sweet and familiar. He swallowed, and I could feel every imperceptible change in his body.

I held tighter to him and asked, "What could you possibly be sorry for?"

"I'm getting blood on you."

I laughed. "Only you would apologize for something like that, Golden Boy."

His eyes were open again, and they locked on mine. He

wasn't laughing. He shook his head. "I meant I was sorry for kissing you."

With his forehead pressed against mine, the sight of him filled up my vision. There was nothing else in that moment, but him. And he . . . he reminded me of music. Of the way singing made me feel. Like I was falling and flying, freedom and fear.

Without thinking it through, I said, "Don't be. I'm not."

11

Cade

Max led me back inside the bar, and it took all of five seconds before Milo was at my side whistling. "Damn, *hermano*, I think you took that promise to get pissed a little too seriously."

I rolled my eyes and said to Max, "This is my *friend* Milo. Milo, this is *Mackenzie*."

That was for calling me Golden Boy.

Her head swung around to face me and she asked, "Are you looking to get in another fight tonight?" Her cheeks were flushed, and her eyes sparkling.

"No, I just like seeing you angry." She pressed her lips together and glared, but a smile was poking through within a few seconds. God, when she looked at me like that I forgot completely about the splitting pain in my head.

When I turned back to Milo, he was looking between Max and me, grinning. "You bastard, did you knock out all four commitments in one go?"

I was still leaning on Max, a little because I needed to and a lot because I wanted to. Her face angled up to mine and she asked, "What is he talking about?"

"Don't worry about it. He's drunk."

I, on the other hand, had sobered up completely. I tried not to look disappointed as I removed my arm from around her shoulder.

"Thanks, Max. I'm good now."

All I wanted to do was get home and take a long, cold shower, followed by a really hot one to ease the stiffness in my back and arms.

"What do you think you're doing?" she asked. Her hands came up to rest on her hips . . . hips that I'd held in my hands before this all went down.

"I'm just going to head home and get cleaned up."

Milo said, "Uh, Cade, you live at least twenty minutes away and your face is leaking. I think we should get you cleaned up here."

Max's fingers found my chin, and she drew my face down toward hers. "I'm going to get a first aid kit. Don't you dare leave."

I was too tired to argue, so Max disappeared, and Milo led me toward the bathroom at the back of the bar.

"Damn, Cade. Who knew you liked the feisty ones?"

I wasn't sure if I liked "feisty ones," but I liked her. A lot.

There was an obnoxiously long line for the bathroom, and everyone was either too drunk or too rude to care that I was bleeding. I leaned against the back wall, tilted my head back against the brick, and closed my eyes. In a shocking turn of events, Milo kept his mouth shut until Max returned.

She said, "Bad news. Our first aid kit is pretty much empty."

I opened my eyes and focused on her. Shoving off the wall, I swayed slightly. Max caught one arm while Milo caught the other.

"I'll catch a cab home," I said. That was a lie. I didn't have the cash for that, but it would make them happy.

Max scoffed, "Good luck finding a cab in this neighborhood."

Milo offered to run to a drugstore and buy some stuff, but I insisted that it was too much trouble.

"Really, guys, I'm fine. I'll splash my face with some water, and then head home. It's not a big deal. I feel fine." I moved toward the bathroom, but Max darted around me and placed a hand on my chest.

She was chewing on her bottom lip, wrestling with something. Her lips pulled into a straight line, and she looked up at me. "We'll go to my place. It's only a few blocks from here."

I didn't have to see Milo to know he was grinning behind me as he said, "That sounds like a *great* idea!"

I brought my hand up and covered hers that rested on my chest.

"Max, I'm okay, really."

She glared at me, and I got the feeling that she was rarely told the word no. With her hand on my chest and mine on hers, I was all too aware of how much my body wanted to say yes.

My brain knew better.

She stepped closer to me and lowered her voice. "Listen, Golden Boy, I'm trying this new thing where I don't act like a raging bitch all the time. That means when a guy gets his ass kicked for me, I have to show a little compassion. It doesn't come easy to me, so help me out."

Huh. One day . . . we'd known each other one day, and she'd already picked up on the fact that I had difficulty saying no to people, especially people that needed my help.

I *was* supposed to do something out of character, though most of the things I did tonight were a little out of character. And it wasn't like I didn't try to say no.

"Okay." I sighed. "But only if you take back that part about me getting my ass kicked."

She laughed. "All right, I'll give you that. But I totally softened him up for you."

"Yeah, remind me not to make you mad when you're smoking."

There was a moment of awkwardness where we'd both already agreed, but neither of us stepped back or stopped touching the other. After a few seconds, she cleared her throat, and her hand dropped from my chest.

I said good-bye to Milo, and ignored the thumbs-up he gave me over Max's head. I waited while she slipped on a coat and grabbed her things. She explained to one of the other bartenders what had happened. I thought maybe they wouldn't let her leave, but after a short conversation, she was back at my side and ready to go.

She smiled up at me, and I was nervous. With all the pain and fatigue, who would have thought I'd have room for something like nerves?

"Come on," she said. "You're covered in blood."

"Too gross for you?"

"Either really gross or really hot. I'm not sure which."

She didn't wait for a response before turning and pushing her way through the crowd toward the door. I followed at a slower pace, sure again that this was a dangerous idea.

Her attacker and Benny were gone when we returned outside, and someone else had taken up the bouncer's post at the door. That was probably for the best, because if I'd seen the guy who attacked her, I couldn't be held responsible for my actions. I kept seeing her face, pale and in pain, and his hand on her throat. Just the memory had me ready to fight him all over again.

She linked her arm with mine and asked, "You okay?"

I nodded. I didn't need her for balance anymore, but I wasn't about to deny the chance to touch her. It felt natural, like we were any other couple returning home.

We were silent for the first block or so, but when I looked over, I could see the glazed look in her eye, and knew she was replaying the event in her mind. I doubted she wanted to relive it any more than I did.

"So you're a musician?" I asked.

She nodded but didn't reply. Her gaze was fixed on the sidewalk, and from this angle I could see red marks on her neck from his hands. I wanted nothing more than to stop and hold her in my arms, but I knew that wasn't her style. I doubt she'd ever been the type for hugs and comfort.

So I settled for distracting her.

"I've written a couple of songs, you know. Not because I want to be a musician, but just because the music helps organize my thoughts."

I followed her around a corner, and though she kept her face down, I could see a small smile form on her face. "Will you sing me one?"

"Not a chance."

"Oh, come on!" She wrapped both hands around my arm, and pushed her bottom lip out in a pout. It was so damn convincing I actually considered it for a moment, but the only song I knew by heart cut a little too close to said organ.

Tonight was the night for forgetting about Bliss, and it had been going remarkably well until now. Singing a song I wrote about her was the last thing I wanted to do.

"Maybe another time," I said.

"I'm going to get it out of you," she said.

I had no doubt that if anyone could, it would be her.

The silence of the street swallowed up my thoughts, and that was fine by me. I was happy to just walk with her, no thoughts or troubles to get in the way.

We passed a twenty-four-hour Laundromat, and she slowed to a stop in front of a glass door with a set of buzzers. A staircase trailed upward on the other side of the door, and she pulled the door open without a key.

"No lock?"

She shrugged. "It's broken. I've been asking the landlord to fix it for weeks."

I looked at the door while she started up the stairs.

"You know, I could probably fix it. My grandfather was a locksmith."

She called back from the middle of the staircase, "Is there anything you can't do, Golden Boy?" I could think of one thing. I seemed to be incapable of finding a girl who wasn't taken.

I let the door swing shut behind me, and climbed up the stairs. We went up two flights and down a hallway before stopping at the last door on the left. She pulled her keys out of her coat pocket, and hesitated for a moment.

She took a deep breath and slid the key in, turning until it clicked. Her apartment was dark as we entered, and she threw her keys on a small table next to the door.

"Hang on a sec."

She left me by the door to turn on a lamp a few feet away.

The light revealed an apartment that was simple, bare, and lifeless. I followed her into a tiny living room crammed with a futon and a boxy-looking love seat. There were no pictures, no knickknacks, nothing that gave any insight into the tempting creature that had entered my life this morning and hijacked it completely.

"How long have you lived here?" I asked.

She laid her purse down beside the couch and said, "Almost two years in this apartment, but I've been in Philly twice that long."

Then why did she live like she might pack up and leave any day? There was nothing but furniture here. The only thing I saw that was even the least bit personal was a guitar case propped up in a corner.

"Take a seat, and I'll grab some bandages and stuff."

She started shrugging off her coat, and then sucked in a sharp breath. Her arms dropped to her side, and her face scrunched up in pain. I leapt to my feet. Her eyes were clamped shut and her teeth dug into her bottom lip.

"What is it, Max? What's wrong?"

She whimpered slightly, and turned her back to me. She held her arms out to me like she wanted me to remove her coat. I took a hold of her collar, and started to pull.

"Ah," she whined.

The lining of her coat was wet with blood and leeched to her back.

"Shit, Max. Why didn't you tell me you were hurt?"

Her voice was small and uneven when she answered, "I didn't think it was that bad."

It may not have been, but the blood had started to congeal, and taking off the coat was going to make her start bleeding again. She shifted, and even that small movement made her groan. I kept one hand on the collar of the coat and placed the other on her shoulder. "See if you can slip your arms out."

I tried to keep the garment still, but she winced a few times as she maneuvered her arms free. I guided her to lie down on her stomach on the futon.

She took a deep breath, and exhaled slowly.

"Just rip it off, Cade."

I knelt beside her and pushed a lock of hair out of her face. She didn't look nearly as brave as she sounded.

"As much as I like the idea of ripping off your clothes, I think I'd better not."

Her cheek was pressed flat against the futon, and she was only at half sass as she said, "Your loss."

I had no doubt about that.

"Hang on a second."

Her kitchen was as minuscule as the living room. I started opening cabinets, looking for a bowl. Max said, "You know you could just ask and I'll tell you where to look."

"It's more fun this way. Who knows what I'll find."

I found a large plastic bowl, and pulled it down. I turned on the tap and waited for it to get warm. I heard her laugh, and then groan on the other side of the couch.

"I hate to break it to you, but you won't find any dirty little secrets in there. Expired milk, maybe, but that's about it."

I filled up the bowl and found a washcloth in a drawer by the sink. I returned to the living room and asked, "Where might I find some of these dirty little secrets, then?"

She smiled and said, "I'm taking those with me to the grave. Sorry, Golden Boy."

I folded down the top part of the jacket, and she flinched.

"Sorry."

"It's okay," she whispered.

It didn't sound okay. I dipped the cloth in the warm water and wrung it out. I said, "Tell you what . . . I'll trade you a secret for part of my song."

I squeezed a little bit of water at the area where her skin met the lining of her coat, and started gently pulling it back.

She said, "Deal," and then swallowed a groan. I added more water, cleansing the skin as carefully as I could. The more I saw of her back the angrier I became. Her skin was already purpling in places, and I felt each scratch as if it was on my own skin. I inhaled sharply, and it felt like my lungs had been filled with fire. I couldn't see straight through my rage, and I wanted to go straight back to the bar and find that guy. He wasn't bleeding nearly enough.

I squeezed the washcloth in my fist and said, "Let's hear a secret then."

We both needed the distraction.

She took a deep breath and said, "I was a cheerleader in high school."

12

Max

You were a what?"

I always enjoyed shocking people with that, and it helped to distract a little bit from the pain.

"You heard me, Golden Boy. I was a cheerleader."

His hands paused in pulling the jacket from my back, and I was thankful for the reprieve.

"I'm trying to picture it," he said. "But I just . . ."

He trailed off and I asked, "What? Can't imagine me in a cheer skirt?"

"No, that's an image that I can conjure all too easily."

"Of course you can. Men." I rolled my eyes, but I didn't mind so much. There was something empowering about knowing that I could attract a guy like him. Even if he had no idea the crazy he was getting himself into.

"But seriously . . . a cheerleader?"

That seemed like a lifetime ago. A different me.

I hated thinking about the past. Every time I did, I felt heavy, like gravity had doubled and instead of just holding me to the Earth, it flattened me.

I couldn't explain why, but the words flowed with him. I said, "I spent a long time pretending to be something I wasn't."

He started pulling at the material again, and I could feel the stretch of my skin followed by the trickle of fresh blood. He wiped the cloth over the cut tenderly, but my skin was so sensitive. I tried my hardest to keep from flinching when he touched me, but I failed a few times.

"At least you stopped pretending. A lot of people don't."

Had I really? I'd just traded one kind of pretending for another.

I needed a distraction . . . from the past and the pain. I clenched my eyelids closed, and said, "Your turn, Golden Boy. Sing for me."

He dipped the washcloth in the bowl again, and I listened to the droplets falling as he wrung out the rag. The water was warm and soothing on my skin until he started pulling at the material again. I held my breath, and heard him start to sing.

His voice was strong and clear. He sang quietly, but the deep notes rumbled in his chest, and it gave me chills.

"No matter how close, you are always too far
My eyes are drawn everywhere you are."

His knuckles brushed my bare back, and my muscles tensed and shivered like a plucked guitar string. My breath caught in my throat, and I barely felt him pull my coat the rest of the way off.

He rewet the rag, and I waited for him to start singing again, but he didn't. He sponged at one scrape, and then another . . . silent.

"Is that all I get?" I asked. It wasn't nearly enough.

"As bizarre and . . . stimulating your cheertastic confession was, I'm going to need a little bit more before I start baring my soul."

I could hear the smile in his voice. The greedy bastard.

I gave an exaggerated sigh. "I can't think of what else to tell you."

"I believe the word *dirty* was thrown around earlier."

I was unnerved by how scared I was at the thought of spilling my secrets to him. Normally, I could care less what people thought of me, but with him it was different.

"I got my first kiss from my babysitter's son when I was five and he was seven. He kissed me and then pulled my hair."

He chuckled, and dabbed at a scrape just above the waistline of my skirt.

"We have different definitions of dirty."

I smirked and added, "To this day, nothing turns me on more than when a guy pulls my hair."

There was silence above me, and his hand stilled against my back. I would have killed to see his expression.

He cleared his throat, stood, and put a few feet between us. "Bandages?" he asked.

I'd reduced him to one-word communications.

"Bathroom cabinet. At the end of the hall."

I bit down on my lip but couldn't stop the wide smile that stretched across my face. I told myself that there was nothing wrong with a little harmless flirting between Cade and me as long as it didn't cross beyond that. Mace flirted with other girls all the time. Neither of us was the jealous type, so it was cool. And Cade would be out of my life after tomorrow anyway.

He took several minutes to return to the living room, and by then I'd convinced myself that being here alone with him wasn't a big deal. Our kiss wasn't a big deal. The nauseatingly goofy grin on my face *wasn't a big deal*. I deserved to relax and loosen up after the day I'd just had.

It was harmless, really.

"I found some ointment, gauze, tape, and scissors. I figured that would be better than individual bandages, since there are so many scratches. The good news is none of them are very deep. There are just a lot of them."

"Sounds fine. Now where's the rest of my song?"

He knelt beside me, and I could just see out of the corner of my eye the way his dark hair fell onto his forehead as he bent over me. I closed my eyes as he began rubbing the cool ointment on my skin.

"About that . . ." he began. "I really don't—"

"Come on, Cade. A deal's a deal. Besides . . . I'm in pain."

I lifted my head a little and gave him my best pout over my shoulder.

He glanced up at the ceiling and shook his head. "You're dangerous."

I liked danger. And this . . . this was addictive. Making him want me.

It was because it was wrong, because we were so different, that it felt so exhilarating. I laid my cheek against the cushion and closed my eyes, enjoying the luxurious feeling of his fingers coasting across my back.

"You might as well start again from the beginning," I said. "So I get the full effect."

It took a while for him to start singing, like he had to talk himself into it. But when he did, his voice was just as intoxicating the second time around. It was rich and resonant, and it rooted into my soul.

> *"No matter how close, you are always too far*
> *"My eyes are drawn everywhere you are."*

He paused again, and I thought he wouldn't go on, but then he pitched his voice higher, and I melted at the sound.

> *"I'm tired of the way we both pretend*
> *Tired of always wanting and never giving in*
> *I can feel it in my skin, see it in your grin*
> *We're more. We always have been.*
>
> *"Think of everything we've missed.*
> *Every touch and every kiss.*
> *Because we both insist.*
> *Resist."*

They were only words, but their effect on me was just as strong as the kiss we'd shared earlier in the evening. The anticipation of his touch was almost as exquisite as the contact itself. I had to concentrate to keep from arching up into his hands. He began taping gauze across sections of my back, and I lived for the moments when his finger would smooth the tape down and graze my skin.

> *"Hold your breath and close your eyes*
> *Distract yourself with other guys*
> *It's no surprise, your defeated sighs*
> *Aren't you tired of the lies?"*

His volume had grown, and I felt nailed down by his words, trapped by his hands. I knew this song wasn't for me. It couldn't be. We'd only met today. But just because the song wasn't *for* me, didn't mean it wasn't about me.

> *"Think of everything we've missed.*
> *Every touch and every kiss.*
> *Because we both insist.*
> *Resist."*

I could feel his breath against my bare skin as he sang, and my whole body tensed. I couldn't even pretend I wasn't affected anymore. It took all my concentration just to keep breathing.

> *"No matter how close, you are always too far*
> *My eyes are drawn everywhere you are."*

He placed the last bandage, smoothed down the tape, then his finger continued on, tracing the line of my spine. My skin broke out in goose bumps, and I tried to smother a moan into the cushion, but he had to have heard.

> *"I'm done. I won't ignore.*
> *I won't pretend or resist."*

His hand settled at the base of my back. The last line was half-sung, half-spoken, and I was half-mad with desire.

> *"I want more."*

13

Cade

I was playing with fire, touching her like this. My hand was resting just above the curve of her behind, and I swear she arched her hips back into my palm.

My voice was low and rough as I said, "All done."

If I were a superstitious man, I would think I'd angered Milo's alcohol gods because I was having a very *inconvenient* reaction to our closeness.

I moved my hand, and was ready to make a quick getaway, but she sat up and said, "Wait, let me do you."

I tried to keep a straight face, I really did. But no male in my condition, whether he's fifteen or fifty, could hear those words and not react.

She rolled her eyes and said, "Your head, Golden boy. The one that's *supposed* to do your thinking."

God, she was so different from Bliss. I could envision completely how this scenario would have happened with her. It would have started with a lot of blushing and mumbling and probably would have ended with something broken or on fire.

Max was honest. Unafraid. She was so comfortable in her skin.

And it was sexy as hell.

"Let me get a new cloth."

She stood and took the washcloth and water into the kitchen with her. I sat on the couch, and did my best to adjust myself so that my predicament wasn't glaringly obvious.

I'd tried to talk her out of the song because I thought it was a bad idea. I thought it would bring up memories of Bliss, but it didn't. In fact, singing it hadn't made me think of Bliss at all. I could only think about Max, and that caused an entirely different problem than the one I'd expected.

I kept my eyes focused forward when she returned because I didn't trust myself not to touch her again. She pulled one of her knees up onto the couch, and slid closer to me. Her knee pressed against my thigh, and all I wanted to do was grab her other leg and lift her over onto my lap.

I searched for something, anything, to distract me, but there was nothing in this apartment to look at. There was only us and the electrifying heat that filled the space between us.

Her fingers touched my chin, and she turned my face

toward her. She was staring at a wound on my forehead, so I had a few seconds to drink her in without getting caught. Her cheeks were flushed, probably from the pain, and her lips pulled down into a frown as she surveyed my injury. And her eyes were the kind of light blue that you only see on wild, untouched beaches.

"I should have taken care of you first. You're still bleeding a little."

I was? It didn't even hurt anymore. There were too many other things on my mind.

Her fingers shifted on my chin, brushing across the stubble that I hadn't bothered to shave this morning. Her eyes met mine for a flicker of a second before she pulled away and began dipping the washcloth in the water.

I watched her small hands and delicate fingers as they wrung out the rag, and then folded it into a small rectangle. She slid even closer when she turned back to me, so that her knee was almost resting on top of my leg. I was already facing her, but her hand found my jaw anyway. She cleaned the area around the wound first, and then started dabbing at the cut just along my hairline.

She used the hand on my jaw to tilt my head down slightly to give her a better look. It pointed my eyes straight to the delicate architecture of her collarbone, which had been the last place I'd kissed her.

I was dying to pick back up again where I left off.

That must not have been enough to give her a good look because she shifted, and rose up on her knees next to me. Her chest was level with my gaze, and her body swayed toward mine.

I closed my eyes and thought about multiplication tables and recited lines from plays that I'd been in over the years. Her breath fanned across my forehead, and I could feel the warmth of her skin only inches away from mine. She stopped dabbing and just pressed the cloth to my forehead, probably to stop the bleeding.

Her voice was low and warm when she said, "You wrote that song for a girl?"

"Is this you implying that I'm gay again?"

She laughed, and I wanted to sweep her into my arms, lay her down on this couch, and map out every bit of her skin with my mouth. I wanted to taste every tattoo, and know what they meant to her. I wanted to unlock the secrets that lay behind her guarded expression.

"No, I just mean . . . was she a girlfriend?"

I shook my head. "No, she wasn't. By the time I decided to do something about it, she was already with someone else."

"So you gave up?"

This was not what I wanted to talk about, but I guess if it kept my mind off of kissing her, it worked.

"There was no point," I said. "I couldn't compete."

"Bullshit." She pressed down a little harder, and jerked my face a little closer to her own. "You're Golden Boy. You're good at everything. You're sweet, gorgeous, and probably stop to help little old ladies cross the street. If you can't compete, the rest of us are completely fucked."

I smiled. Hearing her say I was gorgeous was a pretty good consolation prize.

"The other guy is British."

She tossed her head back and laughed, and my eyes caught on the smooth line of her neck.

"Yeah, you're shit out of luck, Golden Boy."

It felt good to be able to laugh about this with someone. I hadn't even been able to do that with Milo or any of my friends back home. This morning losing Bliss had seemed like a weight shackled to my feet, and now it felt like what it was—a memory.

She was still smiling when she lifted the cloth from my forehead.

She hummed and said, "Looks good."

She sat back, and the hand on my face dropped to my thigh. She used it to brace herself as she reached for the gauze. Sweet Jesus.

I searched for something, anything to say. "It's been an . . . interesting day."

Considering I'd only met her this morning, and I was ten miles past fascinated into obsessed territory, yeah. I'd say the day had been pretty damn interesting.

"Tomorrow will make today look like a cakewalk," she said.

She cut a piece of gauze, and raised back up on her knees to place it on my head.

"Why do you hate the holidays so much? Do your parents go way overboard?"

She pressed tape to the edges of the bandage and started smoothing it down, and her other hand rested on my shoulder for balance.

"It's hard to explain."

"I think I can keep up."

She reached for the rag again and started cleaning more blood off my face. With her eyes focused on her work, she said, "The holidays bring up bad memories for us. My parents think if they pretend enough and have enough decorations and food that they won't think so much about the things they don't have."

"And that doesn't work for you?"

Her eyes met mine for a few seconds.

"Nothing works for me. But music."

I brought my hand up and placed it over hers that rested on my shoulder

"I'm sorry."

She looked down at me, and her eyes searched mine. "Normally, I hate it when people say that, but . . ."

The damp rag skimmed across my cheek to the cut on my mouth. Her eyes were dark, and her lips parted. She dabbed at the cut carefully. I watched the movement of her throat as she swallowed.

Slowly, so slowly that it felt like a dream, her hand turned so that the backs of her knuckles trailed across my lips. Her eyes were open and clear. We were both sober. One of my hands found her hip, and her chest brushed against my shoulder as she leaned over me.

I could feel her breath on my lips, and her eyes were dilated with desire. She bit her lip, and I held in a groan. Her eyes dropped to my lips, and the rag dropped to the floor.

Then her phone rang.

She jumped back so quickly that she was across the room

before I'd released the breath that had been caught in my chest.

She picked up her phone, and her expression was blank as she said, "It's my boyfriend."

I swallowed, but my mouth still felt as dry as the desert.

The universe was doing us both a favor. I didn't want to make her into a cheater. Kissing her earlier had been bad enough.

"I should be going anyway."

I crossed to the door as quickly as possible, and she called back to me, "Cade!" I pulled the door open wide, and looked back at her. She held the phone in her hand, ready to answer. She said, "I'm sorry."

"Don't be. I'm not." She took a small step toward me, and I turned. "I'll see you in the morning."

14

Max

This was a catastrofuck of colossal proportions.

I hit accept and said, "Hi, babe." The sound on his end was garbled and booming. He must have been in some kind of club because the music was blasting. "Mace?"

"Maxi Pad!"

And . . . he was drunk.

"We've talked about this, Mace. There are funny nicknames, and there are atrocious ones. That one is the latter."

"Maxi . . . Come meet me at Pure."

Shit, if he was there, he'd probably been popping pills rather than downing beer.

"I can't, Mace."

"Yes, you can. Christ, Max, this shit is awesome. You have to come try it."

Just as I thought. I wasn't judging him. I'd done too many screwed-up things over the years to do that, but I didn't have room for that kind of stuff in my life. If I dealt with my pain that way, there would be no reason to put it into my music instead, and then I'd be left with nothing.

"Listen, Mace, I had a really rough day at work."

"I'll take your mind off of it." His voice was gravelly and slurred. His voice normally made me weak in the knees. Not tonight. I wasn't up for any kind of solution he had to offer.

"No, Mace. I'm just going to go to sleep."

"Fuck, Max. First, you bail on me this morning."

"My parents are in town, and *you* bailed on *me*."

He didn't even listen to me, just kept right on talking. "Now, you won't even come out when I won't see you at all tomorrow."

I couldn't deal with this right now. It took all of my control not to just hang up the phone.

"I can't, okay? We'll talk when you're sober. Good night."

I clicked the phone off and sank down onto the couch. I pressed the cool phone screen to my heated cheek, and placed my other hand on the cushion beside me. There were so many thoughts running through my head—thoughts about Mace and Cade. But it had been a long, emotional day. I wasn't stupid enough to let myself make a decision in the heat of the moment. Even if I could still feel Cade's hands on my back, and his face beneath my fingertips when I closed my eyes.

Catastrofuck. Definitely.

All I wanted to do was take a shower, but then I'd screw up the bandages on my back. Instead, I shucked off my clothes and fell into bed and oblivion.

He tugged on my hair, and I felt the pull run down my spine all the way to my toes. He pulled my head back, and his lips came down on my neck. He dragged his mouth softly down the column of my throat, and then his teeth grazed my collarbone.

I moaned embarrassingly loud.

He rewarded me with another nip of his teeth.

I burrowed my hands underneath his shirt, and dug my fingers into his lower back. His hips pressed forward into mine, and I could feel his muscles flexing beneath my palms.

He left my collarbone, and nosed aside my shirt, kissing down my sternum. His tongue dragged across one of the branches on my tattoo, and I felt like I was burning alive. His stubble scratched against my sensitive skin, and my legs went weak.

"Please," I begged.

"We shouldn't," he whispered.

I pulled his mouth to mine, determined to convince him. I wrapped an arm around his neck, and a leg around his hips, and pulled him into me. He steadied himself with one hand against the wall, and the other on my ass.

"Yes," I hissed between kisses.

His kiss was intoxicating. Slow and fast. Soft and hard. I melted into him, happy to follow his lead.

He pulled back again. "You're sure?"

Dear God, yes!

I nodded, and he spun me from the wall onto a bed. His hands ran up my legs, raising goose bumps and making me squirm. His fingers hooked around the fabric of my panties and pulled them down gently. My shirt was already gone, disappeared somewhere in the frenzy. He pressed his hips into mine, and my eyes rolled back in my head. Then the whole world rolled, and I was astride his hips. His messy hair looked so good against my pillow, and his brown eyes were so dark they were nearly black.

He slipped his hands underneath the frills of my skirt, gripped my thighs, and said, "Ride me."

What was it about a nice boy saying naughty things that was so damn hot?

I threw my head back and groaned.

"Max."

"Oh God," I whimpered.

His hands traced my jaw, then gripped my face hard.

"Max, are you okay?"

God, yes.

I was so far beyond okay that I couldn't even string together a sentence.

Hands gripped my shoulders, and the world spun. I opened my eyes, and I was no longer on top. Cade was hovering above me, entirely too far away. I reached a hand out toward his jaw.

That was odd. His stubble was gone. He'd shaved.

I hooked my hand around his neck, and pulled him closer.

He resisted, only for a second, but it was enough to give me pause. I blinked. My mouth was dry, and my head felt foggy.

His eyes were on my lips, and his expression pained. "Max . . ."

He pulled away from me, but I kept my hand wrapped around his neck. His movement pulled me up into a sitting position.

His took me in, and his eyes went dark. He exhaled sharply. "Oh fuck me."

That was the plan, but his voice sounded strained, not seductive.

He averted his eyes to the ceiling, and plucked my hand from the back of his neck. I pulled my hand free, and let it run down his chest.

He didn't pull my hand off of him this time, but he said, his voice low and gravelly, "Golden Boy nickname aside, I'm not a saint, Max."

His body was stiff next to mine. I rubbed at my eyes, and slowly the world started to resurface. I was in my bed. In my apartment. Light filtered in through the window, and Cade was sitting on my bed, *fully clothed,* staring at the wall like it was Hitler.

Oh holy Hell, I was dreaming. I'd just put the moves on him in my sleep! I covered my mouth with my hand and racked my brain to try to remember if I'd said anything that would give me away.

When the shock wore off, I let my hand drop to my chest, where my fingertips touched bare skin.

I looked down and had to resist the urge to scream.

I WAS NAKED.

Like, gave him a look at my full-tree tattoo, naked.

Like, curl into the fetal position and die of mortification, naked.

I jerked the covers from my waist up to my chin. Beside me, Cade let out a long breath, and his shoulders relaxed.

As calmly as possible I asked, "What is going on?"

Inside, I was anything but calm. Only a sheet and a few measly articles of clothing on his part separated me from him, and my mind was still fogged with dream-induced desire. And to be honest, I was a little offended that he managed to look away.

A small, crazy part of me wanted to drop the sheet again and see how long his resolve could last. Cade pushed himself to his feet, and moved all the way across the room.

He said, "I knocked, but you didn't answer. I was outside, and I heard you groan. It sounded like you were hurt or sick." He looked back at me, and now I knew how he'd managed to look away from me . . . guilt. He hadn't even done anything wrong! I was the one having pervy dreams about him, and I didn't feel the least bit guilty. He said, "I swear, the door was unlocked, so I came in to check on you. I swear, I wasn't trying *anything*. I'm sorry."

I wondered if I dropped the sheet now if he would try something. My body was wound so tight, I felt like I'd been dangling off the edge of a cliff for hours. And I *wanted* him to try something. I shook my head. I was so turned on that just the brush of the sheets against my chest made my breath catch in my throat.

No. Bad Max. You're with Mace. Focus.

I must have forgotten to set my alarm before I went to bed.

The alarm had been important, but for the life of me, I couldn't remember the reason. I looked at Cade, and his eyes focused on the sheet fisted in my hands and held in front of my chest. A chill ran down my back, raising goose bumps. I shifted and *may* have turned my bare back toward him *slightly*. I saw his eyes go to the curve of my spine, and he swallowed.

The devil made me do it.

And by devil, I mean my uterus.

He took a step toward me, and I smiled gleefully for a few seconds.

Then I remembered why my alarm had been so important . . . and why he was even here.

Thanksgiving.

Thanksgiving *plus* my parents.

Thanksgiving plus my parents plus me *naked* in a room with Cade.

That equaled disaster.

My seduction plan forgotten, I slid off the bed, careful to keep the sheet wrapped around my body. "Shit. What time is it?"

He pulled his phone out of his pocket. "Almost nine."

SHIT.

Right on cue, the buzzer on my apartment rang. I heard my mother call through the door. "Mackenzie, sweetie!"

And then, because I was the dumbass who couldn't remember to lock her apartment, I heard the door swing open, followed by another "Sweetie?"

It was like one of those God-awful zombie movies, where you can hear them coming and you have nowhere to go. You just have to make peace with getting your brain eaten.

Mom was the zombie, and if she walked in here to find me naked with a boy, even a Golden Boy, both our brains would end up barbecued.

"Um, just a second, Mom!"

Shit. I went to run my hands through my hair, but forgot I was holding a sheet, which then slipped.

Cade made a noise in the back of his throat, and turned away. My hormone-riddled body really liked that sound, but this was *not the time*!

Shit. Shit. Shit. Shit.

I must have uttered at least one of those out loud because Cade said, "It's okay. I'll go out and talk with them while you get ready."

"You don't understand! If you come out of my room, and then I go take a shower, my parents are going to assume you and I are sleeping together."

"So don't take a shower. You look beautiful just how you are."

His eyes slipped down to take in my sheet, and he didn't even look sorry. Where had all that guilt gone?

Down girl. Still not the time.

"I smell like smoke and alcohol and sweat, which is just as bad. Plus, bed head looks just like sex hair."

He stepped up and rested his hands on my shoulders. It was meant to be reassuring, but it was bare skin on bare skin, which didn't relax me at all. As twisted as it was, something about this whole situation still had me turned on. A small part of me *liked* that we could get caught, even if there wasn't really a "we," and no actual sex had been had.

"I'll tell them the truth," he said. "You overslept. I just got here."

"Yeah. Like they'll believe that."

His thumbs stroked my shoulders softly, and my body almost wilted.

"I'll make them believe. I promise."

He stepped away like he hadn't just caressed my bare skin, and I wasn't naked beneath my sheet. His expression was calm and unreadable. It was like he wasn't affected at all.

Were some men of a different species? Did they have different DNA that enabled them to be so much better than other guys?

I resisted the urge to drop my sheet again just to get a reaction out of him. I closed my eyes, and nodded. I kept my eyes closed as he slipped out of the room so that I wouldn't do something stupid. I stood there, frozen and turned on, even after I heard him greet my parents.

It was going to be a long day.

15

Cade

For the second time in this apartment, I had a very awkward problem at a very inappropriate time.

If given the choice between facing Max's parents like this and jumping into an active volcano, I would have to make a serious pros and cons list.

I took a few seconds to focus, even though I knew a few seconds would never be enough to get the sight of Max out of my head. She was exquisite, and my self-control was a thin line at the moment. Even now, I was fighting the urge to go back in there and kiss her, which was not helping me fight the other problem I had going on.

I shook my head to clear my thoughts, adjusted myself as best I could, and walked down the hall into the living room.

Please God don't let Max's mother try to hug me.

Max's mother gave a shrill squeal when she saw me. "Cade! I didn't know you were here."

She was wrestling a turkey out of a cooler, and left it to come toward me for what I could only assume was a hug.

I moved like she was one of the Philadelphia Eagles coming in for a tackle, and darted around her.

"Here, let me get that for you!" I bolted for the turkey in the cooler, and used that as my excuse. I stepped right up to the counter, thankful for the cover that it gave me. When she didn't call me on it, I breathed a sigh of relief and started trying to free the poultry.

The turkey was squishy and smelled like, well, raw meat. It helped diffuse my issue a little bit.

It was a big bird, and it was a tight fit in the cooler.

Tight fit.

Don't go there, brain. You were doing so good.

I said the alphabet in my head to distract me as I pried the turkey free. It took a few minutes, but I was almost completely under control by the time I got the bird loose.

"Where do you want it, Mrs. M?"

Mick had just finished piling the last of their things on the kitchen table. It looked like they had brought a whole apartment with them. She grabbed a large pan, and brought it over to the counter beside me.

"Right in here, if you please."

I did as she asked, then rinsed my hands in the sink.

I still had my coat and scarf on. Time to tell the truth and hope I could sell it. "Mackenzie overslept." I figured throwing out Max's real name might help, considering their refusal to call her by her nickname. "I actually just got here a few minutes before you guys." I unhooked my scarf from my neck, hoping it would lend credence to my story. "She was working late last night, and must have worn herself out."

Don't go there either, brain. Focus.

I slipped off my coat, too, and then realized I had no idea where to put it. Did Max have a coat closet? Her parents weren't wearing theirs. Where had they put them? Our whole story was going to come tumbling down because I didn't know where to hang my coat. There were two doors that could be closets. Or they could be bathrooms or laundry rooms or who knows what.

"So, Mackenzie is getting dressed now?" Her mother's brow furrowed, and I imagined her thinking the things Max had been afraid of.

"I think she might be taking a shower, actually. I told her not to worry about it, but I think she wants to look nice for you guys."

Hopefully she wouldn't come out in sweatpants or something.

"Do you think she wants to take pictures?" Mrs. Miller's eyes lit up like Christmas had come early. Ah, well, that seemed to distract her pretty well.

"I think so. It is our first Thanksgiving together, after all. I think it's something we should commemorate."

I took a chance and opened one of the doors in the living room. BINGO! Coat closet. Day = saved.

I was sliding my coat on a hanger when Mrs. M attacked

me from behind. Her arms went around my middle and squeezed so hard, I thought she was trying to give me the Heimlich.

"I am just *so happy* you came into Mackenzie's life. Even after only a few weeks, you've had such a wonderful influence on her. She never lets me take pictures of her."

Well, damn.

Max was going to be furious.

I smiled and said, "Oh, I don't think I've changed her. She was amazing before me, and is amazing now."

"Mick? Are you listening to this wonderful boy? You could afford to take some lessons from him!"

Mick heaved himself up off the couch and came into the kitchen. "You're making the rest of us look bad, son."

"I'm sorry, sir."

Mrs. M swatted her husband on the arm.

"Don't you dare listen to him, Cade."

"Yes, ma'am."

I sighed. I had a feeling this would be happening a lot today.

I watched Mrs. M putter around the kitchen. I offered to help a few times, but she always waved me off. When she wasn't cooking, she was decorating Max's empty apartment. She'd brought throw pillows and afghans and picture frames. I was beginning to understand that Max was the complete opposite of her parents . . . probably because she *wanted* to be the complete opposite of her parents.

"Where are you from, Cade?"

"Texas, ma'am."

"Oh, where at? We live in Oklahoma!"

"I grew up in Fort Worth."

"And your parents are still there?"

I fidgeted, scratching at the back of my neck.

"My grandmother, actually. My mother died, and my dad isn't really in the picture."

She stopped, her hand still shoved up inside the turkey, and looked at me.

"Oh, honey. Bless your heart."

"It's okay," I said. "I was young. I don't really even remember her. Besides, I have my grandmother. That's enough."

She used her turkey-free hand to gesture me closer. "Come here."

I took a few steps, and she kept waving me closer until I was right beside her. Then with one hand still intimately exploring the inside of a turkey, she wrapped her other arm around me in a hug.

She said, "It doesn't matter if you don't remember your mother. I'm still so sorry for the things you had to face. It must have been difficult."

It was weird, but the awkward turkey hug did make me feel better. I got why Max was so weird about her parents, but I would have given anything to have parents that would show up unannounced and intrude upon my life. Grams was too old to do anything like that, though I'm sure she would if she could.

"Um . . . *what* is happening right now?"

Mrs. M released me and I stepped away from her and the turkey. Max stood at the end of the hallway. I guess she decided against the shower. Her choppy red hair was styled calmer than I had ever seen it. She was wearing a turtleneck sweater that covered her multitude of tattoos. She was wearing less makeup, too. She looked like herself, still, but at maybe 25 percent of her normal vibrancy.

I missed the real her.

"Oh, nothing, dear," Max's mom said. "Cade just told me about his parents."

"Right. His parents," Max said. She shot me a wide-eyed look.

So, I changed the subject. "Mrs. Miller, tell me what Max was like as a child."

Max groaned. Her mother practically cheered.

"I just happen to have baby pictures with me! I keep a photo album with me at all times." Max stalked into the kitchen and threw herself down on the stool beside me.

"Yay. Baby pictures. What a great idea, *sweetheart.*" She laced her fingers with mine, and then lightly dug her fingernails into the back of my hand in warning. All I could think about was what it would feel like to have her fingernails dig into my skin under different circumstances.

I pulled her hand up to my mouth, and kissed the back. Her eyes widened, and she sucked in a breath. I smiled evilly and said, "Oh, *honey,* you can't blame me for wanting to see your baby pictures."

While her mother was distracted in the living room finding the album, Max leaned into my ear and said, "You bet your ass I can blame you. You're not funny, Golden Boy."

"Really? I thought it was hysterical."

"Later, when we're alone—"

"—I like the sound of that."

She laughed loudly in the direction of the living room,

totally fake, and then turned on me. "Don't think I won't murder you, pretty boy."

"So, I was golden and now I'm pretty?"

She took another deep inhale, and I imagined she was counting to keep her anger under control. I liked her like this. With her cheeks pink and her eyes sparkling, she looked like herself despite the major style change.

"I can't help it. It's just so much fun to get you riled up."

"You really want to play that game?"

"Here we go!" Her mother flitted into the room and slid the album in front of us.

The first picture was of the day they brought Max home from the hospital. The nursery was a mishmash of different pinks and had MACKENZIE painted across one wall. Max looked like most babies—small with a pink, pinched face, and no hair. Mrs. Miller had fluffy, curled bangs and looked like something out of *I Love the '80s.*

"Mrs. Miller, I have to say, you don't look a day older now than you did then."

She giggled, and swatted me on the shoulder. "Oh, stop."

Max untangled her hand from mine and said under her breath, "Really, please stop."

Max took control of the album and flipped through the book quickly, giving me barely any time to look at the pictures, but one thing was obvious. Max's parents never let her be herself when she was younger. They dressed her in pink, frilly things that you could tell she didn't like. Her hair was blond and always curled in perfect ringlets.

I leaned into her ear and whispered, "You're naturally blond? It's getting easier every minute to picture you in that cheer uniform." If looks could take physical form, the one she gave me would have been a bitch slap.

She looked picture-perfect in every photo. Like a Barbie doll, and her smile in each was just as plastic. She was beautiful, but sad. She flipped the page, and I was treated to the real Cheerleader Max mid toe-touch.

"And now I no longer have to picture it."

Her glare stayed firmly in place, but her lips curled up at the end slightly.

"Did you play sports?" Mrs. Miller asked me.

"I did, yes. Football and basketball."

Max paused in turning the page and said, "Really?"

"I did grow up in Texas. Plus, I was good at it."

She laughed. "Of course you were."

"I bet you were a great cheerleader."

"Great? Not really. Nearly homicidal? Sure."

I got to see her in a bubblegum pink prom dress and graduation robes. We were approaching the end of the book, and I kept waiting for a more recent picture of her with her new, non-Barbie look. They never came. The album just ended, as if the last few years had never existed. I saw the relief written across her features when she flipped the last page. It was replaced by shock and something else I couldn't identify when she saw a final picture taped to the inside of the back of the book.

It was a family photo, and she looked twelve, maybe thirteen. She had that distinctive preteen glare down pat. Behind her was a guy I assumed was her brother. He had the same blond hair and wore a letterman jacket. On the end was a girl, probably sixteen or seventeen that was the spitting image of Max. Or I guess it was the other way around, since her sister was older.

"Your brother and sister?" I asked.

Something in Max's expression fractured. She spun to face her mother, and her expression was terrifying and terrified.

"No. We're not doing this! Do you hear me? If this is why you came, you can leave." She slammed the album shut, and stormed back into her bedroom.

I expected her mother to act shocked or upset, but she calmly picked up the album and returned it to her things, like she was picking up a book and returning it to the shelf. She walked back into the living room and took down a picture she'd placed on the coffee table, too.

I wasn't sure exactly what was going on, but I knew it had something to do with what Max mentioned about holidays the night before. And whatever it was, it had Max broken up into tiny little pieces that I hadn't glimpsed until just now.

16

Max

I didn't know whether to scream or cry, throw things or col-
lapse to the ground. There was something about my mother
that made me feel fourteen and pissed off all over again. I
hated it, but I couldn't seem to turn it off either. She just
couldn't ever leave it alone.

I didn't need pictures of Alex all over the place to remember her. I saw her on the subway, at concerts, passing me
in the street. I saw her when I closed my eyes. I used to see her
when I looked in the mirror, before I'd changed my hair and
inked my skin. I could see her reflected in Mom's eyes every

time she looked at me, like if she just wished hard enough she could make us trade places and get the good daughter back.

It didn't matter how many times I said it, Mom always tried to make the holidays about Alex. She wanted to talk about the time Alexandria did this or when she said that. Mom brought her up so much that she was like this phantom sitting there at the dinner table that sucked all of the happiness and all the normal conversation into the realm of non-existence with her.

Forget wishing I were dead. Mom made me feel that way already. Hell, she already had the photo album ready to show the world her other blond princess, never mind that I hadn't been that girl in a long time. No one wanted to see pictures of this Max. Just Mackenzie.

What was wrong with letting the past stay the past? Why did we have to drag all our issues with us into the future? I couldn't breathe out there for all the ghosts Mom hauled in with her. I didn't fit in that world, and the more I tried, the more I felt like I didn't fit *anywhere*.

I was lying on my bed, my face pressed into a pillow when I felt the mattress dip. I knew it had to be Cade. Mom never followed me after fights, easier to pretend they weren't happening. And Dad steered clear of all things that involved emotion. I pulled myself up on my elbows and looked over my shoulder to see him seated gingerly on the very edge of my mattress. He'd left several feet between us.

I rolled over onto my back and waited for him to say something. To ask questions.

He didn't. He lay down beside me, still careful to keep a buffer zone between us. He put one forearm behind his head, and stared up at the ceiling in silence. This close I could see how broad his shoulders were. I mean, I'd felt them, but I hadn't gotten a chance to really *look* at him. His arms were muscular and his chest wide. I watched the way his body moved as he inhaled and exhaled. The rhythm was calming.

Watching his chest rise and fall was soothing enough that my anger just kind of drifted away. His eyes were closed and his face relaxed when he said, "I let people go."

I sat up on my elbow and looked at him, but his eyes remained closed.

"Um . . . if you're referencing the Bible and that whole let-my-people-go thing . . . I'm not getting the connection."

One side of his mouth quirked up, and he sighed.

"Last night you asked why I didn't fight for the girl from the song. It's because I let people go."

I had no idea what he was talking about, but I approved, as long as we didn't have to talk about me.

"Always?"

"These days, yeah. When I was younger, I fought and lost too many times."

I wanted him to open his eyes and look at me. This somber, closed-off Cade was disconcerting. I was in a dark enough place by myself, and seeing him like this pushed me even deeper. I never knew what to do in situations like this, so I decided to take his lead and stay silent.

I wasn't thinking about the attraction between us. I was only thinking about comforting him when I slid closer and laid my head on his chest.

Maybe I was thinking of comfort for myself, too.

After a few seconds, the arm he'd had beneath his head

came down around me. His fingertips rested on my hip, and I released a breath I'd been holding captive.

Just when I'd settled into the silence and the comfort of our closeness, he said, "My first memory of my dad is of him leaving. I was five and I asked him not to go. I begged him actually." He breathed out in something that was almost a laugh . . . a sad one anyway. "He was gone by morning. My mom died less than a year later." He closed his eyes, and I could tell he was somewhere else. He wasn't with me anymore. "She had cancer, and it was like she just . . . stopped fighting. I wasn't enough to make her want to stay."

The grief came out of nowhere and knocked me sideways. Tears pressed at my eyes, and my throat burned with the effort of fighting down the emotions. I hadn't cried in a long time, but the thought of Cade as a child, probably just as good and perfect as he is now, facing those things . . . it hurt. I was used to turning a blind eye to my own emotions. I was so practiced in the art that it came easily. But I'd never had to worry about anyone else's. I'd never been close enough to someone for it to matter. It took all of my self-control to push the emotions back behind my walls.

There were so many things to say that sat just on the edge of my tongue. But all of them seemed like too little and too much at the same time. So, I just held him tighter, and kept my eyes closed until the tears passed.

He laughed, but it wasn't the laugh that I was used to hearing, the one that turned all eyes toward him. This laugh was bitter and broken.

"When my dad came home for the funeral, I assumed he would take me with him. I imagined what my room would be like in his new house. I stressed about whether or not his new girlfriend would like me. I was so determined to make it work that time. But he left then, too, and I went to live with my grandma."

I listened to his heartbeat beneath my ear, and all I could think was—how much of a dick do you have to be to leave your kid even after he loses his mother? I'd never been any good at holding my tongue, and now was no exception.

I said, "At least we know douchebaggery isn't hereditary."

I was seconds away from suggesting a road trip to find his father and put the bastard in his place. His hand smoothed up and down my spine like he was comforting me, instead of the other way around.

Then I realized . . . he was.

A lot of things pissed me off about my parents and about Alex's death, but nothing upset me more than the fact that I felt alone in my pain. I mean, I knew my parents missed her. I knew they thought about her constantly, but it was with this happy kind of sadness that was completely foreign to me. When I thought about Alex, it was pure, undiluted pain. It felt like my insides had been rearranged, like I still had internal trauma from the wreck. All these years later, just the image behind my closed eyes of her was enough to make me feel like I was bleeding out. I couldn't understand why everyone else didn't feel this way, and it made me furious.

But I could tell from the way the muscles of Cade's chest and stomach flexed below me . . . he felt it, too. I did the same thing—flexed the muscles of my body like armor. Tendons and tissue were the only things keeping the mess inside me at bay. The only thing worse than feeling this way was putting all those emotions on display for the world to see.

For the first time in a long time, maybe since Alex, I didn't feel so alone.

I took a deep breath and said, "My sister died."

The hand on my back slid up into my hair. Any other time that would have sent my hormones into a rave, but now it was just soft and sweet, and it flipped a switch in the back of my mind that I spent most of my days trying to turn off.

The vision of that day in my mind never wavered or faded. It was as vivid today as it was then. When I let the memories get the best of me, I could almost imagine the blinding headlights, the sound of glass shattering, and the pressure of the seat belt cutting into my neck. I squeezed my eyes shut.

I couldn't hold back the images, but I could hold back the tears.

Cade didn't try to make me talk. He didn't ask questions. His touch remained firm and constant, keeping me tethered here in the present. We lay there, wound together so tightly that I didn't have to keep my muscles tense. I didn't need the armor because he was holding me together.

After what could have been an eternity or a few seconds, Cade whispered, "Pain changes us. Mine made me want to be perfect, so that no one would ever want to leave me again."

I inhaled deeply. "Yours made you Golden. Mine just made me angry."

One of his hands found my jaw, and he lifted my head up enough to face him.

"Your pain made you strong. It made you passionate and alive. It made us both who we are."

A laugh pushed its way past the pain that lived in my lungs, and escaped from my throat. "Golden Boy and Angry Girl."

"We should make a comic book about our adventures."

The laugh came easier then.

It was funny how a guy who'd known me for so little time managed to put me at ease in a way that my parents, friends, and a string of therapists never had.

"Thank you," I murmured. I returned my cheek to his chest but tilted my face up toward his. "For this . . . for today and yesterday. I don't know what I would have done if you weren't here. I know you probably had somewhere better to be—"

"Trust me. This was much better than the alternative. I'm exactly where I want to be." He glanced down at me and gave me a half-smile.

I walked my fingers over his stomach and asked, "And what was the alternative?"

"Spending time with someone better left in my past. I prefer moving forward."

For the first time, moving forward felt like a possibility.

We stayed there in a sanctuary of our own making, at ease without speaking. We'd done all the talking we needed, and slowly I drifted off to sleep with Golden Boy beside me in bed.

17

Cade

A bright light flashed on the other side of my closed eyelids. Groggily, I went to rub my eyes, but something had
my left arm pinned to the bed.

A woman stood over me with a camera in her hand. Black
spots flooded my vision, and it took me a few moments before
I remembered where I was and what I was doing here. The
woman with the camera was Mrs. Miller, and she'd just taken
a picture of Max sound asleep on my arm. There was a little
wet spot on my sweater from her drool.

God, I wanted a copy of that picture.

Mrs. Miller held a finger to her lips and whispered, "I'm sorry. The two of you just looked so sweet that I couldn't resist." This was officially the weirdest day of my existence. "Dinner is ready. Mick and I will wait for you two to get freshened up."

She tiptoed out of the room and closed the door on her way out.

Time to wake the sleeping dragon.

In sleep, Max looked younger, softer. She had long eyelashes that rested against her cheeks. Her nose was small and turned up slightly at the end. Even sleeping, she had the sexiest lips I had ever seen. Full and slightly puckered, it was like they were calling to me. And I couldn't stop thinking about her saying she wasn't sorry I kissed her.

Not that it mattered. She was taken.

I was doomed to always be attracted to the girls I couldn't have.

Plus, what she'd told me earlier . . . it couldn't have been easy. I could tell how raw the memories left her, and the last thing I wanted was to take advantage of that tenderness.

I was about to nudge her awake when her eyes opened, and she caught me staring at her. She blinked a few times and then her eyes narrowed on me. She sat up and slid to the complete opposite side of the bed.

"What are you doing?" she asked.

Whatever closeness we'd gained earlier didn't appear to have carried over through her nap. The walls were back up and I was still on the outside.

"I swear it's not as creepy as it looks."

"Said the serial killer to the police."

Her hair was messy and closer to how it usually was.

I said, "I was about to wake you up. Your mother just said dinner is ready."

"My *mother* was in here?"

I was coming to enjoy that wide-eyed exasperated look she got every time something concerned her mother.

"She might have taken a picture of us."

She grabbed a pillow, and I narrowly blocked a swipe to the face.

"You let her take a picture of us?"

I grabbed the pillow when she went in for a second swing, and used it to pull her closer. "I didn't *let* her. I woke up to the flash."

"Seriously?" She made a noise that was part groan/part growl and buried her face in her hands. "Kill me now."

I kept the pillow between us as a buffer and said, "It's almost over."

"You've not been to one of my mother's Thanksgiving dinners. It's only just beginning."

She slid off the bed and went to the bathroom to splash her face with water. I followed and did the same. It was frighteningly domestic as we both tried to maneuver around the small space without bumping into each other. I was struck by the oddity that I had known this woman just over twenty-four hours. And twenty-four hours from now, we would likely go our separate ways, never to hear from each other again.

I swallowed, and she looked at me from the bathroom door.

"Well, are you coming?"

"Yeah, right behind you."

CORA CARMACK

We were ambushed with another photo attack as soon as we entered the living room.

"Mom! Seriously?"

Mrs. Miller's eyes reminded me of those commercials about abused pets—designed to make you feel bad. "I'm sorry. Cade mentioned earlier that you were okay with pictures, and I—"

"Oh did he now?"

I was in trouble. She laced her hand with mine and squeezed a little harder than was comfortable.

"Oh, you know, *sweetie.* I told your mom how upset you were that you overslept because you wanted to look nice for them. We talked about how nice it would be to have pictures to commemorate our first holiday together." Mrs. Miller snapped another picture while I was talking to her daughter. "Mrs. M, don't mind Max. Maybe we should just save the pictures until after dinner."

"Of course, and for the last time, Cade. Please call me Betty. Or Mom."

Max smiled widely at me, but I had a feeling it was more like those predators on the Animal Channel, baring their teeth in a show of aggression. She leaned up, smiling all the while, and said quietly, "If you call my mother 'Mom,' I'm going to replace that turkey in the oven with your head, okay?"

I smiled back, and curled a hand around her cheek. "I'm calling your bluff, Angry Girl." Max was glaring at me, but I could tell she was glad to be back in normal territory. Normal, of course, being our attempts to piss each other off. I called to her mother in the kitchen, "Mrs. Miller—I mean

136

Mom—your daughter says the sweetest things sometimes. I think it would shock you how romantic she can be."

Max laughed low in her throat. Her eyes glinted. She placed her hand over the one on my cheek and said, "It's on now, Golden Boy. You're going to be sorry."

"I can take it."

And if this is what made her feel better, less vulnerable, then I could.

There was a feast on Max's table, and her living room was looking decidedly more lived in. Max waited until we were seated at the table to launch her first attack.

"Oh, Dad, I know you usually say grace, but do you think we could let Cade? He's *very* religious, and I know he would be so happy to do it."

I smiled and shook my head. She was going to have to try a lot harder than that to throw me off.

"Mick, I would be happy to say the prayer, but I would never want to change your holiday traditions."

Max's dad waved a hand. "Nonsense. Pray away, son."

I smiled at Max and took her hand. I pressed a chaste kiss on the back and then reached for her mother's hand on my other side.

"Dear Heavenly Father, we thank you for allowing us to be together today. Thank you for guiding Mick and Betty safely here to Philadelphia that we might join together as a family to eat and give thanks. More than anything, I thank you for bringing Max and I together. It feels like *only yesterday* we met, but she has changed my life in so many *interesting* ways. Sometimes, I feel like our relationship is too good to be real.

I pray that you will continue to bless us all and may our day be filled with food and fun and fellowship. It is in your holy name we pray, Amen."

As soon as the prayer was over, Max tugged her hand from mine. Max's parents held hands a little longer, glancing at us, and then sharing a knowing look. While they watched I leaned over, and placed a kiss on Max's cheek. There was no harm in taking a few liberties with my role, especially since this gig only lasted through the end of the day. I whispered, "You're gonna have to do better than that, Angry Girl."

She waited until her parents weren't looking to flip me off, but we were both smiling.

I said, "Why don't we make a toast?" The Millers were against alcohol, but I figured the sweet tea would work. I held up my glass and said, "To new beginnings, new family, and a promising future."

Max looked queasy, but she took a drink when the rest of us did. Mrs. Miller placed a hand over her heart and said, "Cade, I'm sure Mackenzie has made it no secret that we haven't approved of some of her boyfriends." Max snorted, and I took that to mean that *some* meant *all*. "But I have to say, you are one of the most pleasant, put-together young men that I've ever met."

Mick paused in carving the turkey to say, "Yep. Looks like our Max is finally learning how to pick 'em."

I saw Max's spine straighten out of the corner of her eye. She was looking at her father in shock, no doubt because he'd *finally* used her nickname. I'd only known them a day, and even I knew how big a deal that was. As I watched Max, the shock gave way to confusion and then finally anger. Her eyebrows pulled together, and those full lips flattened into a line. She did one of those long, slow inhales, and I couldn't blame her.

We should have stopped it all then, put an end to the charade. I thought of standing up, faking an important phone call or an illness. But then Max decided to take her anger out on me. And because I cared about her, I let her.

"He is pretty wonderful, isn't he?" Her tone was sugary on the surface with poison laced beneath. "Especially when you consider where he was just a year ago."

Uh-oh. I didn't like the sound of that.

"A year ago?" her dad asked.

"Oh yes. A year ago he was in a really bad place. Weren't you, honey?"

I narrowed my eyes at her. "I suppose."

"You suppose? Oh, honey, don't downplay how far you've come. You worked so hard to overcome your . . . addiction."

Her mother choked on her tea. I closed my eyes to stay calm.

One of Max's hands was curled into a fist on the table, and I covered it with my own. I turned to her parents and put on my best smile. "Max likes to exaggerate. She thinks it's *funny*." I shot her a look and searched for an excuse that would smooth things over with her parents. I looked at her father, whose eyebrows had drawn together in a suspicious ridge. He was wearing an OU T-shirt, which gave me the only idea I had. "The addiction Max is talking about really isn't that big of a deal. I used to spend a lot of time playing fantasy football, an unhealthy amount really. Max hated it, but I've managed to cut it out." I could feel her urge to roll her eyes, but she kept her tight smile. I returned it and said, "For her."

It was a thin excuse, but I was banking on the South's universal love of football.

Mrs. Miller said, "Forgive me, but I'm so confused. I thought you'd only been together a few weeks?"

I opened my mouth to lie again, but Max beat me to it.

"Oh, we have," Max said. "Cade was head-over-heels for me a long time before that though. He just kept asking and asking and asking me to go out with him. It was a little creepy at first."

I gave her a grim smile. "I am persistent."

Her dad said, "And we sure are glad. We were beginning to think Max would never meet someone."

Max frowned and added, "It did get kind of *obnoxious* there for a while. Almost disturbing. You were practically *stalking* me."

Her dad finished his last slice of turkey and said, "Don't mind her. You have my permission to stalk her anytime."

Max closed her eyes and whispered under her breath, "Unbelievable."

I smiled and said, "Why don't we take some pictures before dessert?"

18

Max

I excused myself under the pretense of freshening up for those godforsaken pictures, and fled to my room.

I swear this guy had to have like supernatural powers. He had that mind-control power like the people on *The Vampire Diaries*. Or some scientist had experimented on him as a child, and now he had, I don't know, extra potent pheromones that bent other people to his will.

It would explain why he was so damn likable.

Stupid magic sweat.

I sighed and turned to close my door, but Cade slipped in before I could.

"You're looking even angrier than usual, Angry Girl."

This guy had the worst timing in the world.

I closed the door, and left him for the comforting expanse of my bed. Maybe I was still sleeping, and this all had been one horrible, confusing, *awkward* nightmare.

"What are you doing here?"

"Just visiting my sweet, loving girlfriend."

I threw a pillow at him in lieu of a reply.

He caught it easily, and then leaned back against the closed door, staring at me. The guy was straight out of a preppy GAP catalogue.

And I liked it.

What the hell was wrong with me?

"Do you want me to leave?" he asked. "I can make an excuse."

There was no way my parents would accept an excuse. My mother was like an octopus, and he was pretty damn wrapped up in her tentacles already. But his sincerity made something pinch in my throat, and I had to look away from him again. How did he always know exactly what to say?

Supernatural. Had to be.

"Max, it's not worth it. Lying just puts off the inevitable. Sooner or later, they're going to have to accept you the way you are."

I laughed bitterly. "Well, they've gone this long without accepting it. I'm sure they could squeeze in another twenty-two years."

I heard the floorboards creak as he walked toward me.

"Max . . ."

I sat up and swung my feet over the other side of the bed,

so that my back was to him. I'd already spilled enough of my secrets today. I wasn't doing it again. And I needed to get this all under control before I snapped.

"It's fine. We'll just finish out dinner, and then it will be over. I'll tell them in a week or two that we broke up. They'll get over it."

Doubtful. Something told me I'd hear about Cade as the "one that got away" for the rest of my life.

He said, "Just tell them I chose fantasy football over you. Your dad seems like the kind of guy that would buy that."

"How flattering."

He laughed, "You know I'd always choose you over football, Max."

I looked at him over my shoulder and asked, "Are you sure you're from Texas?"

He smiled and said, "Truce?"

I nodded.

He threw the pillow he was holding, and it nailed me right in the face.

"Now, a truce."

I rolled my eyes.

"Stalker."

"Liar."

"Jerk."

"Loving girlfriend."

"You suck at insults."

"You cringed when I said *loving,* so it counts."

"Golden Boy."

"Angry Girl."

I smiled, feeling a lot less angry. He was good at that.

We returned to the living room, and though dessert was painful, it wasn't excruciating. Cade chatted with my parents, so I didn't have to. Cade was also exceptionally good at keeping them on innocuous topics that wouldn't erupt into the arguments that normally typified our holiday dinners.

He was exactly what our family had been missing . . . well, since Alexandria's accident. She was the good one, the one who always knew what to say and how to act. She was the ingredient that made our family work, and she was gone. Having Cade here made it easier to remember her without hurting.

When Mom brought out the pumpkin pie, she wouldn't let anyone have a slice until they'd said something they were thankful for. Dad was thankful for the good food, and Mom was thankful that they got to be in Philadelphia for the holiday.

I wasn't even lying when I said, "I'm thankful Cade could be here today."

He had an arm around the back of my chair, and his hand came up and touched my hair lightly.

My mother said, "What about you, Cade? What are you thankful for?"

His eyes stayed fixed on mine. His hand brushed the side of my neck where my bird tattoos were hidden by my turtleneck sweater. He said, "I'm grateful that the past is the past, and the future is ours to make."

I blinked, and thought *pheromones.* I mouthed, "Show off," then slid him my piece of pie (which I also didn't like). Somehow, Mom never seemed to remember that.

Mom asked, "Anyone want coffee with their pie?"

"I do," I said.

Mom stood, and Cade joined her. He cupped my shoulder and said, "I'll get it."

"I take it—"

"One cream, two sugars. I remember."

Seriously, this guy was good.

I watched him as he fiddled with my coffeemaker and chatted with my mom. The guy was too selfless . . . too everything. There had to be something wrong with him. Guys like him didn't exist. And if they did, one had certainly never been interested in me.

19

Cade

The rest of the night went quickly, and before I knew it, we were saying good-bye. Mrs. Miller hugged me tightly, and Mr. Miller shook my hand.

"Say we'll see you again soon, Cade. Christmas?"

I looked at Max, and she shrugged and said, "Sure, we'll talk about it."

We'd be "broken up" before then. I wondered how she would actually do it. She should make me the bad guy, that way she wouldn't get any flack over it.

"Have a safe flight tomorrow," I told them. Mrs. Miller

hugged me again, almost like she was assuring herself I was real. Then they walked down the stairs and left. I closed the door and took in Max's apartment. Her mother had insisted on leaving behind all the dishes she'd bought, along with some pillows, an afghan, the Christmas tree, and who knows what else.

It wasn't empty anymore, but it was still lifeless because it wasn't Max.

"Well, Angry Girl . . ."

"We survived," she said.

I wasn't ready to leave, but I didn't have another excuse to stay.

I had one more reason to keep us together, but I was pretty damn certain it was a bad idea. When I'd agreed to do all of this, she'd promised me a date.

It had seemed harmless before—an innocent attraction. I had thought it would get my mind off of Bliss, and it had. I had thought of it like a date with a safety net, because we both knew it wouldn't go anywhere.

But I didn't know that anymore. Well, maybe my mind did, but the rest of me didn't. Any date between us now wouldn't be harmless, and it sure as hell wouldn't be simple.

So as much as I wanted to, I didn't mention the date.

She said, "Thanks for putting up with all of this. After what I've put you through, I probably *should* have paid you. You could have put it on your résumé—expert boyfriend."

"Hey, I got some pretty great food out of it. I think that's enough for most guys."

"Food and sex," she said.

Cue awkward silence. Her cheeks flushed prettily, and I

let the silence go on for a little longer, just because I liked seeing her out of her element.

Finally, she threw her hands up, exasperated, and said, "What? It's the truth! Are you implying that you don't think about sex constantly, Golden Boy?"

"Oh, I definitely think about it." I was thinking about it right now, and it was not making leaving this apartment any easier. My eyes, as usual, were drawn to her lips, and I had the sudden urge to ruffle her hair so that it was closer to her normal style. I wanted her out of that ridiculous turtleneck, so that I could see her creamy skin and the art that enhanced it. God, was it only this morning that I'd seen her tree tattoo in its entirety? I could still picture the bare branches and twisting roots. I wondered what it meant to her. I wondered what it would be like to trace the lines with my fingertips. With my lips.

She cleared her throat, and I realized I'd been standing there staring at her, imagining her naked for who knows how long.

I coughed. "Well, I should probably go."

Go beat my head against a wall. Go jump in front of a moving car. Go get a life. Any of the above was appropriate.

"Right," she said. "Um, thank you . . . again for all of this."

I shook my head and smiled. "It was nothing. I'll see you around, Angry Girl."

I opened the door and stepped out into the hallway. She said, "Good night Cade."

I only let myself look back for a second, and then I said, "Good night." I walked down the flight of stairs and out into the street. Chinatown was fairly busy, since the restaurants were all still open on Thanksgiving. I took one last look at the door to Max's building, and then promised to forget it.

I refused to let myself want what I couldn't have. I wouldn't go through that all again. I said, "Good-bye, Max," and set off for the nearest subway stop.

I was too lazy on Friday to get out of bed. I lay there until far too late in the afternoon to not be pathetic. Eager to accomplish at least *something* during my day, I dialed my grandmother's phone number.

I'd lied to Bliss about her being ill because I knew Bliss wouldn't question it. Grams had gotten sick around the beginning of our senior year—pneumonia—and it had scared the shit out of me. She was all I had, and I'd thought I was going to lose her. I was twenty-one, and my entire life had revolved around partying like most kids in college. But that's not how I wanted our final months in college together to be. That was around the time when I made myself start getting serious about the future. That was around the time I started having feelings for Bliss, too.

It took her to the fourth or fifth ring to answer, probably because it took her that long to get to the phone. She was old . . . and as she liked to say "slow as molasses."

She answered, "You got me."

I'd never heard anyone else answer the phone like her.

"Hi, Grams."

"Oh, Cade! It's so good to hear from you. We all missed you terribly yesterday."

I closed my eyes, surprisingly affected by the sound of her

voice. It must have been the discussion of my parents yesterday and all that time with the Millers. Family was fresh on my mind.

"I missed you, too, Grams."

"How was Thanksgiving with Bliss, dearie?"

I hadn't told Grams about any of the stuff that had happened with Bliss. I'd told her I was having Thanksgiving there because I couldn't afford to come home, and I didn't want her insisting on paying for the trip. Her retirement check barely covered all her bills, and she'd done enough for me. I hated lying to her, but it was a necessary evil.

"Oh, you know Bliss and me, things are always interesting."

I heard her raspy laugh on the other end. "Oh, I bet."

Grams had met Bliss during the second show of our senior year. We went out to dinner after the play, and on the way out of the restaurant, Bliss had walked into a glass door. Grams told me afterward that she knew I loved Bliss because I didn't laugh at what she called "the funniest damn thing I've ever seen."

God, I missed her. And Bliss. I missed a lot of things.

"So everyone made it yesterday?"

"Oh, yes, yes. The little ones asked after you."

Every other holiday, some aunts and uncles and cousins joined us. It didn't make for a very big family gathering, but I suppose I had more than a lot of people do.

"I wish I could have been there. I can't wait for Christmas."

I wasn't sure yet exactly how I was going to afford to go home for Christmas, but I would. If I had to take out more loans on top of my school ones, I would. It wasn't like I wouldn't be paying those back for a century anyway.

Someone knocked at the door, and I said, "Hey, Grams, someone is at the door. Can I call you back later? I want to hear all about how yesterday went with the family."

"Of course, honey. Tell Bliss I said hi."

I swallowed and said, "Uh-huh. Love you. Bye."

A second round of knocks came as she said good-bye and hung up the phone.

Through the door, a voice called, "*Hermano!* You in there?"

"Just a sec, Milo!"

I rolled off my bed and pulled a T-shirt over my head. I padded barefoot toward the door of my studio apartment, and undid the dead bolt.

I yawned and pulled the door wide.

I was in pajama pants, and Milo looked like he'd raided Urban Outfitters. He said, "Whoa. Either you had a really late night or are currently having a really early one."

"Sadly, neither."

Before I could invite him in, he'd already passed by me and plopped down on the futon in my living room.

I laughed and closed my door.

"This isn't still about that Bliss girl, is it?"

It felt good to be able to say, "No, it's not about Bliss."

"Don't tell me you've already gotten your heart broken by some other *chica*. I only left you alone for a day."

"No, no broken heart. Just an unavailable girl."

Milo stretched his legs out in front of him and nodded. "Ah, you know the cure for that don't you?"

"What?"

"An available girl." Laughing, I made my way to the fridge and held up a beer in offering. Milo nodded, and I grabbed one for each of us. He said, "I'm serious. I happen to have it on good authority that you picked up a phone number the other night. Forget the unavailable girl . . . both of them . . . and call the blonde from the other night."

That wasn't a bad idea.

Dating was the solution to my Bliss (and now Max) problem.

"Okay, I'll do it," I told him.

I picked up my phone to find her number, and he said, "Whoa! Whoa! Don't do it now, *hermano.* You've got to give it a few days. You know the rules."

I rolled my eyes. Right . . . Milo had rules for just about everything—drinking and dating being the two most prominent.

"Fine," I said. "I'll call her tomorrow."

He made a face and said, "Eh, better make it the day after. That girl was all over you at the bar. We don't want to encourage too much clinginess. The day after tomorrow will be much better."

So Sunday afternoon, with Milo obnoxiously watching from my sofa, I called Cammie. I pulled out my cell, found her in my address book, and hit send quickly, before I could change my mind.

She answered on the second ring.

"Hello?"

"Cammie?" I asked.

"Yes?"

I said, "This is Cade." Then I couldn't remember if I'd

actually told her my name at the bar, so I added, "We met at Trestle a few nights ago."

"Oh." I could hear the smile in her voice. "Hi, Cade."

"Hi."

Milo whispered, "Set the date up for this weekend. Give her plenty of time to get nervous about it."

I rolled my eyes, but asked, "What are your plans this Friday night, Cammie? And whatever it is, can I steal you away from it?"

"Steal me? I think I'd go quite willingly."

She giggled.

Now I just needed to figure out where we would go. And how to get her there. If I were still back in Texas I would have picked her up, but I didn't have a car, and it seemed odd to pick someone up for the subway.

"Excellent," I said. "It's a date. I'll call you back in a few days to let you know what we're doing."

20

Max

My phone rang so early the day after Thanksgiving that it should have been labeled cruel and unusual punishment. I reached out toward my nightstand, knocking off who knew what until my fingers finally closed around my phone.

"What?" I grumbled.

"Good morning, sweetie."

Ugh . . . it was way too early for this.

"Hi, Mom."

"Your father and I are at the airport. Our flight has been delayed."

Oh no. If she said that they were going to stay even longer, I would go crazy. I had to get back to the band and back to work, and I had reached my crazy quota for the week.

"I'm sorry, Mom. There's no chance they'll cancel it, is there?"

"Oh, no, honey. Just something about the pilot's plane being late the night before, so they're required to give him so much rest. We'll be back in Oklahoma by this evening." Thank God. "But your father and I were talking, and we just wanted to tell you again how much we liked Cade."

I was pretty sure that was already abundantly clear, thanks.

"You know, we've been worried about you. Your father and I had a lot of difficulty with your decision to drop out of college." A lot was an understatement. I wouldn't be surprised if they discussed having me committed as mentally unstable. "But we came around." After a year of fighting, yeah. "We've been helping you pay your rent so you can afford to spend time doing your little music thing." God, I was going to break out in hives if she called my career and lifelong dream a "little music thing" one more time. "It's just . . . you've been here so long, and your father and I were starting to feel that perhaps it was time to face the facts and grow up."

No. Please no. I was so close. I could feel it. The gig next weekend at The Fire was going to be huge for us. We were even doing a live recording of the set.

It wasn't like they didn't have plenty of money. They both had high-paying jobs, and the insurance money from Alex's death had made our already wealthy household even wealthier. They gave me five hundred bucks a month to help pay my student loans from those pointless two years at UPenn that they'd been the ones to insist upon. You'd think when they were the ones pushing me to go to college, that they would have at least paid for it. But since they hadn't helped Michael, they didn't help me. Some bullshit about making my own way. Too bad it had only ever been their way.

Five hundred to them was nothing, and to me it was the difference between doing what I loved and dreaming about doing what I love. I just needed a little more time.

"What does that mean?" I asked. "You're going to stop helping me?"

"Eventually, yes." Shit. I was going to have to double my shifts at the Trestle. Between that and my job at the tattoo parlor, I would have zero time for singing, much less writing my own stuff. "We were going to talk to you about it while we were here, but then we met Cade."

"What does Cade have to do with it?"

"Well . . . you're obviously getting your life together. You're dating a nice, respectable boy and finally starting to take things seriously. Your father and I are so glad you've left behind the negative influences you were spending time with before. So, since you're obviously trying, we're going to give you a few more months."

"A few?" I asked.

"Well, we're going to play things by ear. But as long as you keep taking your life seriously, you don't need to worry about it."

AKA . . . as long as I kept dating Cade.

I wanted to scream.

At her.

At the world.

At myself. For being too damn cowardly to tell her exactly what I was thinking. I should have told her the truth about Cade. I should have told her that she was full of shit. I *had* been taking my life seriously.

I had been taking my life seriously when I left college. Just because I was not taking a familiar road or doing something that made sense to her didn't mean I was naive or ignorant.

It meant I didn't want to be a mindless office worker who daydreamed about what life could have been if things had been different.

It meant I was willing to make sacrifices and work two jobs and kill myself to get it all done.

It meant I was brave.

I *wished* I had been brave enough then to tell her those things.

I wasn't.

Instead I kept my mouth closed and listened to her prattle on about a charity event she was hosting right before Christmas and how Michael was doing, and how perfect his wife, Bethany, was.

The more she talked and the more I stayed silent, the more nauseated I became. Finally, I couldn't take it anymore. I lied and said, "Mom, there's someone at the door. I have to go."

"Oh, sure, honey. It was good to see you. Tell Cade we said hi and we'll see him at Christmas."

"Mom, I'm not sure he'll make it to Christmas."

"And why not?"

"Well, he has his own family to see, plus it's not exactly cheap. He has tuition and loans to pay."

Like all the rest of us.

"Oh, your father and I will just take of all that. He can stay for a few days and then go on to Texas. We'll pay for it. I won't take no for an answer."

I was *so* glad she didn't mind throwing money at someone she'd just met.

"We'll see, Mom. I really do have to go."

I hung up and threw my phone somewhere on the floor. I pulled the covers over my head, and hugged my pillow, but the damage was done. I was too worked up to go to sleep.

I took a long shower. I made a complicated lunch that was supposed to occupy my mind, but didn't. I went for a run. I played my guitar. I tried to write a new song.

I did that for two days.

Distraction. Failure of said distraction.

Different distraction. Different failure.

Repeat until insane.

The whole time my phone sat there, taunting me. Cade was one call away. Or a text if I was feeling particularly cowardly.

One question could solve so many of my problems. Or delay them anyway. Wasn't that what life was? Taking the good while we could get it, and delaying the bad as long as possible.

Cade was good, and he could help delay the bad. Win-win, right?

Except for the part where I had to degrade myself to do it.

How much was I willing to sacrifice for the money my parents were giving me?

I knew . . . I could feel it somewhere in the space between my heart and lungs that this wasn't a hopeless dream.

Anything that felt this good and consumed me so completely couldn't be hopeless. I thought of all the gigs I'd have to cut back on if I didn't have that money. Any one of them could be the one that puts us on the track of making music for a living, but if the gigs never happened, neither would our break.

I'd just finished thinking that I wasn't afraid to make sacrifices.

Could I sacrifice my own pride, bend to my parents, and pretend to be something I wasn't if it meant following my dream? It wasn't as if I had to actually *be* someone else. I just had to pretend . . . for a little while.

Five hundred bucks a month. I suppose people had betrayed themselves for less.

I made it to Sunday evening before I went back to my room and fished my phone out from under the pillow I had stuffed it under to dampen the temptation. Before I could analyze what I was doing, I scrolled through my old texts and found Cade's number.

Hey. My band is playing this Friday at The Fire in Northern Liberties. You should come.

I tossed my phone down on the bed, and then pressed the heels of my palms into my eyes.

Why did I feel like I'd just hit my self-destruct button?

I was just inviting him to see us play. That didn't mean anything. I still had a whole week to make up my mind.

My phone started ringing, and I jumped to answer it.

Oh, it was Mace.

He probably wanted to do something tonight . . . or spend the night, now that my parents were gone. I just . . . I wasn't feeling up to being around people.

I hit ignore.

Cade's reply came a few minutes later.

What time?

I spent most of the next week avoiding Mace. We saw each other at practice, and we grabbed dinner beforehand a few times, but I just kept telling him I had to work, which was true. And when I didn't have to work, I told him I wasn't feeling well, which wasn't true, but oh well.

When the day of the gig arrived, we were set to meet that afternoon to load up our equipment from Trestle. Spence had a van we used to transport what we needed. When I arrived, Mace wasn't there, and Spence was outside smoking.

He inhaled, and on the exhale said, "You look like shit."

I did. "Thanks, douche rocket."

I hadn't slept well the night before because I knew I was going to see Cade the next day, and I still hadn't decided whether I was going to ask him about Christmas.

"I'm just saying . . . we need you to look hot for tonight and you look like you're auditioning to be an extra on *The Walking Dead.*"

"I've had a shitty couple of days, okay?"

"Right. Mace said you've been sick the last few days." Spence made air quotes with his fingers when he said "sick."

"Stay out of it, Spence. And don't you worry. I'll be good by tonight. I'll look so sexy you'll be dying to get back into my pants."

"You know I'm always dying to get back in your pants."

I rolled my eyes. "Har-har."

He smiled, and took another drag on his cigarette.

"You sure Mace is coming?"

"Why wouldn't he be?"

He shrugged. "Maybe he took one look at you in that out-fit and decided not to show after all. Or maybe he found out about the preppy boy you were making googly eyes at last week at the bar."

I flicked his cigarette and it went flying out of his mouth.

He said, "Hey! I was using that."

"I was *not* making googly eyes at anyone. You're delirious."

"No, love, I'm observant. There's a difference. But keep your secrets. Fine by me. Just wait to cut Mace loose until after tonight or we'll have problems."

I twisted the key and opened the heavy front door to Trestle. He followed me inside the darkened, lifeless bar, and I said, "No one is cutting anyone loose. You're way off on this one, Spence."

I flipped on the light, and he shrugged. "I wasn't wrong when I thought you were about to toss me to the curb. I doubt I'm wrong this time."

Sometimes it was really obnoxious being friends with an ex. He liked to bring it up all the time, but I knew for a fact that he was way past over me. The guy had a different girl every week. He liked to say he was practicing for the groupies we'd eventually have. I liked to call him man-whorrible.

My pocket buzzed.

Mace had texted.

Can't make it 4 set up. Sry. C U 2night tho.

Are you fucking kidding me?

I hit dial, and it went straight to voice mail. I called a sec-ond time. Same thing. At the tone, I said, "You better have

the best damn excuse in the world, Mace. Tonight is important. Don't you dare be late!"

Spencer was holding both of our guitars, smirking when
I hung up.

"Maybe it's not Mace who is getting tossed to the curb."

21

Cade

It was undoubtedly the worst idea ever, bringing Cammie to Max's show. But my desire to see her play overruled any common sense I was still holding on to. I'd been in midconversation with Milo about date ideas when I received her text. I didn't even hesitate before saying yes.

Cammie and I met up Friday night at a restaurant close to the venue. She was wearing a little black dress that fit her slim body perfectly. It also probably cost more than my entire wardrobe . . . maybe my whole apartment. When we'd met at Trestle her cheeks had been bright pink. I'd assumed she'd been flushed from alcohol. She'd also been the dictionary definition of *giggly*. Again, I thought alcohol.

Apparently, I was wrong on both accounts. That was just Cammie, cheeks drowning in blush and lungs made of laughing gas.

I went through all the motions of a date.

Pulling out her chair.

Ordering wine.

Small talk.

Cammie was nice enough, and very pretty, but a bit predictable. She ordered a salad and kept tossing her blond hair back and forth so much I was surprised she didn't have whiplash. She giggled not just when stuff was funny, but to fill the silence.

There was a lot of silence on my part.

"So, my professor was completely unreasonable, and wouldn't even consider letting me retake the test, when really the entire misunderstanding was his fault. You'd think for the amount of money we're paying for his class that he would be a little better at communicating, right?"

Silence.

Cammie giggled.

I cringed.

I had to work on replying faster.

"Right. You'd think."

She smiled and tossed her hair again. "I'm sorry. I'm probably boring you with all my talk about school."

"Oh, no, not at all!" I said.

"Oh good. Because you know, I ran into the same professor at happy hour hitting on a girl my age. Can you believe it?"

I said as fast as humanly possible, "I cannot!"

"I mean, the guy was like forty. I suppose if I were a different kind of girl maybe he would have let me retake the test, but honestly. I wrote a letter to the dean about the professor. Maybe he'll get fired. At the very least, my grade will get changed. Daddy is friends with the dean. They've been golfing together for ages."

"Oh, is that so?"

"Oh yes. You know, I almost went to another school so that I could 'make my own way,' and all that, but in the end, I thought . . . why not take advantage of every opportunity I'm given?"

She kept going, but I was having trouble listening. I liked to think that I probably made it longer than most before tuning out. I was sure that there was a really cool person underneath the designer clothes and the manicured nails and the most obnoxious laughter known to man, but tonight I didn't have the patience or attention span to find her. My body felt almost electric at the thought of where we'd be heading next.

I'd spent an embarrassingly long time Googling Max's band Under the Bell Jar. I learned that they'd named themselves after a Sylvia Plath novel, which made me think of Max's threat to stick my head in the oven on Thanksgiving, and I died laughing. The bass player and Max were the original founding members, and it looked like Max's boyfriend was a more recent addition. His name was *Mace*. As in the stuff sprayed into the eyes of rapists and muggers. Or the ancient weapon used to bludgeon people to death.

He sounded like a real keeper.

I was snapped out of my reverie when the waiter came by

with the check. My stomach clenched as I slipped a ridiculous amount of cash into the plastic folder. Maybe I shouldn't be dating, not if I wanted to have the money to go home for Christmas.

I pulled out Cammie's chair and offered her my arm.

She giggled.

God help me.

"I'm so glad I met you at that god-awful bar. My friends dragged me there, and I wanted to leave as soon as we got there. Well, until I met you."

Awesome. That meant she was probably going to hate the place we were heading.

"So, tell me again about this band," she said.

I'd been on the website enough to be able to parrot back to her, "They're a local Philly band that blends rock and folk music. They're supposed to be pretty good."

"Cool."

Giggle.

Giggle.

Giggle.

Dear God. I had to keep talking.

"Yeah, I've not heard them play before, but I know someone in the band. I think it's going to pretty awesome. Do you like music?"

She started talking about Lady Gaga and I sighed in relief. That should last us at least until we walked the block and a half to The Fire. Then hopefully it would be loud enough there to drown out her inane giggling.

When we got to the door, I paid the cover and slipped

happily into the darkened bar. I found us a table, and then escaped to get us both drinks. As I was leaving, Cammie was looking worriedly at her barstool like it was going to give her Ebola. They had a great selection of local beers. I got Yards ale. Cammie wanted a cosmo. The bartender looked at me like I was crazy. This wasn't really a cosmo kind of place, but he went off to make it anyway. While I waited for our drinks, I pulled out my phone and texted Max.

Here. Have a great show!

I didn't expect a reply, since she was going on soon, but I got one almost immediately.

Thanks. You should come backstage afterward.

Huh. We hadn't talked once since her original text, so I had assumed she'd only invited me to be nice . . . or to make more money, but she seemed to genuinely want to see me again. I'd thought of all these strategies for talking to her again, and it looked like I wasn't even going to have to use them. That made it ten times harder to accept the drinks from the bartender and return to Cammie, who giggled when I sat down with what would probably prove to be the worst cosmo in history.

To her credit, she winced when she took a drink but didn't complain. I kept flicking my eyes back to the stage, waiting for the concert to start. I managed to keep up a halfhearted conversation with Cammie about her plans to study abroad.

"I just can't make up my mind where I want to study though. Australia would be amazing. Or London. But I think Paris is my favorite right now. Then again, it changes once a week."

"I have a friend who is backpacking overseas right now. I lose track of where she is, but last I heard she was somewhere in Germany. She's pretty much been all over the place, taking trains and staying in hostels."

"Hostels? Seriously? What if she gets chopped up into pieces or something like that movie?"

I smiled. "I don't think they're actually like that."

"Still," she said, flipping her hair, "I don't think I could ever stay there."

It was official. I had given up hope of excavating a normal person underneath all the spoiled. The evening wasn't a complete bust though, because at that moment a shrill whine came over the speakers, and I saw Max fiddling with her microphone up on stage.

She was wearing the same flower in her hair as the day I met her. Surrounding the white petals were riotous red curls that were even more out of control than I remember. Almost as if she was trying to make up for the day she'd spent tamed down for her parents. She wore these short leopard print shorts over black, sheer stockings with red heels that made her legs look incredible. She had on a white, ripped tee that hung off her shoulders, showing the angles and architecture of her body. She looked effortlessly cool.

Her pale skin practically glowed under the lights, and her white shirt was just transparent enough that I could see the outline of her black bra beneath. I liked it until I remembered *everyone* could see that same black bra. She slipped the guitar strap over her head and looked more at home than she ever had in her apartment.

She stepped up to the mic, her red lips brushing against it as she said, "Hello, I'm Max and this is Under the Bell Jar."

I wanted to cheer, but I restrained myself to clapping like the rest of the crowd. "This first song is called 'Better,' and it's the song that gave us our name."

She stood back from the mic as she started to play, and for the first time, I noticed the other people around her. On bass was a guy who was the oddest mix of punk and nerd that I'd ever seen. He had on a sweater vest and a bow tie with metal spikes. He wore glasses that didn't look like they were just for show, but his hair hung long and grunge-band shaggy. At the back, between him and Max, was her boyfriend from the coffee shop. Mace. He played the drums, his eyes were fixed on Max the entire time.

I couldn't blame him.

I wasn't sure I'd be able to take my eyes off of her either. She smiled as she played the opening progression, and I could see the moment when the rest of the world ceased to exist for her. Then she sang, and the rest of the world disappeared for me, too.

> "I pick a smile and paint it on
> Smooth the cracks, right the wrongs
> Try to push some life into my eyes
> I've lost my soul under all the lies."

Her voice was low and raspy but had this sweet tone that was at odds with the rest of her. The music picked up slightly and the drums got louder.

"It's better this way,
Better that no one sees
It's better this way
Better when I'm not me

"I'll be better
Better
Better."

Her eyes were closed, her rose petal lips right up against the mic. As she repeated the word, she wavered between desperation and anger and shame. It was one word, but I could feel her emotions so clearly, as if she poured them directly into me.

"Better
Better

"I'm drowning under the weight of these
Can't tell apart all the different me's
The bell jar drops, the air gets thin
Nothing gets out, but nothing gets in

"It's better this way
Untouched under glass
It's better, I say
This way I'll last."

The song slowed, and her voice went into her higher register. It was heartbreaking and honest, and I understood her better in that moment than ever before.

"It's Better
Better
Better

"Better
Better

"I'll Never
Never
Get past the pressure
Never, never
I'm my own oppressor

"No one does it better."

She smiled grimly, and I swear she held the whole audience in the palm of her hands. Everyone was leaning forward, me included. She strummed a few more notes, humming slightly, and the music faded out to just the beat of the drums and bass as she chanted a few more times.

"Better
Better."

22

Max

If this was what drugs were like, I understood how people got addicted. No matter how many times I did this, it never got any less exhilarating. The nerves and the fear and the hope and the hurt and the healing—my soul was a galaxy all its own when I was onstage.

I had tried a million things in an attempt to piece my life back together after Alexandria's death, to make the world feel right-side-up again. Music was the only thing that worked.

When the last notes of "Better" were over, I knew without a shadow of a doubt that I would do whatever it took to keep this. Maybe it made me weak. It definitely made me selfish and a liar, but if there was any way I could convince Cade to continue the charade just long enough so that my parents didn't cut me off completely, I would do it.

I found him in the crowd after our third or fourth song. I swear I'd scanned the entire bar for him twice already, and I was beginning to think he'd left. Then I saw him at a table in the middle of the room with the same blonde he'd talked to at Trestle. It was completely irrational, but I felt a spike of irritation that he'd brought her. It was soothed by the fact that every time I glanced at him, he never took his eyes off of me.

We started one of our Rilo Kiley covers, and I couldn't keep myself from making eye contact with him.

> *"And it's bad news, baby I'm bad news*
> *I'm just bad news, bad news, bad news."*

He raised an eyebrow at me, and I nearly laughed into the microphone.

The song fit us, and I'd been thinking of him when I picked it for the set list. It was all about the ways a relationship could go wrong when one of the people in it was like me. Toxic.

A walking corpse . . . that's how the song put it. That was me, but despite how often I told myself that seeing Cade was a bad idea, I was too selfish to stop myself.

I tried to communicate those thoughts as I sang, tried to warn him as best as I could.

I should not have noticed the way his eyes followed my movements or the way his posture straightened every time

I looked at him. I should not have cared. I should not have looked into his dark eyes. I *really* should not have licked my lips between lines, because I could see from here his chest rise and fall. I wanted to feel bad about encouraging whatever *this* was between us, but I didn't.

"Bad news, bad news . . ."

The song ended, and I looked at Spence to make sure he was ready for our next song, one of ours. He gave me a look, and his eyes shot out toward the audience. I didn't have to look to know he was glancing at Cade.

I didn't have to guess what his mental lecture was either. I was completely qualified to give one to myself. Beyond all the normal levels of stupidity that this thing qualified as, it was the highest rung of stupid to allow it to distract me during a set, especially if I only had a few more months to do something significant with my career before my parents cut me off. I needed every song to be as awesome as it could possibly be. I couldn't afford to mess up one verse, one line, even one note.

I kept my eyes off Cade through the rest of the set. I worked the stage, flirting with Mace and Spencer. I leaned down to touch a few guys in the audience, flirting with them, too. Funny how onstage, the more broken and messed up you are, the more entertaining people find you. The audience's favorites were the songs I'd written in my darkest, angriest moments. Air that kind of aggression anywhere else but onstage, and people would stare or talk or lock you up.

When we sang our last song, one of Spencer's originals,

the applause was loud enough to drown out even my thoughts for a few moments.

I breathed in their excitement. *This* was living. I might be a walking corpse everywhere else, but not up here.

The spotlight operator swept his light across the stage while each of us waved. When the light came back to me, blinding, the beauty of the moment disappeared, and I lost my breath.

The flash of headlights.

Crunch of metal.

Screaming tires.

Then spinning, spinning, spinning.

Out of control and unending.

I stood there frozen until Mace hooked his arm around my neck. Sweat coated his skin and mine, too. He pulled me off the stage, and I waited until we were backstage and out of the view of the crowd before I shrugged him off.

I grumbled, "Bathroom," hoping that this time he would take the hint. This time I made sure to go into a stall, so that he couldn't follow me. I kicked the door closed behind me, and resisted the urge to light up. I wanted this place to invite us back, which meant I shouldn't go smoking up their bathroom, even if it would make me feel better.

So, I pretended.

I imagined the flick of the flame, the smell of the smoke, and the filter against my lips. I inhaled slowly, remembered the relaxation it normally brought me, and then exhaled. I concentrated on pushing out the memories with it.

Spencer had told me once, on one of Alexandria's birthdays actually when I was a complete wreck, that we should live like we smoke—inhale the present and exhale the past. Something about it had stuck with me. I only smoked on rare occasions these days, but I lit up an imaginary cigarette almost every day. I didn't need the nicotine, just the motion, the breathing.

My phone buzzed in my back pocket.

Great show, Angry Girl. You still want me to come back?

Did I?

Maybe it made me a bad person, asking him to do me this favor despite all the confusing feelings between us, but it didn't change anything. I still needed him, and if he was willing to let me use him, I would.

Yeah, Golden Boy. Whenever you'd like.

When I exited the bathroom, Mace was waiting. Spencer had disappeared somewhere, so it was just the two of us.

"Are you done being a diva?"

I rolled my eyes. "Needing a few seconds alone after a set does not make me a diva, Mace."

"Then what about the fact that you spent all week blowing me off?"

I didn't have an answer for my behavior, not a good one anyway. So I turned it back on him. "What about the fact that you spent all day today ignoring *my* calls *and* flaked out on setup?"

He tossed his head to get his black hair out of his eyes. He shoved his hands in the pockets of his leather jacket, completely closed off. Face blank. He said, "I told you, something came up."

A drop of unease rippled through my chest. He was lying about something.

"Want to tell me what that *something* was?"

He punched a fist forward in his pocket and clenched his jaw. He shook his head and shrugged. "You have your secrets, and I'll have mine."

"The difference, Mace, is that my secrets don't affect the band."

"Jesus, I've got zero fucks to give about this band, Max. You know I'm only here for you."

Unbelievable. In some demented part of his brain, he must have thought that sounded romantic because he stepped toward me and slipped his hands over my hips. I shoved him back hard.

"If you knew *anything* about me, you would know that this band is my life."

"Oh, it's clear you care about this band more than you care about me, about anybody."

"Damn right, I do."

He tugged on one of his gauges and ran his thumb under his nose. He got up in my face and said, "You're a real piece of work, you know that?"

I'd known that for a long time.

"Says the guy with pinpoint pupils. What are you on? Couldn't wait until after the set?"

He closed his eyes and groaned. "I get it. You're mad about this morning. I'm sorry." His hands came up to my jaw, and he continued, "Can't we just—"

I shoved him back again and felt his fingernails scrape my jaw.

"No, Mace!" My voice was explosive, and I made myself calm down and lower the volume. The last thing we needed was for someone to hear us arguing back here. "Just . . . I can't do this right now, Mace. Let's take the night off, and we'll address this all later."

"Later, yeah, I've been hearing a lot of that recently. I'm sick of waiting for later."

Damn it. I didn't have the energy to deal with this right now. I tried to reach for him, to appease him, but he back-pedaled away from me. "I don't know what the hell you want from me, Mace."

His face screwed up in anger and he said, "I'm not sure I want anything from you anymore."

He blew out the back exit into the alley, and it didn't bode well for our relationship that the thing that irked me the most was that he left Spence and I alone to pack up once again.

Inhale.

Exhale.

Inhale.

Exhale.

"Does that really work for you?" I turned to find Cade leaning against the door. He was wearing a black button-down shirt with his sleeves rolled up to his elbows. You knew you were in bad shape when just the sight of a guy's forearms distracted you. The week of not seeing him had done nothing to quell my attraction to him.

Bad news.

"Sometimes," I said. "At the moment, it's doing a fat lot of nothing."

One side of his mouth lifted up in a half-smile, and he asked, "Do you want me to leave?"

I wasn't sure whether he had heard enough of the fight to

know that it was about needing space or if he was just better at reading me. I wasn't calm, not in the slightest, but I trusted him not to push.

"No, that's okay. I'm okay."

Inhale.

Exhale.

He pushed off the wall and stepped inside the room, closing the door behind him.

"I'm really glad I came," he said.

I nodded, and because I was a glutton for punishment, I asked, "Where's your friend?"

He laughed and ran a hand across his jaw. My hands tingled, and I pushed them behind my back, far away from him. He said, "She's gone. Thank God. She wanted to leave in the middle. I didn't. We agreed to go our separate ways."

I took a seat on a beat-up old couch in the corner, and he sat a few feet away from me. I slid a little closer.

"I wouldn't have been offended, you know. You could have left."

"No, I couldn't have." His eyes dipped toward my legs just for a second, but I saw it. "I'm sure you hear this a lot, but you were amazing."

My skin warmed, and I basked in his attention like it was the sun. I pulled my legs up on the seat, and settled my chin on my knees. "Feel free to tell me again, as often as you like, really."

He stretched an arm out on the couch cushion behind me, and said, "I could do that."

I leaned back until my head brushed his arm. My blood still pumped too fast from the fight with Mace, and the damaged, angry part of me really wanted to prove how much Mace's anger didn't bother me. I turned toward Cade, and leaned my legs against his.

"So . . . I—"

The door swung open and Spencer came trotting in with two people behind him. A tall, attractive blond guy with a little brunette tucked into his side. I heard Cade's sharp intake of breath a second before the brunette said, "Cade? When did you get back from Texas?"

23

Cade

Bliss.

I swear, every time things get remotely good, the universe puts me back in my place.

"Hey, Bliss. Garrick."

The two of them crossed the room toward us, and Max whispered, "Who is that?"

"Remember the alternative Thanksgiving plans I mentioned?"

"The ones better left in the past?"

I nodded and stood to greet my friends. I shook Garrick's hand, and gave Bliss an awkward one-armed hug.

"I didn't end up going back to Texas. Sorry I didn't tell you. Things changed at the last minute, and I decided to stay."

Bliss asked, "Your grandmother got better?"

I cringed. "Yeah, she's good."

"Why didn't you come over for Thanksgiving, then?" She gripped my arm, and I took a step back out of her grasp. I watched her face fall and could see the pity that she was so bad at hiding. I could just imagine the scenario going through her head—me, home alone and miserable for the holiday. Of course, that had been my plan until Max blew into my life. I opened my mouth, unsure of what excuse I was going to use. Was I sick? I could have been sick.

Then Max said, "He was with me."

She slipped an arm around my waist, and on instinct, I put my arm over her shoulder. She pressed close to me and held out a hand toward Bliss. "My name is Max."

Bliss's eyebrows disappeared underneath her side-swept bangs, and I saw her eyes scan Max's tattoos and outfit. I tried to see what she was seeing, imagine what Max must look like to someone who didn't know her. When I looked at her, all I saw was the black bra that showed through her ripped white shirt, and I decided it was better if I kept my eyes off her for the moment.

Bliss shook Max's hand, a little in shock.

Garrick recovered faster. He greeted her, "Lovely to meet you, Max."

When she heard Garrick's accent, her eyes met mine, and I knew she had put the pieces together. She smiled up at me, and I tried to express my gratitude in a look. Her smile widened, so I thought she understood. "Max, this is Bliss. We

went to college together. And this is her boyfriend, Garrick."
I left out the part where he'd been our professor. Things were
weird enough already.

"It's so nice to meet friends of Cade." She nudged me
playfully. "I was beginning to think he'd never introduce me.
Did he invite you guys to see the show tonight?"

"Actually"—her band mate, the one with the punk bow
tie, stepped up—"I invited them. Garrick is a friend."

Max said, "Oh, I didn't realize you knew Spence."

This Spence was looking between Max and me like the
world had spun off its axis. I didn't blame him. With me in
my button-down and her looking like a rock goddess—we
didn't exactly match. He pinned me with a stare and said,
"And you are?"

Max jumped in. "This is Cade, my boyfriend. Don't act
like I haven't been talking your ear off about him, Spence."

"Right." Her friend nodded. "Cade."

I decided it was time to help Max carry the burden and
asked, "What did you think of the show?" I looked down at
Max and said, "She's pretty amazing, isn't she?"

She leaned up and placed a kiss on my cheek, no doubt
leaving a print of her ruby red lips against my skin. I knew
she was pretending, but damn she was good at it.

"It was . . ." Bliss tore her eyes away from me and smiled
at Max, "It was awesome. You have a great voice."

Garrick said, "How come you haven't introduced us to
Max before now, Cade?"

Max answered, "Oh, well, we've not told many people. We
wanted to take things slow, spend some time with just the two
of us before broadcasting it to the world."

Bliss smiled up at Garrick and placed a hand against his chest. "We can definitely understand that."

My eyes zeroed in on the ring on her finger. He'd done it. He'd proposed, and she'd said yes. I expected to feel some kind of pain, maybe longing, but those feelings never came. There was discomfort, sure, but if anything, seeing the ring on her finger only caused generic emotions—the same ones I felt every time another friend changed their marital status on Facebook or announced they were pregnant. It was the unsettling shock of feeling like everyone around me was moving at a speed I just couldn't match.

That was the first moment, standing there facing them with Max by my side, that I really started to question what I'd felt for Bliss. Shouldn't this hurt more? Or was I too distracted by Max's body next to mine?

I felt like I was standing on a precipice, seconds away from discovering a truth about myself that I didn't particularly want to learn.

Max's hand around my waist squeezed tighter, and I tore my eyes away from the ring on Bliss's hand. I cleared my throat and forced a smile. "I see she said yes."

Garrick beamed, a smile so bright and happy that it was painful to look at. "She did."

"Congratulations," I said. "To both of you. I'm really happy for you."

Bliss bit her lip, then gave me a soft smile. Her eyes went a little glassy. Her voice was soft when she said, "Thank you. That means a lot."

There was a beat. Another one of those moments when the winds shifted, time turned, and life started again in a new direction. I didn't know about anyone else in the room, but I could tell Bliss felt it.

Maybe it was because we were both actors. Maybe it was just because of who we were. But I could see in her eyes that she knew, too. This was the end of a chapter.

We were moving in different directions, and every minute put us another mile apart. Regardless of what my feelings for Bliss had been, there was too much history between us to ever go back to how we were. I'd thought that if I could just get over the pain, then everything else would fall back into place. Well, the pain was gone, but the rift it had caused between us remained.

Funny how four years of friendship could be so completely devastated by one moment of more than friendship. Bliss was the one piece of my old life that I hadn't had to say good-bye to when I moved to Philly. College had been like home to me, the big family that I'd never had. But that home didn't exist anymore. And trying to hold on to it through Bliss wasn't good for either of us.

All the memories and feelings that had connected Bliss and me had frayed until we were connected only by a flimsy, dying thread. It reminded me of an empty theatre after the play had ended, the audience had left, and the crew had cleaned up. The last one to leave turned out all the lights, and left a solitary ghost light in the otherwise darkened space. As we stood there, stiff and awkward, that last thread, that last light, gave way.

Bliss took an uneven breath, and pressed her lips together in a way that I knew meant she was trying not to cry. I took a page out of Max's book and slowly inhaled and exhaled.

"Well, we should go clear our stuff from the stage," Max said. "Cade, babe, do you think you could help? Our drummer had to leave."

I blinked and looked away from Bliss. "Sure. Sure, I can do that."

I looked at Garrick, then Bliss, and said, "It was good to see you both. Congratulations again." I shook Garrick's hand, and this time I gave Bliss a real hug. She pressed her cheek into my chest, and her arms squeezed tight around my middle. She mumbled something that sounded like "Burning out," and then released me. She was blinking rapidly, but I could still see the tears gathering around the corners of her eyes.

"Good-bye, Bliss."

I felt surprisingly numb, like a wound that had been cauterized. Maybe it would hurt more later. Or maybe I was just learning that even the good things from our pasts still only belonged in the past.

"Good-bye, Cade."

Spencer walked the two of them out, and I was left alone with Max. I took a deep breath and sunk back onto the couch.

Max stood above me and said, "I don't even know what the hell just happened, and I'm depressed."

I laughed, which all things considered was far better than the variety of reactions I could have had. "It *was* depressing, wasn't it?"

"You okay, Golden Boy?"

I lifted my chin to look at her, and took the hand that was dangling by her side. I pressed a quick kiss to the back of it, and then let it fall back to her side. "Thank you for that. You didn't have to. And yes, I'm okay. Moving forward, right?"

"That is the goal, boyfriend."

"We're getting pretty good at pretending. Maybe you should be an actor, too."

She laughed. "Not in a million years. I don't like acknowledging my own emotions. Why would I want to pretend to have more just for a lousy paycheck?"

"You don't seem to have any problem expressing emotions when you sing. You're pretty damn great at it, actually."

She looked away, uncomfortable, and said, "To each his own, I guess."

Time for a subject change. I stood, and tried to stretch some of that heavy, melancholy feeling out of my limbs. "Let's go pack up your stuff, Angry Girl."

"Oh, you don't have to help. I was just giving you an excuse . . ."

"Don't be stupid. You know I'm going to help you."

"Yeah, I do."

I followed the sway of her hips across the room. She stopped when she got to the closed door, and turned around.

"I need to ask you something else. Do you want to grab a drink with me after we're done here?"

"A drink sounds like the best idea you've ever had." I smiled. "Though that isn't saying much, considering the kind of ideas I've seen from you."

I expected her to laugh. She didn't.

She just smiled and said, "Yeah . . . right."

24

Max

I convinced Cade that we should head back to Center City to
get our drink, so we'd be closer to where both of us lived
before the subways closed.

He said, "Fine by me. I was going to insist on walking you
home anyway."

I laughed. "Of course you were, Golden Boy."

This also gave me the entire walk to the subway station
and the ride to convince him to keep pretending to be my
boyfriend.

He said, "So, I'm guessing you don't want to talk about
your fight with Mace?"

I raised an eyebrow at him but didn't comment.

"I'm guessing you don't want to talk about that girl getting engaged?"

He sighed. "I guess that leaves your music. How long have you been playing?"

I buttoned my coat all the way up to help block out some of the cold. "Since I was thirteen. Around the time that my sister died."

It shocked me how easily that kind of thing fit into normal conversation with him. With anyone else it never would have come close to leaving my mouth.

"And when did you know that it was what you wanted to do for your career?"

I smiled, remembering. "The first time I was able to play a song all the way through from memory. That was the first time singing really transported me to a different place, you know? It was the best five minutes of my life. I forgot where I was, who I was, and I existed only in the music."

"I get that. I feel the same when I'm onstage. I get to step out of my skin and be someone else for a while. I get to live someone else's problems, which usually get resolved in a much quicker and easier fashion than my own."

I'd never even had a friend that I could talk to like this. I'd lived so long as an island that I'd forgotten what it felt like to have this kind of connection.

"You ever get tired of being yourself, Golden Boy?"

"Sometimes, yeah. What about you?"

He was so honest. He made me want to be, too.

Inhale.

Exhale.

"All the time."

The silence between us was frail, but easy, as we walked the neighborhood streets that led to our subway stop. I surveyed the buildings around us, the uneven sidewalks, the lit up windows for apartments on the second and third floors. I'd walked these streets more times than I could remember, but I'd never really looked around me.

Life was funny like that.

I asked, "Do you think everyone feels that way? Or is there something wrong with us?"

He thought for a long moment, his boots scuffing against the sidewalk as he walked. "I think everyone does. Even happy people. They may not admit it to anyone, but I think they feel it. I think they close their eyes, or go for a run, or take a long shower, so that they can forget just for a second who they are and what they have to do day in and day out. Living is hard. And every day our feet get heavier and we pick up more baggage. So, we stop and take a breath, close our eyes, reset our minds. It's natural. As long as you open your eyes and keep going."

I watched him as he spoke. His eyes scanned the sky, and his breath puffed out as smoke in the cold air. He believed what he was saying. And that made it a little easier for me to believe it, too.

I should have asked him then, but he'd just given me this precious, perfect thought, and I wanted to hold on to it for as long as I could before I had to ruin it. We stayed silent for the one more block it took to reach the subway stop.

We waited about ten minutes for our train, still not saying

a word. We sat together on a bench, sharing the silence, and it didn't feel awkward or unnatural. I didn't want to run or fill up the void or do anything other than what I was doing.

It was . . . nice.

When the train pulled in, we took two of the seats beside each other, and it felt so routine, like we'd been doing this for ages.

I said, "I have something to ask you, but I really don't want to."

He turned slightly, and his knees touched mine. "That sounds interesting."

"It's insane, actually."

He waited, and I tried to just spit it out, but really there was no good way to say it, so instead I buried my face in my hands. I groaned and said, "Money is stupid. It ruins everything."

He hummed. "Tell me about it. I made a promise that I would be home for Christmas, but I get paid so little for my work-study job that I'll be lucky to afford ramen in January if I do."

I sat up but kept my eyes on my hands as I asked, "What if I could help you get home for Christmas?"

"I'm sorry, but I just don't think your boss would be okay with me taking over your dancing shifts at Trestle."

I laughed so hard that everyone else in the train car turned and looked at us.

"God, I would pay to see that."

He nudged my shoulder with his. "Hey, I'm a good dancer."

"How much have you had to drink tonight?"

"Do I need to take you dancing to prove how awesome I am?"

I was tempted to say yes, to take him to the the Garage or some other place, and just lose myself in alcohol and the moving bodies. But I had to stay focused. For so many reasons.

"I'm taking a rain check on that offer, Golden Boy. But . . . I was serious about Christmas. My parents really want you to visit for the holidays, enough that they volunteered to pay for all your flights and stuff."

He kept smiling, even as his head tilted to the side and his brows furrowed. "I thought we were going to be broken up by then?"

"We were . . . but hell, I'm just going to say this. My parents were coming to Philly to tell me it was time to stop singing, to move on and get a real job. They've been helping me with money stuff so that I had time to write and sing, but they were going to stop . . . until they met you. Apparently my dating you is enough to make them believe I'm not a total screwup, and they're willing to keep helping me out for a little while longer. But if I have to tell them we broke up, they're going to cut me off, and with the cost of living here and my debt, it will be almost impossible for me to keep going with the band. So, like a complete coward, I'm asking you to pretend to date me to keep my parents happy."

"Max . . ." His body shifted away from mine slightly. I turned to face him.

"I know it's crazy, but I promise it will just be a few days, just an appearance, and then you can leave and go home for the holidays with your family. You said you needed money for your flight . . . my parents will pay for it."

His eyes searched mine. "I couldn't let your parents do that, Max."

I grabbed one of his hands and held it between both of mine. "It's nothing to them, Cade. I promise. You should see the ridiculous things they spend their money on. I'd much rather they spend money on you."

He placed his other hand on top of mine, and stared at me. "Max, I want to help you, but you have to know how bad of an idea this is. You can't keep pretending for your parents. You'll only resent it. And you know that. The first song you played tonight . . . that was yours, wasn't it? Didn't you learn anything from writing it?"

I felt sliced open, like he'd dissected my mind and my heart and laid it out for everyone to poke and prod. I'd written that song right before I dropped out of college, and he was right.

I hadn't changed at all.

I thought by leaving college I was putting all of that pretending behind me. I thought I had ripped out the roots of that old life and started fresh. Pretending for holidays and other meetings had seemed so insignificant, but it wasn't.

I'd grown right back into that same person.

And I hated that he could see that.

I ripped my hands out of his and stood, even though the train was still moving. "I didn't ask for a therapy session. I'm sorry I can't be perfect like you. Just forget about it."

We pulled into the station, and I walked to the other end

of the car while I waited for the train to come to a complete stop. I heard him call my name as I stepped out onto the platform, but I didn't look back. He caught up to me on the stairs, but I kept going, taking the steps as fast as I could without falling.

"Max . . . wait."

When I surfaced into the night air, his hand caught my elbow and turned me to him.

"Let me go, Cade."

"No."

"What do you mean, no?"

He caught my other arm, and pulled me right up against him.

"I mean that we're not going to have a fight over this."

I said, "You don't get to just decide what we fight about."

"I'll do it, Max."

I blinked and stared up at his face. His dark eyes locked on mine, and he wasn't joking. "Why? You just said . . ."

"I think you have to stop pretending to be something you're not, yeah. Which is why I'll come to Christmas with you if you go as yourself, not as that tame, turtlenecked version of you. That's step one of escaping the bell jar."

My heart was beating so hard I could feel it up in my throat. My lungs felt far away, like they had sunk down into my stomach, and everything in me felt out of place.

"I'd still be lying about you. I'd still—"

"So, it's baby steps. You knock out step one first, and let your parents get used to the idea of who their daughter is. Then you hit them with Mace."

Somehow, in all the chaos, I still managed to laugh. "I've thought about hitting them with mace quite a few times actually."

His half-smile snuck on his face again, and it made me feel a little steadier, a little less out of sorts. Somewhere in my freak-out, his hands had worked their way up from my arms to my neck, and his fingertips now cradled my jaw.

He asked, "So what do you think? Are we a go for Operation Introduce Your Parents to the Real Max?"

"More like Operation Give my Parents a Panic Attack . . . but yeah, we're a go."

"Excellent."

His thumb traced the line of my jaw, and a shiver raced up my spine. I swallowed and wet my lips. "Thanks," I said. "For everything. The walk. The talk. And you know, fake dating me."

He paused for a few seconds and then said, "You know, I seem to remember you promising me a real date the other day."

My heart thumped. I wanted him. I'd been attracted to him before, and now it had only grown. Tonight had been so perfect. He'd said all the right things, and made me think, and pushed me to be myself. Which is exactly why I didn't need to date him. My dating history was toxic, and he was the last person I wanted to taint. We could be friends. I'd needed a friend like him my entire life. He called me on my bullshit and made me less afraid.

And yet, when he looked at me and his skin touched mine . . . friendship was the last thing on my mind.

My phone buzzed, and I jumped at the chance to escape. I pulled away to answer it, but the name on the screen made me pause.

Mace.

The conversation with Cade had put me in a peaceful place that I didn't want to destroy. I hit ignore, but just seeing his name had ruined some of the luster of the evening.

It had been a long day, and all the emotions of it hit me all at once. Maybe all I needed was sleep. I asked Cade for a rain check on the drink, and he volunteered to walk me home. I was happy for the company because his presence kept my mind from dwelling on the things it shouldn't be dwelling on . . . like how things were spiraling out of control with Mace. And the rockier our relationship became, the more disruptive he was toward the band, which meant more than whatever was going on between us.

When we reached my block, Cade held open my apartment building door for me.

"Your landlord still hasn't fixed this lock?" He followed me up the stairs and said, "You should let him have it, Angry Girl. That's ridiculous. It's not safe to leave it like this where anyone can get in."

I kept climbing the stairs and smiled at him over my shoulder. "I know . . . some complete psycho could creep into my apartment while I sleep . . . naked."

We reached my floor and he said, "You're right. I could do that."

I laughed and gave him a playful push. His hands caught my arms, and he pulled me closer to him. My stomach felt like I'd just gone down the drop of a huge roller coaster. I licked my lips and he said, "Really though, please make your landlord take care of the door. If he doesn't, I will."

His face was stern, and it gave me goose bumps.

I tried to play off the way he affected me with humor. I rolled my eyes and said, "Yes, *Master*. Anything else you'd like to order me to do?"

His eyes darkened, and something contracted low in my belly. A whimper built in my throat, and I was seconds away from throwing myself at him when I heard someone call my name.

"Max?"

The clenching in my belly turned painful. Cade's hands loosened on my forearms, and I turned to face Mace.

He'd been sitting outside my door and was climbing to his feet. He lumbered down the hall, one hand on the wall to steady himself.

He was trashed.

I took a step away from Cade and asked, "Mace, what are you doing here?"

"Clearly not having as much fun as you are. You didn't waste any time, did you?"

His normally gorgeous features were twisted into something ugly. His nose scrunched up, and his lips pulled into a grimace.

"Mace, this is my *friend*, Cade. He came to see the show and walked me home."

He twisted the piercing in his eyebrow. "Right. You think I'm stupid, don't you?"

I sighed. "No, I think you're high."

He lurched toward me and said, "And I think you're a whore."

Cade moved in front of me. "Chill, man. We're just friends."

I curled an arm around his elbow and tugged him back. "Don't bother, Cade. He's not good for the band, and he's not good for me. Consider yourself done with both, Mace."

He sauntered up to me. His eyes were red, and his pupils constricted. It was funny how attraction could live and die in an instant. Looking at him now, I didn't feel any of the heat that normally crackled between us. He stood there, high and angry, and I only felt relieved. I stared him down, and he scanned me from head to toe. He drew a thumb across his bottom lip, and said, "I was bored anyway."

I skipped straight past angry into repulsed. What a douchewaffle.

"Go pop some more pills, asshole."

He clipped Cade with his shoulder as he passed and snarled, "Enjoy the lousy lay, *man*."

"Son of a—"

I inhaled and curled my hands into fists. I went after him, but Cade's arms wrapped around my middle and took me captive. He held me back until Mace was long gone and my breathing was under control. As angry as I was, and as much as I wanted to follow Mace down the stairs and give him a swift kick to the junk, part of me was also thankful. I felt like a bird loosed from a cage.

I faced Cade, and he looked even more enraged than I had been.

That guy had the self-control of a saint.

I smiled and said, "How about you show me those dance moves after all?"

I was free. Time to fly.

25

Cade

I was torn.

Part of me wanted to tell her it wasn't a good idea, that she should take the night to cool off and think. Another part of me was already thinking of how she would look on the dance floor. And then in the back of my mind was the tempting thought that I should take her into her apartment and prove that she was anything but boring.

As usual, the responsible choice won out.

"Max . . . it's been a long day. Are you sure you don't want to do something a little less—"

She cut me off. "I want to dance, Golden Boy. I can do that with or without you." She turned that killer pout on me and added, "Though being alone really isn't the safest option." She batted her eyes and smiled. She already knew she'd won.

"When I blow your mind with my dance moves, I expect an apology."

She grabbed my hand and pulled me down the stairs after her. "We'll see who blows whose mind."

We hailed a cab and headed north, into my area of the city. We pulled up outside what looked like an abandoned warehouse in a less than stellar neighborhood. I should know because it was mine. I'd passed by this place numerous times and just figured it was probably abandoned and filled with homeless people.

I asked her, "Did you want to dance or get murdered?"

I paid the cabbie and slid out of the car. Max grabbed my hand and started tugging me toward the warehouse.

"Relax, Golden Boy. I think you'll like this place."

I liked her. Too much for my own good.

I could feel the vibrations from the music before we even entered the building. It didn't look like your typical club. There were couches and artwork painted onto the walls that made it feel like a cross between a friend's apartment and a graffitied street corner. A lot of buildings around the city were covered in murals that spanned multiple stories. There was similar art on the walls here, but it was smaller, and up close you could see all the detail work.

Max said, "Welcome to the Garage."

This place pulsed with the same vibrancy that bled from

Max's every word and movement. It matched her. So yeah, she was right. I liked it.

It didn't feel like normal clubs that were packed tight and reeked of sweat with modern, upscale fixtures. This place had a heartbeat all its own. It had soul.

I turned my eyes back to one of the murals on the wall. It was all black and white and showed people singing and others dancing. It was simple, no color, no frills. But it was beautiful.

Max leaned up to my ear. "My boss at the tattoo parlor did that back when this place opened. He's also the one that did this."

Tattoo parlor. That explained the abundance of art on her body.

She pulled the neck of her shirt down to reveal smooth skin, tattooed branches, and enough cleavage to make my mouth go dry.

"Lucky guy."

Someone shouted Max's name, and I turned to see her jogging over to one of the bartenders. When I caught up he was saying, "Sorry I missed the show tonight, but . . ." He held up the drink he was mixing and shrugged.

"It was a good one," I said,

Max beamed, and the bartender looked between us like he didn't quite understand how we fit together.

His eyebrows were still halfway up his forehead when he said, "I'll try and make the next one. You kids have a good night." He poured us two shots on the house, and then turned to the people next to us for their order. Max used her elbows to heft herself up on the bar and gave him a smacking kiss on his cheek. She didn't look like a girl who'd just broken up with her boyfriend.

At the moment though, her long legs had my full attention. She looked over her shoulder and caught me staring. As she slid down off the bar, she didn't seem to mind. In fact, her smile only widened.

"You ready to be amazed, Angry Girl?"

If her smile as she led me upstairs was any indication, I might have to change her nickname. Going up the stairs behind her could give any straight man a heart attack. Her red high heels gave way to toned calves, glorious thighs, and short leopard print shorts that enhanced her curves. Somewhere out there was an ex-boyfriend with her likeness tattooed somewhere on his body. She was the kind of sexy that begged to be immortalized.

Upstairs was more crowded than the section we'd just left, but there were still couches and mismatched furniture that gave it the same relaxed vibe. There was the main dance floor, and then a second one that was raised up a few feet and featured b-boys freestyling while a crowd of onlookers cheered.

She took a deep breath and closed her eyes. I was getting accustomed to interpreting her breathing. There was the "I'm about to breathe fire" inhale, the "anything involving her mother" inhale, and my personal favorite, the "just been kissed" inhale. As she entered the dance floor, though, her breath was reminiscent of the way she sang. She was relaxed here. Her arms snaked above her head, and her ripped white tee raised to show a strip of skin above her shorts. The last time I'd seen her lower back, it had been covered in bandages and bruises. Now, more than a week later, only the faintest hint of healing scratches remained behind. From here, her skin looked smooth, and I could see the dimples at the bottom of her spine.

A few people slid between us, and I missed the view. She turned, and her eyes found mine. She crooked a finger at me and smiled.

That was the moment I knew for sure that I hadn't been in love with Bliss. I couldn't have been. Because at that moment, nothing could have kept me from going to Max, not even if Bliss had been on the other side calling me, too. I moved through the crowd until she was in my reach. She was twisting and turning and singing along to a song I'd never heard. She ran her hands down her sides to her thighs, and one side of her tee slipped over her shoulder. I wanted to replace the hands on her thighs with my own.

"I'm waiting, Golden Boy!"

Watching her was appealing, but touching her was irresistible. She was even more electric than the music that pulsated around us. I stepped forward right when she rolled her body from her chest down through her hips. When she went to repeat the move, I matched her. Our chests brushed, and she bit her lip.

Every theatre major in college had to take dance classes, and every day in warm-up the professor made us practice isolating different parts of our bodies. The purpose had been to stretch, not dance, but the ability transferred well to this kind of techno music.

Max danced the same way she sang . . . with complete

abandon. I just followed her, keeping our bodies close and matching her movements. She tossed her hair and started to circle around me.

The music changed to something a little slower. I slipped a hand around her waist and pulled her into me. Our hips locked together, and I placed a hand on her hip to guide her into a circular motion. My thigh fitted between hers and hers between mine until we were as close as we could possibly get. She rolled her body to one side, and I leaned the opposite direction.

The air around us was warm and sticky with sweat. She rocked her hips into mine, and I had to clench my teeth to keep in a groan. Moving with her was amazing, but every once in a while she would move in a way I didn't expect. Our hips were so tightly pressed that the friction her movements caused had me seeing stars.

I pressed her backward, and with zero hesitation and no self-consciousness, she dropped her head and body backward in a dip. I kept her steady with an arm around her waist. With her body leaned back, I got a clear view of her tight stomach, the black bra beneath her white shirt, and the delicate column of her neck. I couldn't resist reaching out and running my hand from the front of her throat around the back. I cradled her neck in my hand, and used it to propel her back up to me. She wrapped both arms around my neck, so that her chest was pressed tightly against mine. I simplified our movements because being pressed against her was better than any dance move that would have moved us apart.

I could feel the sweat collecting on my skin, and it glistened on hers, too. I kept one hand curved around her neck and the other ran in a loop from her thigh up to her rib cage. I sighed, wishing that I could freeze this moment, wishing that we were somewhere else. Her face was level with my neck, and her forehead pressed into my jaw. Her breath on my neck was an exquisite torture.

I thought briefly about this being an unwise decision, but I couldn't bring myself to care. I knew from the first time I saw her with Mace that they meant nothing to each other. There was no gravity between them, not like there was between us. No matter how hard we tried to keep ourselves apart, we always wound up right back here.

I thought I had that kind of pull with Bliss, but now I could see that I was wrong. We would have been perfect together, another notch in my pursuit of the "right" life. That's what I was in love with . . . not my friend. Bliss had been exactly what I thought I'd wanted. A friendship evolved into something more. Loving and kind. Sweet and safe.

Max scared me shitless.

And it was so much better.

I could finally say that the past was the past, and the present was so much more appealing. I slid my hand on her neck up until her hair threaded between my fingertips. Her arms tightened around my neck, and her lips brushed my jaw.

I stiffened for a second, worried that I was making the wrong choice.

Almost as if she could hear my thoughts and was trying to shut them up, her teeth grazed my skin, followed by a firm press of her lips.

If this was a mistake, it was the best one I'd ever made.

26

Max

I followed his lead and slipped my fingertips into the curls at the base of his scalp. His other hand slid from my hip to the small of my back and snuck underneath my tee. His hands pressed into my skin, and I was taken back to the night he'd treated my injuries, and how badly I had wanted to do this then.

His face tipped down toward mine, and he breathed, "Max."

There was hesitancy laden in his voice, and I knew what he was thinking. He was about to get noble. He was going to

pull some shit about this not being good for me or me needing time or whatever. He was overthinking something that
was so simple.

So I made it simpler for him.

I shifted up on my toes and kissed him.

His resistance must have been thin, because he was kissing me back immediately. The hand under my shirt slid farther up my back until his fingers met my bra strap. He used
that arm to pull me up onto my tiptoes. It lined up our hips
perfectly, and I moaned into his mouth.

He kissed like he lived—perfectly. His mouth searched
mine feverishly and thoroughly, like he needed to taste every
part of me. Oh how I had underestimated tender kisses. This
kiss was a slow burn that had me squirming against him,
ready to beg for more. He placed a light peck on my mouth,
and then nipped my bottom lip. His mouth pressed harder
against mine, and the kiss crescendoed into something fierce
and addicting.

Even though I didn't want to, I broke away to breathe.
His lips dropped to my neck instead, where he kissed and bit
and sucked, driving me wild. All the feeling in my body was
concentrated on the area where our bodies intersected, so
that the rest of me felt weak and lifeless by comparison. My
legs shook, and for the second time, he was the only thing
holding me together.

Last time it had been because I was in pain.

The only pain I felt now came from the ache in the pit of
my belly that wanted *more*. I pulled his head up from my neck
and pressed my forehead to his.

I wondered if my eyes looked as dilated as his. There was

a good chance that he would say no, but I was too far gone to care about rejection.

"You said you lived close to here?"

I'd been prepared for a fight. I thought he would shoot me down, but his eyes searched my face for a few seconds, which was a few seconds too long for my liking.

Then he nodded, and my uterus did the butterfly or possibly the running man.

I kissed him again because I could. I'd meant it to be quick, but his hands cupped my face, and he kissed me hard. I fisted my hands in his shirt and prayed that he lived *extremely* close.

When he broke away, his voice was husky. "I can't say no to you."

Perfect.

"Then don't."

The door to Cade's apartment clicked shut behind me, and I leaned back against it. The wood was cool against my back, and I shivered. My heart thumped radically in my chest. I felt like my blood had been replaced with Red Bull. He stepped toward me, and I felt feverish.

I searched his eyes, and my stomach dipped like I was falling.

I hadn't even been this nervous my first time.

I hadn't been this nervous *ever*.

He fixed his eyes on me, and desire outweighed my fears. The way he looked at me made my skin sing with electricity. It wasn't just that he made me feel attractive. Any guy on the street with wandering eyes or a good whistle could do that.

He made me feel . . . special, which sounded so damn cheesy that I could choke. It was true though. I knew myself better by knowing how he saw me. He erased the doubt and the fear and the anger. He made me feel like the melody instead of the accompaniment.

"Are you sure?" he asked.

I couldn't quite get a handle on his expression. It was full of wanting, but whether he wanted me to say yes or no was unclear. I had no problem adding a little clarity to the situation. Rather than answering with words, I reached down and pulled the white tee up over my head.

His eyes followed my shirt to the floor. Then he took his time scanning from my heels up to my face. He crossed to me, and I pressed back against the door, needing the support. My whole body tensed in anticipation, but he kept nearly a foot of space between us. He plucked the strap of my bra between his fingertips, and his knuckles grazed my skin. The air in my lungs started to burn. He began to slide the strap over my shoulder, and then seemed to change his mind. His eyes met mine instead, and he gave a dark half-smile. Then he said, "Take it off."

The breath rushed from my chest, and I was so turned on that my fingers went numb. He leaned one arm on the door next to me, so that when I reached behind my back, my chest brushed his softly. I kept my head tilted back so that I could see his face. He was so close, but too far, and the longer he stayed there the more uneven my breathing became. I fumbled with the clasp, unable to force my fingers to cooperate. I was ready to rip it off when the clasp finally came undone, and the straps fell from my shoulders. I leaned back against

the wall, and let my bra drop to join my shirt. The door behind me was cold against my overheated skin, and the peaks
of my breasts hardened.

His right index finger touched the skin just above my
belly button, and my muscles tensed on instinct. He'd found
one of the roots to my tree tattoo, and his light touch followed it until it met up with another line. He followed that
line down to my hip, and then back up to the hollow of my
rib cage. He took his time, tracing each line, and his touch
was so soft that goose bumps rose up on my skin. He danced
over the sensitive skin on my ribs, and I sucked in a breath.

He made a sound low in his throat in response, and I was
going to sink into a heap of frayed nerves and arousal if he
kept at this. Finally his attention turned to the trunk of the
tree that grew up in the valley between my breasts. I arched
my back, desperate for him to touch me somewhere more
substantial. He used two fingers to push on my sternum and
pressed me back against the wall.

"Patience, Angry Girl."

I groaned, and he smiled.

"You don't know how much I've thought about this tattoo.
I want to memorize it so that every time I close my eyes I can
see the way it accentuates your body."

For the briefest of seconds, both of his hands cupped
my breasts, and I moaned in response. But then he slid his
hands up to my shoulders, and held me back against the door.

He placed a kiss on my puckered frown and said, "I
promise to pay this much attention to every part of you."

It was the hardest thing I'd ever done in my life, to sit
there, still and silent, as he traced each branch. The tree

spanned my chest, but always stopped a few inches shy of where I really wanted his touch. I wanted to grab his hands and move them myself, but I liked him being in control too much.

When he finished, my skin was flushed and my breath heavy. My knees grew weak, and my hands clutched at the door behind me. Our eyes met, and his lids were heavy and his pupils dark. I felt intoxicated. Everything in the world but him was blurry. Everything in the world but him disappeared.

"Beautiful," he whispered.

A "please" slipped from my mouth, and he rewarded me by pulling me forward until my chest pressed against his. It was good, but he was still clothed so it wasn't enough. I reached greedy fingers toward the bottom of his shirt, and he lifted it over his head for me.

He loomed over me, one hand perched on the wall on either side of me. It was reminiscent of the night he'd kissed me outside of Trestle, but the view was so much better this time. His chest was broad and tanned, and gave way to rippling lines of muscle on his abdomen. But my hands went straight for the V of muscle that started above his hips and disappeared down into his jeans.

Mace had been fit, but on the skinny side.

Cade was . . . God, he should just stop wearing clothes altogether. I would fully support that. A little impatient, I slipped a finger under the waistband of his jeans and tugged him forward. The first touch of his skin on mine was like lightning. I could feel the charge between us building.

After that, slow became a thing of the past.

His mouth crushed down onto mine. His hands left the door to tangle in my hair, and my back hit the wall with a loud thud. There was nothing sweet or delicate about this kiss. The guy who'd traced the lines on my skin was replaced with someone hungry and desperate. His hands held me in place as his lips conquered mine. I gave myself up to him and wrapped my arms around his neck.

He released my hair, and I whimpered at the loss, but then his hands found my thighs. He bent his knees and curved his fingers around the back of my legs. He lifted, and I wrapped my legs around his waist. I clenched my arms and legs around his body, and I could feel the length of him pressed up against my center. My breath caught in my throat, and his hips bucked into mine. My lower back hit the door again, and I was happily trapped. His tongue traced my collarbone, and I fisted my hands in his hair. He cupped my behind and kept our hips locked tightly together.

His mouth moved down my chest, but he was too tall to reach where both of us wanted him to be. There was a small dining table to the right, and he spun and laid me down across the top. Then he bent and took the tip of one of my breasts into his mouth.

I cried out and arched up into him. His hands slipped beneath my back, and kept me there, my body bowed up toward his mouth. He flicked his tongue over the peak, and then traced a branch on my tree to the other side. The tension in my belly was so strong that I was going to fall apart from this alone.

I used my legs around his waist to pull his hips to mine and begged, "Please." Cade ignored me and continued pressing kisses across my chest. I forced his face up to mine and said, "I thought you weren't able to say no to me?"

He ducked and placed a quick kiss on my sternum and said, "I'm not done exploring this part of you."

I wrapped my arms around his neck and pulled him up so his chest aligned with mine. "Explore that part of me later."

His smile was so damn sexy.

"I like the sound of that, but I also like hearing you beg." I pulled his face to mine and covered his mouth with mine. Between kisses I whispered against his lips, "I like you when you're a little less golden."

He pulled me up off the table, so that we stood in the middle of his living room with my legs wrapped around his waist. For once, this put me looking down at him. I pushed some of the curls off his forehead and gazed down at him.

He was beautiful in a way I wasn't accustomed to. I'd been with plenty of attractive guys, but he was different. He was movie star gorgeous. Untouchable. Just to squash that thought, I touched my fingers to his lips. He was mine for tonight at least, and I was sure as hell going to enjoy it.

"I want you," I murmured. "How many times are you going to make me say please?"

He turned and started moving toward a door that I hoped led to his bedroom.

"I think that one did the trick."

27

Cade

She looked so good spread out on my bed. I hadn't had nearly my fill of kissing her, but I was just as impatient as she was. She uncurled her legs from my waist, and I knelt on the bed between them. I reached for the button on her shorts and slid them and her tights down her legs. Her hips were perfect. Her legs were perfect. And the black underwear that matched her previously discarded bra were pretty damn perfect, too.

Something devious glinted in her eye, and she pushed on my abs until I stepped off the bed. Then she kneeled at my feet, and unbuttoned my jeans. Whatever blood was still left in the rest of my body rushed south. I fisted my hands at my sides to try to stay in control, but when my jeans and boxers hit the floor it was a lost battle. Her mouth was heaven and hell all at the same time, and the tables of control turned so fast that my head was spinning.

"God, Max."

I groaned and laced my fingers into her bright red curls. I couldn't make up my mind what I wanted more. Part of me wanted to take our time, while the rest of me wanted to screw going slow. There would be time for all this later.

It was torture pushing her back, but I just couldn't wait any longer. I pulled her up to stand in front of me, and slid her underwear down over her hips. She was so gorgeous that it hurt to breathe. She sat on the bed and scooted back toward the pillows. I wanted to follow, but I made myself stop and grab a condom from my nightstand. Then I crawled toward her until my body hovered above hers. I hesitated, knowing how powerful the press of our bodies would be. Her eyes were closed in anticipation, and she was biting her kiss-swollen bottom lip. I pressed my lips against hers and sucked that bottom lip into my mouth before lowering myself into paradise.

I started slow, mostly because I was trying to memorize the way she felt around me. I hated that she'd been with that asshole, Mace. I hated that he'd seen her like this, but I was happy to know that she was mine now. I took her hands from around my neck, and laced our fingers together. I pressed her palms down into the mattress at the same time that I rocked my hips into hers. Her mouth opened in a silent cry, and she tilted her head back. I wanted to hear her, so I did it again, harder.

She bit her lip, and let out the smallest whimper. Each time I pressed into her, her reaction was a little less inhibited. I ran my hands from her knees, down her sweat-slicked legs, to the curve of her bottom. I snapped my hips forward and pushed up on her hips at the same time. She twisted and arched beneath me, moaning my name. The sound of it nearly pushed me over the edge, but I made myself slow down.

"Max."

Her eyes fluttered open, and she looked at me from under half-lowered lashes. I pressed a kiss to her forehead, and then rocked my hips again. Her eyes closed, and I slowed my movements again.

"Look at me, Max."

She whimpered but did as I said. The next thrust made my vision go spotty, and though her body contorted underneath mine, and she tried to tug her hands free from my grasp, she kept her eyes open.

There was too much pleasure, too much want, too much beauty beneath me. There was too much everything. The world seemed to expand to accommodate the power of that moment. Something shifted between us—small and ineffable—but we ceased to be whatever we had been before and became something new.

I saw the same wonder in her eyes that I felt in my chest.

Then I saw the fear chasing on its heels.

I saw her start to close off, and knew I needed to do something. I took hold of her hips and flipped us over so that she was on top, so that she was in control.

Her eyes were closed, and when she opened them that flicker of fear was gone. She smiled and pressed her palms into my abdomen. She shifted her hips over mine, and breathed. "I had a dream about you like this once."

Damn.

It was my turn to groan, and the thought of her dreaming about me was so sexy that I had to grasp her hips and still them until I got myself under control. She leaned over and kissed me. The press of her breasts against my bare chest didn't do anything to help me, but it was too good to push her off. After a minute, I lifted my hands and let her move again. She sat up and raised her arms above her head to tangle in her hair.

The sight of her like that was the most erotic thing I'd ever seen, and I didn't think I would forget it as long as I lived. It also made it hard to hold on. I slid my hand to where our bodies met to help her along, and she slammed her hips down hard on mine in response.

If I were an artist, I would paint her just like this. She reminded me of the spirits and nymphs that populated so many of Shakespeare's plays. She was wild and free and inhumanly beautiful. The only other time I'd seen her this vibrant was when she was onstage.

Her legs squeezed around my hips, and her hands dropped back to my chest. Her fingernails scraped down my stomach, and I bucked up into her. She threw her head back, and I pressed my fingers harder against her. Then she moaned, and my world was awash in color and heat and . . . God, she was so tight.

Her eyes met mine, and they shone dark and glassy. I sat up and held her to my chest. Her body convulsed around mine, and I pressed my forehead against hers as I gave in to the pull.

I don't know how long we stayed there, wrapped around each other, foreheads pressed together, gaze locked. It could have been minutes or years. All I knew was that I never wanted to move. Our bodies fit perfectly together, like a lock to a key. I kissed her, soft and slow. I didn't want to think past the feel of her skin or the curve of her hips or the smell of her hair. But for now, I would settle for lying side by side with her in my arms.

28

Max

I was relaxed and numb and glorious.

Until I wasn't.

Until the glow faded, and I was assaulted my all the thoughts that my mind had been too preoccupied to think before. His arms were tight around me, secure and comforting and caging all at once.

Sex had never been like that for me. It had always been about bodies and sensations and simplicity. Sex with Cade was confusing. It was adding one plus one and getting an answer other than two. It was more than it should have been, and it threw my world off balance.

Cade got up to go to the bathroom, and I slipped my panties back on, and then went to the living room to hunt for my shirt. Cade's place was the opposite of mine. He had pictures of friends and family on walls and bookshelves. Those shelves actually had books on them, along with mementos and keepsakes that apparently meant enough to him to bring all the way to Pennsylvania with him. His place felt homey. It felt nice and comforting, just like him.

Unease flitted around my chest, but I pushed it down. I tiptoed back to Cade's room, and my nerves started to rattle. I stared at the rumpled sheets on his bed and just couldn't make myself get back inside it. Cade was wonderful. Mind-blowingly wonderful. Tonight had been one of the most intense moments of my life.

But that was the problem.

We'd known each other ten days. I looked at the clock, and it read 3:00 A.M. Make that eleven days, but still . . . eleven days. There at the end, he'd looked at me in a way that no other man ever had. I couldn't even put into words what that look had done to me.

It wrecked me, completely.

It was so honest and raw that it made the rest of my life feel fake and insignificant in comparison. Everything was changing too fast. Even now, thinking about it, I felt like something in me was disintegrating faster than I could hold it together.

I jumped when Cade's arms wrapped around my middle. His chest pressed into my back, and he placed a few kisses down the side of my neck. His touch was almost enough to deflate my worries, but they stayed there, lurking at the back of my throat, making it harder to breathe. Even so, my body was at ease with his. I leaned back into his arms.

His lips hovered next to my ear, and he whispered, "Have I told you how gorgeous you are?"

I swallowed. "Not in a few minutes."

"Mmm . . ." The scruff on his jaw tickled the sensitive skin of my neck and he said, "As long as you know."

He was too good for me. That much was abundantly clear. He was sweet and thoughtful and generous in every way. He never missed an opportunity to reassure me or compliment me or touch me. I wasn't used to that kind of affection. I shied away from it in every other part of my life, but coming from him I soaked it up like rain on arid ground.

I was tired of thinking, so I turned in his arms and wrapped myself up in his embrace. His chest was still bare, but he'd slipped on a pair of pajama pants that hung low on his hips. I pressed my cheek to his chest and looked down. Seeing our bare feet facing each other pulled something in my chest, and my breath caught in my throat. The intimacy of this embrace made me panic, but at the same time, the thought of moving out of it was painful.

He tugged me down onto the bed and pulled the covers over us. I concentrated on breathing normally as he slipped an arm over my waist. He reached over me to turn off the lamp beside the bed. In the dark, he pressed a kiss to the back of my neck, and I shivered.

I felt like crying.

I just . . . this wasn't my life. Things like this didn't happen to me, and if they did, it never lasted. Girls like me didn't get guys like Cade.

Maybe it would take a week, maybe less, but I would end up screwing this up. It was what I did. The only thing I was better at than destroying things was singing, and with my behavior today, I was beginning to realize I was in danger of destroying that, too.

More than anything, I didn't trust myself. With Mace I'd been obsessed with him a few weeks ago. I liked him enough to go through this elaborate scheme just to keep my parents from scaring him off. Then boom, I woke up and couldn't care less about our relationship.

That was how I worked. Or rather . . . how I didn't work.

I couldn't do that to Cade. What if we got together, and I woke up one day and wanted out? I liked him more than I liked myself, so I'd probably end up sacrificing my own happiness to keep from hurting him. It would be just like all the years I played at being Alex to keep my parents happy. But instead of blond curls and cheerleading, it would likely mean kids and a minivan.

I may not have been the most self-aware person in the world, but I knew enough to know that if I let myself care about him, I would sabotage my life to better his.

Or I would sabotage it all just because I could.

Or maybe I wouldn't have to sabotage it. Cade was obviously getting over that Bliss girl. Now, she . . . she made sense with him in a way I never would. What if being with me was just a phase, an overcorrection after things didn't work out with her?

How long would it take for him to realize that I wasn't really what he wanted? And how badly would it hurt when he did?

I felt sick from my stomach to my soul.

I waited until Cade's breathing evened out, and I was certain that he was asleep. Then I slipped out of his arms and slipped on my shorts. I'd only wanted a little space to think, to breathe. But the minute he was no longer touching me, my blood pumped faster, singing *run, run, run* with every beat. I looked back at him, the hard lines of his body, the relaxed expression on his face, and I did just that.

I grabbed my heels and my purse and opened his front door as quietly as I could. It was nearly four in the morning. I couldn't walk home alone in this neighborhood, but I couldn't stay either. I was minutes away from a meltdown of ugly proportions.

So, I called Spence to pick me up. He lived in Northeast Philly and had a car. Despite the late hour, he answered on the second ring. I sighed in relief at hearing his voice, and tears pricked at my eyes.

Shit.

"Spence, I'm so sorry, but can you come pick me up?"

His voice was groggy, but he didn't hesitate before he said, "Yeah. Yeah, of course. Where are you?"

I gave him the cross streets, and he told me he'd be here in about ten minutes. I ended the call and pressed the phone to my chest.

I knew what I was doing was awful, but if I was preventing a bigger tragedy did that make it so terrible?

I needed to stick with my intuition. Cade deserved better than me. And I couldn't give him what he needed. He needed a girl who could commit to him with the same care and complete abandon that he gave her. That wasn't me. I was broken and patched and missing pieces. I couldn't give him all of me, because I didn't even have that. There was a piece of me still on that highway, a piece of me buried with my sister. I'd left shards all over this city, and he didn't deserve to have to clean up that mess.

And he wouldn't want to . . . not when the luster wore off and he got a good look at the girl he'd caught. Then he'd see me for what I really was . . . toxic. And he would want nothing to do with me.

I sat at the top of the stairs at the end of Cade's hallway. I wrapped my arms around my middle. The muscles of my body were tense, once again trying to hold myself together by sheer force. I remember the way his arms had wrapped around me tonight and that time on Thanksgiving when he'd been the one to hold me together.

And I lost it. My vision swam with tears, and I held my breath, like that would keep the tears at bay, too. I shuddered and pressed my face into my knees. For the first time in nine years, the first time since Alex, I couldn't push the tears down. I couldn't control them. I cried. I sobbed. The emotions ripped free from my chest, taking pieces of me with it.

It was four in the morning. If I couldn't cry now, when could I?

So, I let the guilt wash over me, and I said good-bye to something beautiful and terrifying and delicate that I'd held in my soul for a few short hours. I said good-bye to something that should never have been mine.

A door swung open on the floor below me, and laughter floated up the stairs. I tried to wipe my eyes, but I was too far gone and not fast enough. Cade's friend Milo and a pretty girl were at the bottom of the stairs, staring up at me.

I ducked my head and scooted close to the wall so they could get by. The girl walked past me in silence, but Milo sat down beside me.

I pressed my lips together and tried to concentrate on breathing.

"It's Max, right?"

I didn't think I could speak without crying, so I nodded instead.

His eyes took in my appearance, and I knew I must have looked like a complete wreck. He sighed. "Did you at least leave a note?"

I looked at him in shock.

"What? You're out here at four in the morning, crying, with major sex hair. It doesn't take much to put things together. All I'm asking is if you told him why?"

God, I didn't think I could feel lower than I already did.

Wrong.

My phone buzzed. Spence.

I knew it was terrible, but I wasn't changing my mind. I looked at Milo and shook my head.

"Tell him I'm sorry."

Then I ran, leaving behind the best thing that could never happen to me.

I stayed in bed the next day until the sun was on its way down again.

He didn't call.

It wasn't that I wanted him to, but I just thought . . . I don't know what I'd thought.

He let people go. He'd told me that. He didn't fight for

the last girl, and he didn't fight for me. If I was honest, a small, terrified part of me had been counting on that. If he came for me, I didn't think I would be able to say no. And this was for the best. I had to believe that or I'd never be able to get out of bed again.

I was saving us both.

So I kept busy, passing the time as best as I could.

I hadn't told Mom and Dad anything about "breaking up" with Cade. It didn't matter anyway. By the time I'd battled off the depression enough to call Mom, they'd already booked both of our flights.

I would tell them something when I got there—he was sick or a family emergency or something. Hell, maybe I'd just tell them the truth.

What did it matter anymore?

I didn't have that much longer until I left for Oklahoma, and this all came crashing down. The important thing was squeezing in as much rehearsal time as possible before then, especially now that we had to find a new drummer to replace Mace.

Music was what mattered now. The only thing that mattered.

29

Cade

The bed was cold when I rolled over, and already I had a sinking feeling. I didn't know if it was how quiet she was as we went to sleep or the way she'd clung to me in that hug, but I just knew something wasn't right. Though she'd lay right beside me, she'd felt miles away. Even so, I got up and checked the bathroom.

Empty.

I tried the living room and the kitchen.

Empty.

I called her name, and it only echoed back at me.

Empty.

That was how I felt, too. I sat on the bed, numb, but not really surprised. I should have listened to what my brain had been telling me all along. It was obvious just from looking at Max that we came from different worlds. I was naive to think she could ever be happy with someone like me. And I was naive to think it had only been physical attraction. It was so much more than that. All I knew was that I was pretty damn tired of having my heart handed to me in a blender.

Eventually the emptiness was filled up by anger, and I ripped the sheets off my bed and threw them down. They still smelled like her, and I refused to let her linger in my life the way I'd done with Bliss. If she didn't want me, fine.

I was probably dodging a bullet anyway.

I stayed calm as I stripped the bed. I grabbed a laundry basket and dumped the dirty clothes already in it to make room for the sheets. I checked the clock.

7:21 a.m.

That wasn't too early to go to the Laundromat.

The sooner she was out of my life the better. I had to keep moving forward. One foot in front of the other.

But where was the damn detergent?

It wasn't in the bathroom, where I normally kept it.

I checked the kitchen and my closet, and all the while the muscles in my neck and back grew tenser until they were as hard and unforgiving as stone.

I searched my bedroom, but instead of finding detergent, I found Max's sheer black tights.

I stared at them while my control unraveled. I wanted to throw them in the trash. I wanted to return them. I wanted to keep them. I was a mess of wants, none of which mattered, because *she* didn't want *me*.

I picked up the lamp beside my bed and threw it against the wall. I watched it shatter, and wished I had the satisfaction of seeing myself break that way. It was worse, when you couldn't see or touch the part of you that was in pieces.

The anger only made me feel worse. It gave way to guilt too easily, and after a few days, I was left feeling even emptier than before.

Over the next week, I didn't spend much time at home. I couldn't. Every time I touched my door, laid something on my table, or slept in my bed, I saw her. I could still smell her on my pillow even after washing my sheets. Or maybe the memory was so ingrained that I thought I could. I saw her behind my closed eyes while I tried to sleep at night. So I avoided home as much as I could. One night with her had tainted it.

I put in more hours at the library, stayed longer after class, and volunteered to help with random stuff around the theatre department. *You need someone to organize that storage room that no one has opened in years? Sure!*

You need someone to build that prop? Gladly!

I made it my goal to be the best in every assignment, in every class. To be perfect. And as such I demolished my midterms. I just had to fill my mind with enough things that there wasn't room for her. That was the plan at least, but Max was larger than life and tended to beat out the other stuff no matter how hard I tried. And when classes ended for the holiday, there was nothing left to keep my mind busy.

Near the end of the week, I came home to find Milo sitting on my couch, eating a bag of my potato chips. I hadn't told Milo what happened because I didn't want to relive it more than I already had.

I said, "You know . . . I gave you that spare key for emergencies, not so that you could come in here and mooch my food."

He swallowed the graveyard of chips in his mouth and said, "Where the hell have you been all week, Winston?"

I threw my bag in a chair and shrugged off my coat. If he was going to try to get me to some bar or club or anything, I wasn't up for it. I headed to the kitchen and said noncommittally, "Around."

He stood but didn't follow me into the kitchen.

"You all right?"

I opened the cabinet to get a glass, and said, "Yeah, why do you ask?"

"I saw her, Cade."

My whole body tensed, and I nearly dropped the glass I'd gotten from the cabinet. I took a deep breath and opened the fridge to grab the pitcher of filtered water.

I let the fridge block my face as I asked, "Her?"

"Quit bullshitting me, *hermano*. Be real with me."

My hand shook as I poured the water.

"What? We had sex. She left. It's not that big of a deal."

"Not that big of a deal? I will call bullshit on that so many times that the word *bullshit* will lose all meaning."

I sighed. "What do you want me to say?"

I took a drink and set my glass on the counter.

He shrugged. "Well, you could start by telling me how it was."

I saw red, and was halfway across the room before he cried, "Whoa, man! Kidding!" My ears were roaring, and Milo was standing on the futon with an arm stretched out between us. "I think I've proved my point about this being a big deal."

I exhaled slowly and rubbed a hand across my face.

"You want me to say I'm miserable? Fine. I'm miserable. Are you going to make me take some more dumbass shots? Because that's not going to cut it. Just drop it."

Milo whistled. "It's about time you got angry."

"And getting angrier by the second."

He asked, "Did you go after her?"

I took a deep inhale and exhale, but that only made me think of Max.

"No, I didn't go after her. What's the point?"

"The point is to call her on her bullshit like I'm doing for you."

I shook my head. "I think her leaving was a pretty clear indication of how she feels."

She knew I wouldn't go after her. She knew I didn't chase people. And she'd left anyway. That was a pretty glaring indication that it was over as far as I was concerned.

I was done with this conversation. I returned to the kitchen and took a long drink of my water.

"She was crying, Cade."

Time stuttered.

"She what?"

Milo stood in the door to the kitchen, his face serious. I couldn't have heard him right. He said, "That's why I'm here. I've been trying to catch you all week. I came home when she was leaving the other night. The girl was torn up, sitting at the top of the stairs waiting on a ride. It looked like she'd been crying for a while."

Something twisted in my chest, and even now I wanted to find her and comfort her, even if I was the problem.

"Did she say anything to you?"

"Just to tell you that she was sorry."

I sank onto the end of the futon and buried my head in my hands.

Milo continued, "All I'm saying is . . . whatever is between you guys isn't nothing. Girls like that don't cry over nothing."

It hurt to get my hopes up, and they hadn't even been shot down yet. The crash would be infinitely worse.

If I fought for her and lost . . . I just . . . I couldn't. She couldn't stay and I couldn't go after her. We were both crippled by our pasts. And for once . . . I needed to think about myself first.

"You're overthinking this. I'm not saying you need to lay it all on the line, tattoo her name on your ass, or write I love you across the sky. Just talk to her. Feel it out. If you never see her again, you'll always wonder."

If I had overthought a few more things where she was concerned, maybe I wouldn't be in this situation. Besides . . . crying didn't mean she had feelings for me. It could have just been the guilt getting to her. If she had really been upset, she would have come back. She would have called. She would have done *something*.

"I have to go, Milo. I'm working with the after-school program today."

Volunteering was the perfect antidote to how I was feeling. Most of those kids had it infinitely worse than I ever had. One afternoon with them would kick loose all of the self-pity that I couldn't seem to shake. Those kids lived in a stark reality, and it was time I woke up and realized I was there, too. Hoping for the impossible with Max was only going to mess me up more.

"You're being stupid, *hermano*."

No. I thought it was the smartest damn thing I'd done in ages.

30

Max

It was a shit storm of an idea, but somehow I'd managed to bury all of my concerns until I was facing down his door. I had a completely legitimate reason to be here. My parents had already bought the plane tickets, so he might as well have his. Or maybe I just wanted to see him so badly that I didn't care about how it could go wrong.

He had to be angry. I'd slipped out without a note. I hadn't called. I didn't do well with fights—too messy. Fighting was for people who cared, and I made it my policy not to.

So then why was I more worried about the possibility that he wouldn't be angry? That he wouldn't care at all?

I raised my hand, and before I could change my mind, I knocked. My heart slammed against my rib cage, and my mouth went dry.

I was going to see him. If I thought I'd wanted that, craved it, before, the feeling paled in comparison to the spike of anticipation I felt in those silent, waiting seconds. He was under my skin, buried in my thoughts. I could still see him, smell him, and feel him as if it had happened moments ago instead of days. A week.

How could I go so freaking crazy in a week? I'd lost all direction, all sense of what I wanted. My compass just kept spinning and spinning with no true north in sight.

The thought of Cade was the only thing that made me feel steady.

If I could just see him, things would be easier. Closure. That's what I needed. If I could just see that he was okay, I could stop feeling guilty. I could stop obsessing over whether or not I'd made a mistake.

After a few moments, I knocked again.

No answer. Not even a sound on the other side of the door.

He wasn't here. The influx of emotions rocked through me, and I couldn't tell whether I was more devastated or relieved.

"You just missed him."

The voice came from behind me, and I spun so fast that I lost my balance and had to steady myself against the door. It was his neighbor, Milo. The same one that saw me leaving a week ago.

My eyes widened, and my mind blanked.

"I'm just . . . I . . ."

He held up a hand and said, "You don't have to explain it to me."

That was good because I didn't have an explanation. I was hoping I would miraculously know what words to say when I saw Cade. That I wouldn't just hold out the tickets and then run for it. Hell, I still didn't even know exactly what I wanted out of all this.

I cleared my throat and fixed my eyes on his forehead so that I didn't have to look him in the eye.

"Is he . . . how is he?"

Milo leaned against the doorjamb and crossed his arms casually over his chest.

"He's good. *Really good*, actually."

"Oh."

This was so bad. I needed to get out of here. I turned toward the stairs, and Milo stepped in front of me.

"You could ask him yourself. He's at the rec center on campus for that after-school program he does."

I couldn't.

"That's okay. I'll just see him another time."

Milo laughed. "No, you won't. If you don't do it now, you'll never do it."

"What makes you think that?"

"Because I recognize a kindred spirit. It took all you had to do this once. It won't happen a second time. Believe me, I've been there."

I squirmed under his gaze, and he grinned at me. He was

so smug with his assessment of me that I was surprised he didn't suffocate under all that arrogance.

"You don't know what you're talking about. I just came to give him something that belongs to him."

Milo didn't look like he believed me. I didn't know if I believed myself.

"I'll just come by another time."

I turned and bolted down the stairs. For the second time, I ran away from Cade's apartment. And even though I wouldn't admit it to Milo, I knew he was right. So, I turned north toward the Temple campus. I had the whole walk there to either gather my courage or change my mind.

The rec center was easy enough to find, but finding Cade was a different story.

There were so many kids. Hundreds of them. Of all ages and genders and nationalities. They played chess and basketball and learned to dance. The building rang with their cheers and laughter. A group of kids ran past me, screaming excitedly, and I was nearly trampled in the process. I watched them, smiling. Their stumbling feet led my eyes right to Cade.

A large group of children surrounded him and a pretty blonde. Cade and the girl were wearing red T-shirts with the word VOLUNTEER stamped across their backs, and the children hung on their every word.

Cade had his arm stretched in front of his chest, pulling it back with the other arm. The T-shirt he wore was just snug enough to hint at the curve of his chest and shoulders. You could tell from looking at him that he was in shape, but not even I had expected his body to be as gorgeous as it was. Just closing my eyes, I could call it to mind all too easily.

He shook his arms out and said, "All right, guys. Now that we've stretched out our bodies, we need to stretch out our faces. Your facial expressions are very important as an actor. So, let's do a little Lion Face/Lemon Face. Pretend that you've just tasted the most sour lemon in the history of the universe."

The kids puckered their lips and scrunched up their faces. Cade walked around the circle, making a funny face with them.

He stopped beside a boy, maybe seven years old, who was concentrating extremely hard on the face he was making.

"How sour is that lemon, Jamal?"

The boy hopped from one foot to the other, shaking his head, and said, "SO sour, Mr. Cade."

I smothered a laugh into my hand.

"Okay, now I want you to get mad that that lemon was so sour and roar like a lion."

The kids dropped the squished expressions and stretched their faces wide. Their eyes bulged, and their lungs bellowed, and it was kind of terrifying. Such stuff as horror movies are made of.

Cade then proceeded to shout, "Lemon Face! Lion Face!" in quick succession, and the kids switched back and forth with glee. After a few rounds the kids were jumping around and screaming whether they were making lion or lemon faces.

Cade made eye contact with his girl partner and chuckled. The girl looked at him from beneath her lashes in that universal "I want you" way. He stood next to her, and she bumped his shoulder with hers.

Watching them, I felt like the floor had given way beneath my feet.

Milo had said that Cade was good. *Really good*.

Was this why he'd wanted me to come here? My stomach twisted. I looked back at the blonde and wondered what *Really Good's* name was.

This was a mistake. This was his world. All laughter and good deeds and sunshine. This was exactly the reason I'd left. My life was dark, depressing, and decaying in comparison. I don't know what I was thinking coming here.

Had I expected our lives to just fall together? Did I really believe that all our differences and all the baggage piled up between us would just melt away because . . . What? Because I missed him?

Or did I think we could pick back up with our friendship like nothing had changed?

Everything had changed.

I'd never thought of myself as naive, but I supposed there was a first time for everything. I took one last look at him. His smile was so gorgeous that it was painful to watch. I was seconds away from turning. I just wanted to soak up a few more moments. Then his eyes met mine.

He blinked, like maybe he was seeing things, and his smile disappeared. That was all the insight I needed. I turned just as I heard him say, "Amy, can you take over?"

I darted between two rows of tables with kids playing chess.

"Max!"

I picked up my pace and pushed through a set of double doors. I could hear him behind me, and I contemplated darting out into traffic. That would have been easier to face. Instead, I took a deep breath and made myself turn south and continue as calmly down Broad Street as I could.

The next time he said my name, it was quiet, and it sent a quiver down my spine. "Max." I had a feeling I would regret it, but I didn't have it in me to keep running. I schooled my features and turned to face him.

"Hi, Cade."

His expression gave nothing away as he asked, "What are you doing here?"

Straight to the point then.

I fumbled with my purse, glad that I'd prepared at least that much.

"I came to give you this. Milo told me you were here." I held out an envelope and snatched my hand away as soon as he took it. I swallowed and said, "My parents had already bought your ticket. They got a refundable one, so I thought, um, I thought you could just change it from Oklahoma to Texas."

He didn't open the envelope, not even to look at the ticket inside. He just stared at me, his jaw set firmly and asked, "Is that all?"

In my head, I saw that blond girl touching him. That's the second blonde I'd seen him with, both much more his type. Both the kind of girl my parents wished I was. If anything, this visit proved that I was right.

"That's all," I told him.

"Then why did you run?"

I did run, didn't I? How embarrassing.

Because I was on the verge of doing something very stupid . . . like thinking I had made a mistake. Or thinking I stood a chance.

"Because you were busy. I was going to go grab a cookie from that food truck on campus, and then come back." I was going to go stuff my face. Attractive. *Good save, Max.* "You should get back, though. I didn't mean to take you away from the kids." And Amy. I kind of wanted to maim Amy.

Silence grew up between us like weeds, and I didn't know what else to say. I should turn around and leave. I should cut my losses, burn the end of the rope before it frayed further, but I couldn't.

What if this was the last time that I saw him?

"I should go," I said, except I didn't leave. My feet had grown roots and burrowed into the concrete. "Um . . . it was good seeing you."

His eyes searched mine, and I could see the distrust in them, like he was puzzling out my words, trying to decide if they were genuine.

I didn't blame him.

Half the time *I* wasn't even sure if I was genuine.

His expression was guarded in a way that it never had been before. Wearing a mask was my defense mechanism, and I hated that I had pushed him to it.

Whatever connection we'd had was long gone. I just needed to accept that.

I pasted on a smile and said, "Good-bye, Cade."

31

Cade

"Max, wait!" I didn't really know what I was saying until the words had already left my mouth. "What time do we fly out?"

She turned, and something I couldn't decipher flickered in her eyes. I'd been trying so hard to remain ambivalent, to not let her presence get to me, but I just couldn't.

The look of shock on her face was pretty spot-on for how I felt. The moment the words left my mouth, I regretted it. But for some reason when she asked, "We?" I didn't back out.

I looked at her wide blue eyes and said, "If you still want me to go, I'm in. I made you a promise, and I'm going to follow through." Even if it killed me.

She crossed her arms over her chest, and surveyed me. I kept my face passive and my body relaxed. I didn't want her to think this was a ploy to get her back. It wasn't. This charade had been really important to her, and if she thought she needed me to face her parents, I wasn't going to let her down. I was afraid if I didn't go, she'd keep right on pretending.

"You would do that for me?" she asked.

I was a little afraid to examine what I was willing to do for her.

I weighed my words carefully before saying, "We made a deal. I would do it for anyone." I swear she winced, and I had to bite my tongue to keep from telling her the truth.

She swallowed and nodded. "Okay, then. Um, thanks. We fly out Sunday morning at eleven."

"Okay. I'll come early, and we'll catch a cab to the airport."

"Right, well, I'll see you Sunday then."

I watched her go for few minutes before returning to the rec center.

Bad idea didn't even begin to describe what I'd just done.

Over the next few days, I kept finding myself being drawn back to that airline ticket. Sometimes I would just stare at the numbers—dates and times and flights—until they stopped making sense. Other times I would hold the ticket in my hands and concentrate, as if I might be able to feel her intentions behind it just by touching it.

Was it just a ticket? Or did it represent something more?

I was sitting on my couch, holding the ticket, when the phone rang.

I looked at the caller ID and smiled. Talking to a friend from back home was exactly what I needed.

I hit accept and held the phone to my ear. "Rusty, if you're calling to bitch about how much being a grown-up sucks, don't expect a pep talk because I've got nothing."

Rusty laughed on the other end, and just like that, all the time and miles between friends had been erased.

He said, "Tell me about it. Can we go back in time and tell our past selves to flunk a few classes so we can go back to being in college?"

"Hey, I *am* still in college."

"Ah, grad school doesn't count. That's like college 2.0—all of the work and none of the fun."

"And working full-time is so much better?" I asked.

"Hell no. Yesterday someone spit coffee at me. Okay, so on the counter in front of me, but still I watched liquid arch from a stranger's mouth toward me. This is my life."

We laughed, and then the line went quiet.

After a few seconds, he said, "Now that I've buttered you up with laughs, I'll get straight to the point . . ." *And so the other shoe drops.* "Bliss. I heard about the engagement. I'm sorry, man."

I picked the airline ticket back up, and held it as I said, "You and everybody else on Facebook."

"How are you doing with it?"

I said, "Okay."

And I was just fine . . . where Bliss was concerned anyway.

"Cade . . ."

"I am, Rusty. I promise. I mean, I saw them a week or two ago, and it was awkward as hell. And depressing, because I'm pretty sure my friendship with Bliss is DOA. But I'm okay. There's actually this other girl."

I hadn't told anyone about Max. I'd liked feeling that she was this awesome secret that I refused to share with the world. But she had my mind so twisted up that I had to tell someone.

"Another girl, huh?" he asked. "What's she like?"

"A total mind fuck, that's what she's like."

Rusty said, "I like the sound of her already." He would. "So you're together?"

"Not exactly."

"Are you about to be?" he asked.

I looked back at that damn ticket and said, "Um . . . I doubt it."

"*Were* you together?"

"Sort of."

"Damn I'm confused, and I'm not even part of it."

"Tell me about it."

"If I'm reading between the Cade lines, I'd say you still want to be with her."

"I don't know, man. I do, and I don't. She's amazing, but she's got a whole baggage claim to herself, man. If I'm honest, she stands to screw me up way more than Bliss ever did."

"This is why I don't date girls."

"Not a solution I'm willing to take, man."

He said, "It sounds like you've already made up your mind. You know this girl isn't good for you."

I did know that, but it didn't stop me from thinking about her constantly. I had to keep reminding myself of how it felt waking up alone that morning just to stop myself from calling her.

"You're right. I just want life to be simple again, you know?"

That's what I'd seen in Bliss. I knew it now. A life with her would have been simple and nice and safe. Complication free.

"Good luck with that, Winston. Life isn't ever simple. Not until you're dead."

The phone call went on for a while after that, but my mind stayed stuck on those words. We talked about what other friends were doing and the possibility of getting the gang together for New Year's.

But I thought about how I'd spent twenty-two years chasing after a life that I'd convinced myself I'd wanted. A simple, predictable, perfect life. But it still had yet to become any of those things. I'd been accumulating talents and accomplishments, marking them off this unwritten checklist that had been in the back of my mind since I was a kid. But what did it all add up to?

The truth was . . . none of that kept people from leaving. Nothing could, if the person was determined to go. The only question was how long you were willing to chase them.

Rusty had to get to work, so we wrapped up the call with promises to talk again soon. I had hoped talking with him would give me perspective, but I still didn't know what I wanted, and my thoughts were more knotted up than ever.

32

Max

I refused to be nervous about spending time with Cade. Not when I had so many other things to worry about, but thoughts of him kept creeping into my head.

He'd ruined me.

Before I'd been like ice—cold and cutting and solid. But for weeks, he'd been thawing me out, and I hated it.

There was no control like this, no protection. And I had fewer than twenty-four hours until the end of the world. Also known as family Christmas.

Home was the lion's den. My scars were always more sensitive there because that's where I'd gotten the wounds. Now more than ever I needed my armor.

So today was about strengthening my resolve.

My mom had called seventeen and a half times today already. The half because one of the phone calls lasted so long that classifying it as one call just didn't seem fair.

My brother and his wife, Bethany, had arrived yesterday, and I could feel the pretentiousness creeping through the phone just hearing them in the background.

I still hadn't packed my bags. I had two sets of clothes folded and ready to go—my traditional holiday garb of turtlenecks and scarfs . . . or my normal clothes. As much as I wanted to make Cade happy, this wasn't a decision that I could make lightly.

When I came home from my shift at the tattoo parlor, I reached out to tug open the door to my building, and it didn't budge. I blinked, and then pulled again, but nothing changed.

I stepped back and looked around my street to make sure I'd gone to the right building. There was the Laundromat next door, which meant I was in the right place. I stepped forward and yanked on the door again. Nothing.

The door was locked.

The door to this building hadn't been locked in ages, almost a year, I was sure.

I fished out my keys, and it took me a few seconds to even remember which key worked on this door because it had been so long. What had made the landlord fix it now? I'd given up bugging him about it months ago because nothing worked.

Unless he hadn't been the one to fix it.

I froze with the key halfway to the lock. Would Cade have done that? Even though we were . . . well, not whatever we had been.

I weighed the probability in my mind of who could have fixed the door. Between my bum of a landlord and Golden Boy—the choice was obvious.

My heartbeat sped up faster just thinking about the possibility.

Maybe it didn't mean anything. Maybe it wasn't even him.

But what if it was and what if it did?

I thawed a little bit more.

I shook my head, and focused on my keys. When I found the right one, I shoved it into the lock a little too hard. Then I went upstairs and faced my packing options. I took a few turtlenecks, just in case, but for the most part I packed my normal clothes, the clothes I thought Cade would have approved of.

When I couldn't hold back my nerves about tomorrow or my fantasies about Cade being the one to fix my door, I went to bed for the night, hoping I could stay strong . . . against everything.

My head was pounding, and it sounded like I was underwater. The world was so far away and too bright after so long alone in the dark. A light shined in my eye, and I flinched. A face hovered over mine, and my heart turned over in my chest.

Alex.

It had to be.

I tried to say her name, but my tongue felt like sandpaper, and my throat burned with the effort. All I managed was a whisper.

"Don't try to talk, Rest your vocal cords."

The voice was male, not Alex's. My world chose that moment to sharpen, to emerge from the blur of my vision. I licked my lips. They were sticky and tasted like pennies.

Two fingers pressed into my wrist, and the man startled rattling off numbers to someone else I couldn't see.

I registered the steady rumble of an engine, and whatever I was lying on swayed slightly.

I was in an ambulance. They were taking me away.

I panicked, and tried to sit up, but my shoulders were strapped down. I was trapped again. I bucked and squirmed, and a sharp pain shot up my leg. I tried to scream, but nothing came out.

Empty.

The pressure in my head increased until I thought it might explode.

I mouthed Alex's name again and again, even though I couldn't say it.

"You're going to be okay," the paramedic assured me. "We got to you in time."

No. No, they hadn't.

They were too late.

I saw the paramedic pick up a syringe, and then my world went fuzzy again. The panic subsided, but the memories did not.

It all came too late.

I woke up, gasping, my arms and legs slick with sweat and stuck to the sheets. My dreams were always worse around the holidays, but that had been the first in a while. I'd been too preoccupied with other things of late for my old demons to show their heads. I guess it was too much to hope for that they'd finally ended.

I tried to go back to sleep, but now the accident was fresh

in my mind. Every time a car passed outside, the lights reflected through my window, and I shot up in bed, afraid another dream was starting.

Finally I decided that sleep wasn't going to be a possibility. I got up, and took a long shower. I used the time to clear my head, and focus on what I needed to do on this trip.

The end goal was music. That was what I had to remember. Music was my constant. As eager as I was to see Cade again, I couldn't afford to be distracted. Not by him, not by the past, not by anything.

I used the extra time to straighten my hair, a rare occurrence for me, but it kept my hands busy. Mom called twice to make sure I was up, and the second time I just put her on speakerphone and let her chatter on, interjecting the occasional "Yes," and "Really?" to keep her going.

I pulled a scoop-neck shirt over my head, and looked in the mirror. The tattoos weren't blatantly on display, but they definitely weren't hidden. I closed my eyes and tried to imagine how my parents would react.

But for the life of me, I couldn't picture it. Or maybe I didn't want to.

I was grabbing my coat and scarf when a knock sounded on my door.

Cade.

My head was spinning.

"Just a second!"

I leaned a hand against the nearest wall and took a second to calm myself and fortify my walls.

Don't think about him. Think about music.

I imagined a quick cigarette, but it did little to calm my nerves. Finally, I just grabbed the doorknob, and pulled.

He stood on the other side of my door, leaning against my doorjamb in a way that was so comfortable and sexy that I thought I had to be dreaming.

I pinched myself, but nothing changed.

So much for not thinking about him. All the emotions I'd narrowly kept in check this week hit me hard and fast. I tried to swallow it down, but it was just too much.

The expression on his face was unreadable, and I couldn't seem to get my brain to process the fact that he was standing in front of me. It took all of my brainpower to utter, "Hi." Then the rest of my thoughts fizzled out completely.

He pushed off the door, and stood in front of me with his hands in his pockets. My traitorous eyes traced from his arms to his shoulders to the straight edge of his jaw before I managed to get myself under control.

If just seeing him could affect me like this, how was I ever going to survive the holidays with him at my parents? I looked up, and he smiled like there was no painful history between us, like he wasn't dying just from being in such close proximity. It took all my strength to resist touching him, and he stood there, the picture of ease and comfort.

I stared, battling with myself until he cleared his throat and said, "You ready?"

Not even close.

33

Cade

When she opened the door, the sight of her undid me. Her hair was longer and so blond it was almost white. Her normal curls were gone, and it fell in long, straight sheets. My heart sunk because I thought she'd tamed her hair color to appease her parents. Then she turned to the side to gesture me in, and the light hit her hair through a window. It was not white, but a very pale purple.

She smiled, and she seemed genuinely glad to see me.

"The hair looks great," I said.

The top half of her hair was pulled back so that it didn't

cover the birds on her neck. Her clothing wasn't outrageous, but it was still her. More importantly, it didn't feel like she was hiding.

She shrugged. "You told me to be myself, so I am."

I didn't have to fake the smile that spread across my face.

Max moved toward the couch and fiddled with her carry-on, giving me the chance to take her in completely. She looked nervous, but I was sure it was just about seeing her parents.

I was a mess inside. I couldn't make up my mind whether I wanted to turn around and walk out the door, or pull her into my arms and kiss her. I settled for behaving as naturally as possible.

I didn't know what to say, so I settled for being useful. As soon as she had zipped up her duffel bag, I leaned around her and took it. My chest brushed against her back, and she stiffened.

I moved back quickly, but the damage had already been done. She moved away from me to grab a few more of her things.

"Are you nervous?" I asked.

She looked up at me, her blue eyes wide and questioning. Her eyes made this so much more difficult.

When she didn't answer, I added, "About your parents?"

She breathed a laugh and said, "Only enough to throw up."

It was good to hear her laugh.

"Oh, is that all?"

I followed her out into the hallway and waited while she locked her apartment. Over her shoulder she said, " I should warn you, my sister-in-law, Bethany, is the Antichrist in panty hose."

I laughed, and she whipped around to face me. She looked so surprised. I could only imagine what she had expected out of this trip. Maybe she thought I'd try to get her back. Probably she just expected me to be broken up over what she'd done.

I was sick of being that guy.

There was no reason I couldn't act normal. I was an actor for God's sake.

She said, "You laugh, but I'm serious. Spending time with her is like taking a cheese grater to the brain."

"It can't be that bad."

She gave me a look and said, "When she married my brother, she insisted on having white doves released when they kissed. They got married in Oklahoma. She's lucky someone in the audience didn't stand up and open fire."

"So she's a bit crazy, but aren't all women like that about their weddings?"

We emerged onto the street and she added, "She told me I wasn't allowed to be a bridesmaid because my skin tone would clash with the dresses she'd chosen."

I winced, but she wasn't done. "Yeah. She was also runner-up for Miss Oklahoma like eight years ago, and she still maintains that the pageant was fixed, and she should have won."

A cab was waiting for us at the curb, and I opened the door for Max to slide in first. "I get it. Don't leave Max alone with Bethany or the sister-in-law might lose her waving hand."

As we set off for the airport, the conversation became forced. It was harder to pretend when we were in such a small space and had a cabdriver as an audience. She twisted her hands nervously in her lap. One hand wandered up to the skin of her neck and brushed across the birds on her neck.

Before I could stop myself I asked, "Why birds?"

She looked like she'd forgotten that I was there completely. I wished I was capable of the same. She worried her lips with her teeth and I said, "Sorry. You don't have to answer that."

"It's okay. It's pretty cliché. Before there was a bell jar, there was a cage." She curved her hand around her neck and said, "I got these when I dropped out of UPenn. The first time I tried to stop pretending. They were supposed to keep me looking up and moving forward. Now they feel like a lie."

I reached out and pulled her hand away from her neck. I ignored the shock of warmth and said, "It's going to be okay, Max."

I released her hand, and she wrapped both arms around her middle, like she was holding herself together.

"You're really dreading this, aren't you?"

"You have no idea. My mother is so hard-core about Christmas. She's like the love child of Mrs. Claus and the Terminator. If you even look like you're not filled with Christmas cheer, she'll be shoving eggnog and cookies and Christmas carols down your throat." She laughed, and it felt forced, but I could tell she was ready for a subject change, so I went with it.

I shrugged and said, "I like eggnog."

She groaned, but her frustration gave way to a smile. Each new smile looked a little less faked, and I made a silent goal to put her completely at ease. I was a masochist. I was just as bad as that crazy monk in *The Da Vinci Code,* only her smile was my whip.

"So, um." She fidgeted with her hands. "I should have said it before, but thank you for showing up. . . . I'm glad I won't be alone."

"You're welcome."

I thought that would be the end of it, but her cheeks flushed and she continued, "And well, we don't have to . . . that is, if you're uncomfortable about pretending to be together, we don't have to really do anything, um, couple-like."

I forced a smile. I'd been thinking of that almost constantly. Part of me thought I should avoid couple behavior at all costs, but another part of me saw it as a golden opportunity.

"Pretending won't bother me." Maybe saying it out loud would make it truer. "It's not a big deal. Acting is what I do."

She nodded, her lips pursed into a straight line. "Right, of course, I just wanted to . . . offer."

Max's anxiety continued to build so that by the time we boarded the plane, she looked ready to turn around and go back.

She gestured for me to take the window seat, and she sat on the aisle, leaning as far away from me as she could. She kicked off her shoes and pulled up her knees, like she was at home sitting on her couch. When we were high enough in the air that we could use electronics, she pulled out her phone and tucked her earbuds in. I could hear her music from here, and I wondered if it helped to drown out her fears.

I closed my eyes, leaned my head against the window, and tried to do some drowning of my own. It didn't take long before my head drooped, and I drifted into a peaceful nap.

What felt like moments later, a movement against my

shoulder jostled me awake. I lifted my head up from the window, and my face itched from where it had been pressed against the plastic window cover. I blinked, and looked over to find Max's cheek perched on my shoulder.

Her brows were knit together, and her eyes clenched shut. She took short, sharp breaths, and every few seconds her expression would contract in what looked like pain. She mewled and pushed her face into my shoulder. She looked like a completely different person—vulnerable and in pain.

When she muttered "Alex" in her sleep, I placed my hand on her cheek.

A few other passengers were starting to stare. I put my face close to hers, and whispered, "It's a dream, Max. Wake up."

Her hand fisted in my shirt, and I wrapped an arm around her, pulling her close.

"Sssh. You're okay. I'm here. Just wake up."

Her eyes flew open, and she flinched back.

"It was a dream." I kept repeating that sentence because I wasn't sure she heard me. Her gaze darted around us, but when she realized where we were, she released her grip on my shirt.

"You okay?" I asked.

She pressed her lips together and nodded. She closed her eyes and took a deep, shuddering breath. She tipped her head back toward the seat, but my arm was still around her. When her neck touched my bicep, her eyes met mine.

34

Max

My emotions were still on overdrive from my dream, and having his arm around me sent my heart sprinting. I stared at him, tracing the line of his nose and the curve of his cheekbones with my eyes. His face had the stubble that I loved so much, and his eyes were still heavy from sleep.

He smiled, and a familiar warmth uncurled low in my belly. I wet my lips, and his eyes cleared. I couldn't make myself look away. Confusion crept into his expression, but he didn't break our gaze either. I wanted him to know how badly I felt, but I didn't know how to put it into words. I didn't know if it even mattered to him. He shifted in his chair, and his arm weighed heavier around my shoulders.

God, I was so confused. I was Alice in Wonderland, tumbling down the rabbit hole for a second time. I was lying with my head against his arm when a flight attendant tapped me on the shoulder to ask if I'd like a drink. I gave a polite nod and by the time I looked back at Cade, his arm was no longer around me, and he was looking down. My earbuds were still dangling around my neck, music blaring. I turned down the volume and opened my mouth to say something. What I was going to say was a mystery, but if I stayed silent any longer I was going to spontaneously combust. I took a deep breath, and he spoke before I could.

"The past is past, Angry Girl."

I snapped my mouth closed, and after a moment, I nodded.

He pressed his lips together in something that was meant to be a smile, but there was no life in it. And his eyes were distant, like he was looking past me.

For the first time I felt positive that he was acting.

Suddenly, the thought of spending days with him didn't make me nervous. It made me sad. There were many parts of my life that I wanted to leave firmly in the past, but now I was pretty sure he wasn't one of them.

Once again, I was too late.

35

Cade

I hated how easy it was to put on a mask in front of her. I'd been pushing her to be herself, and I wasn't any better. All I wanted to do was grab her and kiss her.

But I had to listen to my brain instead of my heart. It was the only way I could survive this trip. The new hair color softened her somehow, but her eyes were lined with terror. It was so unnatural to see fear written across the face of a girl who was so fearless that for a few moments she had felt like another person entirely.

So, I told her what she needed to hear. Even though it shredded me.

She relaxed, but only a little. She spent the rest of the flight fidgeting and checking the time. The closer we got to landing, the more frenetic she became.

The plane's descent turned rapid, and Max tensed up. Her hands clutched the armrests, and her eyes closed. She pressed her head back into the seat, sat very still, and took deep breaths. I had the urge to put my arm around her again, but I fought it off.

I asked, "Is it the landing that has you nervous or what's waiting for us on the ground?"

She didn't open her eyes as she answered, "I choose option C."

"Both?"

She nodded. She licked her lips and explained, "I just feel like landings last about one minute longer than I can handle. And frankly, as far as this trip is concerned, I'd prefer we just stay in the air."

She didn't get her wish. The sound of the wind roared in the cabin as the plane came in for a landing. Her hands turned white on the armrests, and her lip turned a vivid pink as she bit down. I knew, logically, that she was nervous, but the tension in her neck and the way she worried her bottom lip reminded me of other things entirely, and I had to look away.

The wheels touched down, and she pressed her hands into the back of the seat in front of her, grimacing as the plane slowed down. When it was over, she released a long breath and wilted back into her chair. I waited for her to perk back up, but her eyes stayed closed, and her hands still gripped the armrests.

"You're looking a little green, Angry Girl."

I was expecting a response like "You're looking like you wanna get punched, Golden Boy."

Instead, she stayed silent. When she did open her eyes, she just stared at the people ahead of us unloading their things and pressed her palms into her thighs. I didn't see her fear anymore. I didn't see anything really. She was blank, like she had just shut down completely. It was torture seeing her this way. Maybe I shouldn't have made her do this.

I decided then . . . no matter how painful it was or what it cost me, I'd help her get through this in whatever way I could. Even if I never saw her again afterward.

I carried both of our bags off the plane, and Max was quiet as we left the terminal for the arrivals area. She pulled out her cell with numb hands to call her parents. We walked side by side until suddenly she was no longer there. I looked back, and she was standing still as a statue, looking as if she might scream or pass out or both.

When I got closer she groaned, "They didn't."

"Who didn't?" I asked. "What's the matter?" I placed my hands on her arms and her eyes snapped to mine. For a few seconds neither of us said anything, and I knew I'd crossed a line. I pulled back, and put another foot between us.

Her face went soft, and she said, "I'm sorry."

I thought she meant for her reaction to my touch until she stepped behind me and began buttoning her coat. She fastened it all the way up to her neck, and threw on her scarf, too. She undid the clip holding back her hair so that it fell around her face.

She still looked beautiful, but I knew what she was doing. "Max . . . what is going on?"

She tamed her appearance with the same ease and efficiency that she had before her parents' arrival on the day we met. I turned and looked behind me, but I couldn't see her parents anywhere.

"Damn it, Max, we talked about this . . ."

"I know." Her eyes met mine, and they weren't blank anymore. "They sent Bethany and Michael to pick us up. I just can't start with her. I can only fight this battle once."

The minute she had hidden all the things that made her Max, her body relaxed and all the tension that had plagued her disappeared. I had the sinking feeling that I wouldn't see my Max again for the rest of the trip. Not that she was mine anymore. Or ever had been really.

"I promise I'll do it, Cade." She sounded more like she was trying to convince herself than me.

I sighed and said, "Okay, fine. Let's go meet the Antichrist."

She squared her shoulders, like she was preparing for battle. I followed her glare across the terminal to a couple dressed in business attire, and I recognized the man as an older version of the brother I'd seen in her mother's photo album.

The couple started toward us, linked at the elbow. Her brother was in a suit, his tie loosened slightly. The woman on his arm, Bethany, looked to be mid-to-late twenties. She was wearing a red dress and black heels that looked more appropriate for a cocktail party or a political campaign than picking someone up from the airport. She had long, flowing blond hair that reminded me of Sleeping Beauty. She was smiling widely and giving a small wave that I imagined she had perfected during her run for Miss Oklahoma.

Max looked like she wanted to take out all her nerves and fears on a punching bag with blond hair. I could see already that this was going to be a very long trip.

"Mackenzie, sweetheart!" Bethany called. "It's so good to see you! We've heard so much about your little boyfriend that I just insisted that Michael and I be the ones to pick you up. I *had* to see this for myself."

I leaned closer and reminded her, "Breathe."

Bethany's appearance was meticulous, from her manicured nails to her blond ringlets; they stopped simultaneously, as if all of their movements as a couple were choreographed, and stared at Max. Her sister-in-law looked at her from head to toe, and then clucked pitifully. "Don't you look *tired* from your flight."

Max gave a grim smile and opened her mouth. I rushed to cut her off. "It's so nice to meet you both," I said, holding out my hand. Michael shook my hand first. He looked like he could care less what his sister looked like. He was more concerned with the BlackBerry he kept pulling out of his pocket. "I'm Cade. Though it sounded like you already knew that."

Bethany smiled. "Yes, all Betty and Mick have talked about is how much of a"—she paused and looked back at Max— "*good influence* you've been on our Mackenzie. Lord knows she needed someone to whip her into shape. I've been trying for years, but an Ivy League education can only work so much magic."

I returned to Max's side, unsure whether or not to touch her. Her fists were clenched tightly at her side, so I took that as a no. Bethany kept talking. "Now, Mackenzie, don't you worry for a second about that bad dye job. It might be tough, since it's the holidays, but I bet my hairstylist can squeeze you in and get all of *that* taken care of." Bethany's gesture didn't cover Max's hair so much as all of her.

I watched Max inhale and exhale very slowly. This appeared to be another instance where her coping mechanism wasn't quite working. I considered turning her around and walking away. I didn't want to see her put up with this any more than she wanted to deal with it herself.

"Listen, Beth—" She said the name with such malice that I was sure she was thinking of another *b*-word.

I cut in before the conversation could become dominated by four-letter words.

"You don't like her hair lavender?" I asked. "I think it's beautiful."

Max stiffened beside me, my attempt to put her at ease failing miserably.

Bethany smiled. "Oh, bless your heart. That's sweet, but you don't have to coddle her. If there's anything our Mackenzie is it's tough. She can handle it."

Max took a step forward, and I stopped worrying about whether or not it was okay to touch her. I clamped my arm down on her shoulder to hold her in place.

I said, "Do you think we could get on the road? I don't know about Max, but it's been a long trip, and I'm anxious to get settled in."

"You don't have any checked bags?" Bethany looked at the Max's duffle bag and my backpack slung over one arm. "Tell me you don't have your dress wadded up in there."

Max's face went pale. "What dress?"

"For the Charity Gala at the hospital. Your mother has been talking about it nonstop. She didn't tell you to bring a dress?"

Max groaned and said, "I vaguely recall her mentioning something like that, but she didn't say we had to *go*."

"Well you do." Bethany looked pleased at Max's misery. She huffed as if Max had just ruined Christmas. "I guess we'll have to squeeze in a shopping trip in the morning along with a hair appointment. I don't know how your family survived before I came along." Bethany looked up at Max's brother and said, "Are you ready, sweetie?"

He paused whatever he was doing on his BlackBerry and said, "Whenever you are, honey."

The two shared a kiss that left even me feeling like I'd overdosed on sugar.

"Follow us." Bethany turned and trounced away, her curls bouncing slightly with her movement.

'I'm going to kill her," Max breathed. "You're going to find her body chopped up and wrapped in individual boxes under the tree."

"It's scary how much I actually think you might mean that."

We followed at a distance, and I kept my hand around Max's shoulder the entire time. I don't know if she even noticed. She was too concentrated on sending imaginary Chinese throwing stars at the back of Bethany's head.

"She is everything I hate about my family," Max said. "She makes me sick."

I didn't like the girl either, but Max spoke with a kind of venom that worried me. "Every family has one," I told her. "And in a few days, you'll be gone and won't have to see her for another year."

"You don't get it." Without looking away from Bethany, she said, "That *was* me. I was just like her all through high school. I was just as fake and vile and—"

I pulled her to a stop and said, "And now you're not. You beat yourself up because of who you were and because of who you're not and even because of who you are. You've got to stop."

She stared at me, and I could tell I had penetrated her walls, if only for just a moment. Then Bethany turned over her shoulder and called, "You'll have to forgive the car. There was a mix-up at the rental company, and they gave someone else the BMW that Michael reserved. This was the best they could do on such short notice."

"Let's go," Max said. She pulled away and walked a few paces ahead of me all the way to a brand-new Toyota SUV that probably cost more than a new liver on the black market.

Michael opened the front door for Bethany, and placed a quick kiss on her lips before opening the trunk for us. I threw our bags in, and opened the door for Max.

"What a gentleman," Bethany said. "Your taste really is improving, Max."

There was going to be blood spatter all over these nice leather seats if she wasn't careful. Max sat stiffly against the seat, her fists clenched in her lap. I placed a hand over one of her fists and squeezed. I figured the best thing I could do was to get Bethany talking about herself.

Once we were out of the parking garage and on the road, I asked, "So, how long have you two been married?"

"Oh two years this June. We had the most glorious June wedding. Everything about it was just *perfect*."

Michael put the car in drive and said, "Only as perfect as you."

Bethany aww'd, and the two of them looked away from the road long enough to share a quick kiss.

Max made a noise like she was going to hurl and said, "Perfect driver, too."

"Any chance we'll be hearing wedding bells in your future?" Bethany asked.

I couldn't look at Max. I played my role, kept my eyes on the audience, stayed in character, and said, "We're just taking things slow, seeing how things go."

"Oh." Bethany's lips turned down in a pout and she gave Max a look of pity. "Of course you are."

I followed Bethany's eyes to Max in time to see her press her forehead against the window and close her eyes. She pulled her hand away from mine, and began to close herself off again.

I asked, "How long until we get to Max's parents' house?"

"It's about a thirty-minute drive," Michael answered.

"If they don't kiss us into a ditch first," Max said.

36

Max

Mom threw open the front door of their two-story house and squealed when she saw us. The Joker probably had a more realistic smile than I did. When both my parents came into view, Cade's hand curved around my waist, falling just below the line of my coat. I could feel the heat of his fingers through my shirt, and it was like five little daggers of doubt to my back.

This was too hard. My body and my mind and my heart were at war, and my sanity was the collateral damage.

Dad shook Cade's hand, and Mom pulled both of us into a hug simultaneously.

"Come in! Come in! Oh, Cade, Mick and I are just so happy you're here." She released me and hugged him around the neck for a few seconds. His arm was still around me, so I'm sure we resembled some kind of radioactive waste monster that had begun sprouting extra heads and limbs. When she pulled back she lifted a strand of my hair and clucked her tongue. She said, "Oh, honey," and frowned, but didn't say anything further. It gave me a little bit of hope that maybe she could handle the rest of it.

But just a little.

I met Cade's eyes, and his flicked to my mother.

I took a deep breath and said, "Mom?"

"Yes, dear?"

Her eyes met mine. They focused on me in a way they hadn't in years. Normally, she'd look at me for a second or two before glancing everywhere around me. She blinked, still looking at me, waiting for words that I just couldn't seem to pry from my lips.

Instead, I asked, "What room is Cade staying in?"

"Oh, we've put him in the guest room upstairs, right next to your old room."

I looked at Cade, and he gave me a stiff smile.

Every time we took a step forward, I seemed to take a running leap back.

Mom continued, "Why don't you two get settled in. Dinner is almost ready though, so be quick!"

I nodded and went to grab Cade's hand. He stepped out of my reach and gestured for me to lead the way instead. His shoulders were even stiffer than his smile. I walked up the stone pathway through my parents' large, ornate front door, and he followed. He paused in the doorway to take in the high, arched ceiling and Mom's tendency to decorate every inch of available space.

"Stairs are over here," I said.

He nodded, but didn't reply.

The entire way up the stairs, I could hear his heavy footfalls, and each one made me flinch. By the time I opened the guest room door at the end of the hallway, I could feel his emotions like a cloud at my back. He threw our bags down on the bed, and turned to face me.

I normally loved the way Cade looked at me . . . all of the ways. The way he'd looked out in the audience while I sang. The way he would keep his head down on our walks home, but look at me sideways. The way he'd looked at me when I'd been spread out beneath him. I could tell, just by his expression that he believed in me . . . all of me.

But his expression now was none of those things. He didn't look angry . . . well, yes he did. But mostly, he looked sad. And he looked disappointed, an expression with which I was all too familiar. And that indefinable something that I'd always seen in his gaze was gone. So was his belief in me.

I shut the door behind me, and the click echoed through the silence of the room.

"I'm sorry." I seemed to say that to him a lot, more than to any other person in my life except for Alex. "I know I said I would tell them . . . that I wouldn't pretend anymore—"

"You've said a lot of things."

I sucked in a breath, but my lungs still felt empty.

"Cade."

"I just don't understand you." His hands went to his hair,

and he began to pace back and forth in front of the bed. "I thought you were fearless," he said.

A noise ripped from my throat, and even I didn't know if it was a laugh or sob.

"Well, you were wrong."

"You get up onstage in front of hundreds of people and bare your soul. You don't take shit from anyone. You go after what you want. You're amazing. But then when you're here, it's like you're a completely different person."

"Oh, come on. It's an act, a crutch, a mask, take your pick. I project fearless, and you project perfection. It doesn't mean either of us actually are those things."

His pacing changed course, and he came at me. I had to crane my head backward to meet his gaze. "How do you think this is going to turn out? You can't keep who you are a secret forever. What are you going to do? Wear turtlenecks for every visit? Never come home during the summer? Not invite them to your wedding?"

I swallowed.

"I'll tell them. I just need time. I need to prepare them so that they're not so shocked. They're holding money over my head."

He scoffed. "The world holds money over everyone's head. It's a fact of life."

"Like it's that easy. I don't know why you suddenly think you can judge me."

"Because I know you!"

He didn't, not at all. If he really knew me he wouldn't be here. He wouldn't care about me. But I couldn't say that, so I just backed away from him and shook my head. I wanted this conversation to be over, but he wasn't done. He said, "I think you're just scared."

"Of course I'm scared!" My volume got away from me, and I slapped a hand over my mouth, hoping my parents hadn't heard. I took a deep breath and continued quietly, "I'm terrified . . . Always."

Terrified that I'll never make it. That I'll wake up one day to realize my parents are right. Terrified that I've poured my everything into a career and life that will never happen . . . that I've wasted the life that should have been Alex's.

"What are you scared of, Max?"

"Of everything. Absolutely everything."

I didn't say that included him, but I didn't think I had to. I think he knew.

"Is that what you wanted to hear, Golden Boy?"

He sighed, and put his head down. I was used to disappointing people, but I had never wanted it to be him.

He said, "No, not at all."

"Well, I'm sorry to disappoint you."

God, I was. So sorry.

He took a step toward me, and I took three back.

I cleared my throat and said, "I'm going to put my things up next door. There's a bathroom in the hall if you need it. Just pop over when you're ready."

Then I ran.

There were no prying eyes lurking at the bottom of the stairs, so I hoped that meant no one had heard us arguing. As soon as I was safely ensconced in my room, I leaned back against my door and concentrated on breathing.

I hated how afraid I was. I hated the way fear could eat

away at everything until even the constant things in life, like the earth beneath my feet and the sky over my head, seemed like figments of my imagination.

The fear made me feel pathetic and small, but I couldn't get past it.

It wasn't just the money or the risk of angering my parents.

It was a thorn on the dark side of my heart that told me I was inadequate, that there was some measure of what it meant to be good, to be important, and I didn't reach it. As long as no one else saw that thorn, it was a secret I could protect, a wound I could nurse in private.

Talking to my parents would open it up, start the bleeding fresh, make it impossible to ignore.

I pushed my coat off my shoulders and pulled my shirt over my head. I threw my duffel bag on the bed and tore it open. I scrambled for a turtleneck and found a black one. I was pulling it over my head when my door opened.

I couldn't see through the black fabric, but I spun away as quickly as possible, so that my tattoos faced away from the door. I tried to tug the sweater down so that it covered my stomach, but the stupid turtleneck was caught on my head. I said, "Hold on a sec, Mom."

My head pushed through the neck opening at the same time I heard, "It's Cade."

I felt like my heart turned to face him before I did.

I finished pulling my shirt down to cover my stomach, and met his gaze. There were so many emotions in his expression—anger and sadness and desire—but I couldn't tell which one was winning.

My voice was raspy as I said, "Ready."

He didn't move for several long moments, just pinned me to my spot with his intense gaze. Anticipation and want built in me until my knees felt weak. Just when I was ready to give in, he stepped back and into the hall.

Mom called my name a few seconds later. "Dinner's ready!"

I squared my shoulders and joined him at the door. As we descended the stairs, his hand touched the small of my back, and it took all of my concentration not to tumble down the stairs. I faced a potentially life-changing holiday. I could lose my family, lose their support, and lose the life I'd built for myself. And yet somehow, all I could think about was his touch and how much I missed it. As disastrous as this trip was likely to be, I never wanted it to end.

37

Cade

Everyone was seated and waiting for us in the dining room when we came downstairs. This was the first time I'd been in a house that had an actual dining room instead of a table crammed into the kitchen. Her parents were seated at each end of the table, and Michael and Bethany sat on one side, opposite the two empty chairs meant for us. I pulled out Max's chair for her, and then sat down beside her.

The dinner wasn't quite as elaborate as the meal Mrs. Miller had prepared for Thanksgiving, but it was close. I could only imagine what Christmas Day would be like.

"Mick?" Mrs. Miller asked. "Will you say grace?"

I started to bow my head, and then Max blurted out, "Can I say it?"

Even Michael looked surprised.

Mrs. Miller blinked a few times, but smiled. "Of course you can, sweetheart."

She reached out her hand to me, and I took it.

I turned to Max, and held her gaze as I laced our fingers together. Every head lowered, and I followed. But I kept my eyes open and fixed on Max.

She stared at her empty plate as she spoke, as if it might help her find the words.

"Dear God, thank you for this food and for family. For fear and forgiveness." She paused, like she wanted to say more, but just couldn't piece together the words. Finally, she let her eyes fall closed and said, "May our lives have a healthy dose of each. Amen."

A chorus of hesitant amens filled the dining room, and Max stayed staring at her plate. I squeezed her hand and didn't unlace our fingers.

Bethany placed a napkin in her lap and said quietly, "I've never heard a prayer quite like that before."

"That was lovely, sweetheart," Max's mother said.

Max gave a nearly inaudible "thank you," and it was the only thing she said for the rest of dinner. Luckily, Bethany dominated the conversation. She talked about Michael's job, and their house, and how they thought they were almost ready to have kids. I was beginning to understand how she stayed so skinny. She never stopped talking long enough to really eat. Max distracted herself by picking at her food, and I distracted myself by staring at Max.

When dinner was over, Mrs. Miller shooed us into the living room while she cleaned up. And without the distraction of food, the discomfort level grew even higher. Mr. Miller pulled me aside to look at the various taxidermy pieces that were scattered across the living room. I'd grown up in Texas, where there were almost as many taxidermy places as there were churches, but I imagined what it must have been like for other guys that Max had brought home. I pictured Mace staring down the glassy, dead eyes of a twelve-point buck, and had to smother a laugh.

We were standing in front of a wild boar, while Mr. Miller recounted his hunting trip, when I overheard Bethany talking to Max on the couch.

She said, "It's never a good sign when the fighting starts this early. I mean, between the arguing you two did upstairs and the uncomfortable silence between you at dinner, I give it a week, maybe two before you go separate ways." Max was miraculously calm. She stared straight ahead, picking at a stray thread on the arm of the sofa. "You're lucky I kept up the conversation during dinner or your parents would have noticed." Max remained silent. "I know it's hard." Bethany placed a hand on Max's shoulder, who stiffened in response. "But you could hardly expect to snag the first decent guy that looked your way. I'm sure you made some mistakes along the way, but next time you'll know better."

I didn't know what Bethany had against Max, but there was a cruelty in her tone that told me she was enjoying this. I couldn't listen to it anymore. I turned to Mr. Miller and said, "Excuse me for a moment, sir." Then I headed for the couch.

I plopped down beside Max, shocking her out of the statue act she was putting on for Bethany.

I said, "Hey." And because I wanted to shut Bethany up and had been dying to do it since I first saw her this morning, I leaned in and pressed a kiss to Max's lips. She locked up for just a second, but then closed her eyes and kissed me back.

My body roared to life, and I resisted the urge to deepen the kiss. I pulled back and draped an arm over Max's shoulder. I tugged her closer until she was leaning against my chest.

"Sorry, I was getting lonely." I smiled and asked, "What are you two talking about?"

Bethany sputtered, and a slow smile spread over Max's face. It sent warmth to every part of me.

Max said, "I was just telling Bethany how great you were."

"Is that so?"

"Oh yeah, I mean, you're about as *perfect* as they come."

I held back a laugh and said, "Oh no, you're the perfect one."

She leaned her head against my chest, and I wondered if she could hear the way my heart sped up. She said, "I guess we're just perfect for each other then."

I wrapped my arms all the way around her and held her close.

Bethany stood and said, "Excuse me. I'm going to go find Michael. I have no idea what could be keeping him."

No doubt he'd snuck off to enjoy the superior company of his BlackBerry. We watched Bethany stalk out of the room. Max hesitated for a moment, and then turned her face into my chest to muffle her laughter.

"That is officially my favorite Christmas memory ever," Max breathed.

"Why does she hate you so much?" I asked.

Max propped her chin on my chest and looked at me. When she wasn't looking at me, I could pretend that this was all an act. That this was a role like any other. But with her eyes on mine . . . I lost focus.

She said, "I mentioned she's the Antichrist, right?"

"Ah, so this is a battle of good-and-evil kind of thing."

"No, this is a she's-psycho kind of thing."

"I could buy that. She enjoys hearing herself talk too much to not be at least a little bit sociopathic."

Max's eyes fluttered closed, and I realized that my hand was threading through her hair. I hadn't even realized I'd been doing it. I knew what that did to her. I started to pull my hand back, but she laid her cheek back against my chest and wrapped an arm around my waist.

If that wasn't permission, I didn't know what was.

Bethany came back with Michael, and Mrs. Miller brought out a tray with mugs of hot chocolate. I took one, but Max declined. She stayed pressed against me, her head resting over my heart as her family took seats around the room.

I tried to keep my body calm, and my mind calmer as we sat there.

I was tired of questioning what everything meant, so I just gave in. I brushed my fingers through her hair, skimming her neck and her back. I didn't know what she was thinking or if she was thinking at all, but it was peaceful, like a reprieve from the world.

Bethany kept glancing our way, but for once she didn't

say anything. I closed my eyes and leaned my cheek against the top of Max's head. I took the reprieve because we both needed it.

"Michael," Mrs. Miller called to her son. "Why don't we put all those years of piano lessons to work and sing some Christmas carols?"

Ah, there was the Christmas fiend Max had mentioned.

Michael obediently moved to the piano in the corner of the room, and he pulled the cushion of the bench up to look in the hidden storage beneath. He picked up a book.

"The red book," Mrs. Miller said.

He returned the book he'd chosen, and picked up a red one instead.

He flipped through the pages for a few seconds then asked, "Silent Night"?

Mrs. Miller nodded, and he began to play.

Max sat up a little, and leaned her head against my shoulder instead. Everyone began to sing, but my ears only heard her.

> "Silent night. Holy night.
> All is calm all is bright
> Round yon virgin mother and child
> Holy infant so tender and mild
> Sleep in heavenly peace
> Sleep in heavenly peace."

It was amazing how even a song I'd heard a hundred times sounded beautiful and special coming from her. There was something just slightly different in her tone, in her phrasing, that made the song sound fresh to my ears. Her voice was soft and vulnerable, and I couldn't stop myself from turning to face her. She lifted her head up and looked at me. I brushed a hand across her cheek, and she leaned into my touch.

I brushed her hair back, and I could feel her walls dropping. Her fear fled, my anger abandoned me, and certainty crept in. I was certain that we weren't as different as we wanted to believe, certain that she felt something for me, certain that this could work.

She took a breath, and I was certain that she could feel it, too.

Then the music ended, and the spell broke. I saw her retreat back into herself. She slid over on the couch, and all my certainties came crashing down.

I understood that she was unsure, but I just couldn't take this anymore.

38

Max

I kept my distance.

It was the only way I knew to keep my heart.

I knew I couldn't keep him away forever, but I managed it through the rest of Mom's impromptu caroling session. I maintained the distance until it was time for bed. He was in his room, and I was in mine. And I was going to need my sleep to recharge my resolve—both with respect to Cade and to telling my parents the truth.

It was a bad sign for both that I was still wide-awake at 2:00 A.M. when a knocking started on my door.

I was wearing an oversized T-shirt and a pair of boy-short underwear. I thought of rummaging for a pair of shorts to pull on, but whoever was knocking was making enough noise to wake up my parents, so I figured it was better to just answer them.

When I pulled open the door, Cade stormed into my room. Panicked, I peeked my head out the door, but there were no lights on, which meant he hadn't woken anyone . . . yet. I shut the door quietly and said, "What are you doing here?"

His eyes snapped from my bare legs up to my face, and his eyes were blazing.

"You're mad," I said in confusion.

"Hell yes, I'm mad."

"I told you that I would tell them, Cade. I was planning to do it in the morning, in fact. It's all I've been thinking about."

"That's not what I'm mad about."

I barely had time to mutter, "Then what?" before he'd caught my face in his hands and pulled my lips to his.

His kiss was angry and punishing, and I felt it all the way in the marrow of my bones.

"I'm angry that you keep pushing me away when I know you don't want to."

He crushed our lips together again, bruising and beautiful.

"I'm angry that you left me after the best sex of my life."

He turned and pressed me against the door, just like he did that night. I whimpered in response.

"More than anything, I'm angry that I had to wait so long to kiss you again."

Then he poured his anger into me, our tongues battling for dominance. I was so in shock that I didn't know whether to push him away or pull him closer, not that he gave me much of a choice. His hands found my wrists, and he pressed them into the door above my head. He wrung every last ounce of fear out of me until I was weak and panting and absolutely out of my mind with desire.

When he started to pull back, I shot forward and kissed him again. He released my hands, and I grasped the bulge of his shoulders. His teeth grazed my bottom lip in an almost-bite, and I lost it.

All my excuses were buried deep beneath the heat of his body against mine. I pressed my hips into his, and he groaned into my mouth. I couldn't control myself. My hands trailed from his waist to his chest, and he held me tighter in response. I spun us, and started pulling him toward my bed.

His hand slid down to my ass, and his kiss was so devastating and consuming that I wanted to rejoice or scream or cry.

The back of my knees hit the bed at the same time that he pulled away.

His eyes were dark, and his breathing labored. "Whatever stupid reasoning you've got for staying away from me, it's wrong. And I won't stop until I've proven it to you."

Then he left, and I fell back on my bed in shock.

It took nearly five minutes before I could do anything but sit there with my fingers pressed to my swollen lips.

As soon as I heard Mom bustling around downstairs, I pulled myself out of bed. It was still dark out, but even without a sufficient amount of sleep, my strength felt renewed. Maybe

Cade had kissed some confidence into me the night before. Whatever the reason, my heart was eerily steady as I dressed that morning. I put on the scoop-neck shirt that I'd started the day in yesterday.

I pulled my hair around to the side and did a quick loose braid that left the other side of my neck and my birds completely visible. The shirt only showed the very tips of my branches, but the lines were dark enough such that they couldn't be missed. I replaced the plastic retainers with my usual ear piercings.

This moment was years in the making.

I'd spent so much of my life, too much of it, altering myself to please other people. This was my crossroads moment, and nothing would be the same on this new road, including me.

Before I could change my mind, I went next door to the guest room and knocked.

Cade opened the door, already up and ready for the day. His hair was damp and curled around his face. I could smell the familiar, masculine scent of him from here. Last night came rushing back at me, and it took a serious amount of self-control not to throw myself at him.

He said, "Good morning."

His tone was cautious, like maybe I had come to deliver an angry tirade of my own. But I wasn't angry, just . . . on the verge of hyperventilating.

All the calm I'd woken up with disappeared upon seeing him. Somehow, he made it all feel real. My control crumbled, and my throat felt like it was going to close up. He must have seen the freak-out coming because he pulled me into his room and closed the door behind us. I turned my back on him and said, "Just give me a second."

I pressed my palms into my eyes to try to stop the tears that were building there.

"Max . . ." His voice was soft and came from right in front of me.

"I'm okay," I whispered without lowering my hands. I *hated* getting emotional, but nothing was worse than getting emotional in front of another person.

His arms circled me, and I sunk into his chest. My breath rattled in my chest, and I fisted my hands in the front of his shirt.

"You can do this," he said.

There it was . . . the belief. He had far more in me than I had in myself. If nothing else good came of this, at least there was that.

"It won't be easy," he said. Understatement of the year. "But your parents love you, Max." I laughed, even though nothing was funny. My throat was thick with emotion. He brought a hand up and pulled my hands from my eyes. "And if they can't see how amazing you are, they're blind."

I swallowed, and my throat felt raw. I didn't know what I'd ever done to deserve him. I didn't know why he would come anywhere near someone as toxic as me, but I was thankful.

Silence filled the room, but it was the comfortable kind of quiet that Cade and I had had before everything had changed. I didn't say anything because I didn't need to.

He held out his hand, and I latched onto it like I was falling and he was the only thing that could save me.

"I'll be with you every step of the way."

Some of the tightness in my chest eased, and I nodded.

"Thank you," I said.

"I don't know why you're thanking me."

I remembered the way he'd put himself out there last night and said, "You faced your demons, and came out on top. So, maybe I can, too."

He smiled and squeezed my hand.

"Come on, Fearless Girl."

I was far from fearless, but knowing he thought I was provided me with half the courage I needed. We left the guest room, and descended the stairs together.

Dad was watching television, and Mom was messing with something in the kitchen when we came downstairs. Michael was on his phone, and the Antichrist was flipping through a *Better Homes and Gardens* magazine.

Bethany saw me first, and her jaw dropped. God, it felt good to be the cause of that horrendous look on her face. I hoped it stuck that way.

She called, "BETTY!" Her face turned smug, and I thought back to Cade's question the night before. Why *did* she hate me? Probably because, just like my parents, she liked her world nice and neat and clean. I wasn't any of those things, with or without the tattoos.

Cade squeezed my hand, and I took the deepest breath that I could get. Mom came in from the kitchen drying a pan with a towel and said, "Yes?"

Bethany pointed in my direction. I took a few steps until I was all the way in the living room. Cade kept close by my side. Mom's eyes settled on me, but it was several long seconds before she really saw me. She dropped the pan and it clanged against the hardwood floors. Her face passed through a spec-trum of emotions that normally I would have found funny, except that I had no idea which one she would end up landing on. It was like *Wheel of Fortune,* only all the good possibilities had been removed. Dad looked up from the television just as Mom said, "Mackenzie Kathleen Miller, how could you do such a hideous thing to your body?"

It stung, but I kept my expression as blank as possible.

Dad asked, "What horrible thing?" He turned to face me, and I saw the anger wash over him. Out of the two of them, he was the more unpredictable one. He stood slowly, his motions stiff and small. His eyes flitted between my neck and my ear piercings and back again.

"What in the name of God have you done?"

His tone was soft, but clipped. This was the scariest ver-sion of him—still and silent and like the calm before the storm. Mom came to stand by Dad, and he took her under his arm. She turned weepy and mopped at her eyes with the back of her hand.

"Why does she do these things to us?" she asked him.

All my anxiety ignited into anger.

"I didn't do this to you. I made a choice about what to do with my body. It had nothing to do with either of you."

My father exploded. "You mark yourself up like some kind of . . . *tramp* on the street, and you expect it not to bother us?" He didn't raise a hand to me, but he might as well have. It hurt just as bad.

"Mick." Cade's voice cut in, hard and firm. Dad paused, and I could see his embarrassment and fury at having some-one outside the family witness this conversation.

"Son, I think you should leave us alone to deal with this."

Panic crushed me, and I crushed Cade's hand between mine in return.

"With all due respect, sir, I'm not going anywhere."

Mom sputtered in disbelief, and Dad fumed. I didn't want them to hate Cade for something that was all about me. I took a step closer and said, "I know you don't like these kinds of things, but—"

"Don't *like* them?" Mom's voice turned hysterical. "We raised you in the Church. You've been taught since you could speak that your body is a temple, and now you've destroyed it. You *know* what the Bible says about those kinds of abominations."

"The Bible also says to give away your riches, but you guys sure haven't bothered to do that. And I didn't *destroy* my body. There are no needle tracks on my arms. I'm not addicted to anything, nor have I become a prostitute, *Dad*. This is art that means enough to me that I made it a part of myself."

"Squiggly lines mean a lot to you?" Dad barked. "And birds? Yes, I can understand why birds mean a lot to you."

"*Freedom* means a lot to me."

"I'm glad to hear that because you're going to get plenty of it. If that's what you do with the money we give you—mutilate yourself and ruin all your chances of having a decent, respectable life—then we're done helping you."

That news hurt a lot less than I thought it would. In the grand scheme of things, their money meant nothing. It was the least important thing they could take from me.

"You've not been interested in helping me in a long time."

Dad said, "I mean it, Mackenzie. You better hope your

little music thing works out because you'll not get a decent job anywhere else looking like that."

I couldn't stay there anymore without doing something crazy. I gritted my teeth and spat out, "My *name* is Max. *Max.* And that 'little music thing' is my life. I'm tired of you trying to turn it and me into what you want. I'm not *Mackenzie,* and I'm *not* Alexandria."

Mom gasped like I'd slapped her. Even that made me furious. She threw around Alex's name all the time, trying to push photos and old knickknacks on me. But the minute we tried for honesty about my sister and me, I'd apparently taken it too far.

I spun around and went to the table at the end of the foyer where Mom and Dad kept all the car keys. I found the familiar key of the car I used to drive before I moved to Philly.

"Where do you think you're going, young lady?" Mom cried.

"To clear my head. I'll be back when being here doesn't make me sick to my stomach."

Though at the moment, the answer to that felt like never.

It was becoming harder to breath, and I knew exactly where I would go—the same place I always went when I wished for a different life.

39

Cade

I'd almost dragged her out of there several times myself. I knew it would be difficult for her to have it out with her parents, but I hadn't anticipated how much it would affect me, nor could I ever have dreamed her parents would have reacted so badly. I thought parents were supposed to love unconditionally? I assumed they would be mad, scream a bit, maybe cry, then settle down and talk it out like adults. When her father called her a tramp, I very nearly hit a man that was three times my age.

I followed Max out a door in the kitchen that opened into the garage. I expected her parents to come after us, but they didn't do that either. Her parents had a three-car garage. At the far end was a black Volvo that lit up when Max pressed a button on her key. I tried to catch up to her, but she was already opening the car door, and it blocked my path.

"Max—"

"Just get in the car, Cade."

Thank God. I was worried she wanted to leave without me. Needless to say, going back into that living room would have been awkward. I jogged around to the other side and slid into the passenger seat. The electric garage door was already opening, and as soon as it was up, Max peeled out of the garage, tore down the driveway and out into the street. She shifted the car into drive and slammed on the gas.

"Max, be careful, please."

She slowed down a little, but not much.

"I'm sorry," I said. God, that seemed so inadequate. All of this was my fault. "I never should have made you do that. I am so sorry."

She smiled, and her eyes were watery. "Don't be."

"I shouldn't have pushed you. You were scared, and apparently with good reason."

"I always find a good reason to be scared, Golden Boy. I think it's time I got over that, don't you?"

I knew what she was saying, and my heart tried to soar, but I was still too torn up over what I'd witnessed. Anything that made tears form in her eyes was something I never wanted her to have to face. For the first time, I felt afraid of where this was heading, afraid of the depth of my feelings for her.

My life moved at a slow pace. It took months before I had feelings for Bliss. Never before had I felt so intensely and so quickly. Max swept into my life like a hurricane, and I never stood a chance.

She made a sharp left turn, then a right, and another left. We were in subdivision hell, and for all I could tell, it looked like we were back on the same street. She turned right again and dead-ended into a two-lane highway. She made a left, and we drove toward the rising sun. Her knuckles began to relax against the steering wheel. The farther away we got from her parents, the calmer she looked.

"Where are we going?"

She sighed. "To the only place more depressing than home."

Every time I thought I understood her a little bit more, I was proven wrong.

"Why?" I asked.

She looked at me. Her hair glowed in the light of the waking sun. Her eyes were a bottomless ocean that I would give up air to explore. A perfect moment passed, uninterrupted by the world, unhurried by time, untainted by fear of the past or the future. And she answered, "Closure."

We drove for another five minutes until we reached a hill on a deserted stretch of highway. Trees lined each side of the road, and they curved over the highway like a tunnel. At the top of the hill was the sun, and it looked like we'd drive right into it if we didn't stop. It was breathtaking. The kind of scene you see in landscape photos and paintings. Max pulled over into a ditch just before the hill and trees started. She turned off the ignition and sat there, staring for a moment. Her gaze was so intense that I didn't want to say anything. Whatever this place was, it meant more to her than just pretty scenery.

Quietly, she spoke. "Come with me."

She removed the key and shoved it into the pocket of her jeans. She opened the door and started walking along the highway toward the hill. I unbuckled my seat belt and hurried after her. She was silent as she trudged through the knee-high grass. I followed behind her and realized there was a small trail worn into the earth. The grass and weeds bent backward out of our way, and I had a feeling that this path was of Max's making.

Her breath came heavier as the hill inclined, but she didn't slow or waver. She also didn't speak. When we reached the top, my shirt was stuck to my back with sweat, and I'd removed my coat despite the cold. Max had left hers at the house, but she didn't even answer when I offered mine.

The path veered off its straight line toward a rocky outcrop at the top of the hill. Max followed and climbed with practiced ease to the top of the largest rock. I followed, trying to step in the same places that she had. I sat beside her, and our feet dangled off the edge of the rock. We were underneath the cover of the trees, and we could see down both sides of the hill where the highway stretched into the distance.

It was peaceful up here. You couldn't see any glimpse of

the city, nor was there a car or house in sight. I could understand why she would come here. This far away from life, in the middle of nowhere, your soul felt bigger somehow.

She took a shaky breath, pointed to the road, and said, "My sister died right there, while I watched."

All the air rushed out of my lungs, and my soul, which had felt clear and infinite moments ago, was mangled. She'd said it quietly and calmly with no hesitation, but I could see the toll the words took on her. Her hands were knotted tightly in her lap. She was still and stiff except for the swallowing motion of her throat that repeated every few seconds.

"I was thirteen and at some ridiculous sleepover out in the boondocks that I hadn't wanted to go to, but Mom had made me. So . . . as I so often do, I acted like a bitch and pissed off the girl throwing the party. Mom sent Alex to come get me."

She looked up at the purple and pink morning sky and pressed her lips together. "Alex was good about stuff like that. Most teenagers would have pitched a fit over having to come get their little sister on a Saturday night, but not Alex. She was upset about something, and I kept bugging her to tell me what it was. That was when I found out why she was at home on a Saturday night. Mom and Dad had found pot in her room, and she was pretty much grounded for eternity. That's part of why my parents are so crazy conservative now."

Max sniffed and pressed the back of her left hand to her mouth for a moment. Then she reached for the leather cuff bracelet on her wrist and removed it. On the pale skin of the inside of her wrist was a tattoo I'd never noticed before. It read 11:12. Something started to sink in my stomach, and I steeled myself for what I knew was coming next.

"It was 11:12." Her voice broke, and tears started sliding down her face. "I know because I was messing with the radio, trying to find a decent station out here in the middle of nowhere. Alex was talking about how unreasonable Mom and Dad were. The pot was Michael's, but she didn't want to tell on him, so she took the heat. We were nearing the top of the hill, and neither of us was paying much attention. There was a guy coming up on the other side of the hill, and he'd fallen asleep at the wheel."

Max started to shiver, and even though I was sure it wasn't from the cold, I hung my coat around her shoulders. She exhaled and closed her eyes. Her eyes and lips were pressed into straight lines. Her tears reflected the sunlight, and her face looked fractured, rearranged by grief.

Her pitch was higher and her volume louder as she continued, "Alex swerved, but she wasn't fast enough. His car clipped the side of ours at the same time that Alex slammed on the brakes. We started spinning, and then the car was in the air. I remember everything and nothing about the seconds that followed. I screamed and looked out my window at the tree we were flying toward. I looked back at Alex, and there was glass flying everywhere and a hole in the windshield. She wasn't in her seat, but one of her shoes was stuck between the bottom of the dash and what was left of the window. I stared at that shoe for lifetimes before the top of the car slammed into the earth. It had to have been a second, maybe two, but my mind raced into the future. I thought about what I would do, what we would all do if Alex died. I pictured growing up without her, missing her on every birthday and holiday. I saw ten years into the future, and it was terrible."

She shuddered, and her breath came out choppy. She pressed a hand to her chest, like she was physically holding her heart inside her body. I couldn't go another second sitting here doing nothing. I scooted closer and put my hand over the one on her heart. She laced our fingers, and pressed our combined fists hard into her skin.

"My vision went black for a few seconds from the pressure of slamming into my seat belt. I was hanging upside down, and my skin was slicked with blood from all the glass in my skin. I saw her shoe again, and I started screaming. I don't remember if it was words or just noise, but my sister was out there. No matter how I twisted and pulled, I couldn't get my seat belt to come undone. I stopped struggling and started twisting to see if I could spot Alex anywhere through any of the windows. I looked out the side window, and I could just see her bright pink sweatshirt and this mound that had to be her body. She wasn't moving, and I screamed her name as loud as I could. I screamed it again and again, and I kept waiting for her to move or for the guy from the other car to come find her or for anyone to come help. But no one came. I didn't know it at the time, but the guy who hit us ran into a tree, and he died, too. I didn't have a cell phone because Mom had taken it away, and I didn't know where Alex's was. I kept screaming and crying for Alex for I don't know how long, but I was the only living thing for miles. I don't know how long it was before someone came along. When they did, my throat was raw, my vision was spotty, and it felt like someone was squeezing my head as hard as they could. And I knew my sister was dead."

I pulled her into my arms, and she cried until the events of the morning disappeared, until the present took a backseat to the past. And until I knew I couldn't live without her.

40

Max

I felt hollowed out. Like all the pieces of me that I'd been holding together for years had poured out of my skin. Those pieces were broken and jagged and had torn me up for far too long. It was good they were gone, but now I was empty.

I'd never told anyone that story in its entirety. I told the EMTs what they needed to know, and the therapists what they wanted to hear. I still couldn't quite believe that I'd told Cade. I was too afraid to look at his face, to see the knowledge of who I was in his eyes. I concentrated instead on his heartbeat, strong and steady beneath my cheek. All the things my life had never been. I needed something steady, because I wasn't through yet. If I really wanted closure, really wanted to let this all go, there was more.

The morning had become noisy with the singing and droning of insects, and I whispered above it, "I wished it was me that died. That's why I kept coming back here. I was the one who didn't fit, who didn't work. Alex was the good one, and it should have been me. "

Cade took me by the arms and pushed me away from his chest. "What happened to your sister and to you was terrible. It was a tragedy that I wish you'd never had to face, but don't ever say it should have been you. You lived, and despite suffering a tragedy that would have crippled many people, you became a strong, beautiful, talented woman."

I didn't wish that it had been me anymore. Well, not very often anyway. But I was too raw to listen to his praise right now.

I wiped my eyes, stretched my limbs, and tried not to look at him.

The sun was moving high overhead, and I felt like it was shining light on all my secrets, all my flaws, even that dark, hidden thorn at the back of my heart.

"You get it now, don't you? Why I pushed you away?"

The wind was wreaking havoc on my hair, and he reached out and brushed some of it back and over my shoulder.

"I think I've gotten it for a while, Max."

I took a deep breath, thinking maybe this would be easier than I had anticipated.

"So you understand? That's good. We should call and see if we can move your flight to Texas up. You can go be with your family, and I'll try to fix what I've done to mine."

I hopped down off the rock, and he followed.

"Max, I'm not going anywhere unless you come with me."

There he went, sacrificing his own needs for mine. Maybe it was a mistake to let him see me like this. He was so empathetic that he felt the need to help every person in pain.

I turned, heading for the trail, but he grabbed my wrist to stop me. "I'll be okay, Cade. I can handle my parents." At least, I hoped I could.

I went to pull away, but he just pulled me around to face him completely. He was so close, and my body had a mind of its own. I swayed toward him.

"I'm not staying because I think you need me. I'm staying because I want to. I told you last night that I would prove you wrong, and this"—he gestured to the hill in front of us— "doesn't change anything." His brown eyes shone bright and sincere. "I should have come after you when you left that night, and I won't make the mistake of letting you go again."

I closed my eyes. How could one sentence make me miserable and joyful at the same time?

Mournfully, I said, "No you shouldn't have."

He flinched, but he kept going. "There are some things that are worth fighting for, no matter the outcome, and you are one of them."

"Cade . . ."

"I know how different we are. I know that I'm not your normal type. But I also know that you're attracted to me." His hand came up to my cheek, and my traitorous body greedily accepted his touch. "I know that you make me laugh, and that I love hearing your voice, especially when you sing. I know that I haven't stopped thinking about you since the day you sat down beside me at that coffee shop." If I was honest, that was probably true for me, too. "And I know that I hate seeing you in pain, more than anything else in the world."

"Cade . . . I just can't."

I tried to pull away, but his other hand came up to my face, and he held me firm.

"Why?"

"I'll hurt you."

"I'll take my chances."

I pushed away, and this time he let me go. I pointed up toward the hill where we'd spent the last several hours. "Don't you see who I am? What I cause? I'm poison."

His expression turned angry, "You are not poison, Max."

I shook my head, and hated that I was fighting not to cry again.

"I am. I ruin everything good that comes into my life. It all rots around me, and you would be exactly the same way."

"You're wrong. You couldn't ruin me, because everything about you makes me better. You make me take chances and make bolder choices. You make me less concerned with being perfect and more concerned with being real. You make me want to be fearless."

The closer he came, the more nervous I got, and I was fighting the temptation to run. "Would you stop saying that? I told you before. I'm *not* fearless! I'm the complete opposite. I am filled with fear every day of my life, and it chokes me until I can't move or breathe or think without it taking over. It doesn't matter how much time passes, I still feel like I'm hanging upside down in that seat with the world crumbling around me." I couldn't catch my breath. All the walls I'd built over the years had been torn down when I'd told him about Alex, and now there was nothing to keep all the emotions from flooding me.

"I know you're not fearless, but I don't think you let fear rule you as much as you think you do. You fight for your dreams. You don't take shit from anyone. You were brave enough to be yourself, even in front of your parents. You are the most vibrant, beautiful thing I have ever seen."

He stood in front of me, and one of his hands slid inside his coat to rest on the small of my back. Energy crackled between us, and his forehead pressed against mine.

"Close your eyes. Remember what we talked about that night after your concert? Living is hard. It was hard when you were thirteen, it's hard today, and it will be hard again in the future. So, you close your eyes and you breathe. Breathe with me."

I was shaking, but I felt stronger with him in front of me, his gentle breaths fanning across my lips. I breathed until the weight of the world seemed easier to manage. Maybe that was just because I wasn't holding it alone.

I admitted, "I'm so afraid."

"I know you are. But fear lets us know we're alive. It tells me that you care about what happens between us because the mind doesn't waste time being scared about things that don't matter."

"Now open your eyes, Max. You are not poison. I am not better off without you. Look me in the eye and tell me you don't have feelings for me."

I looked him in the eye, but I couldn't say that, because it wasn't true.

"Then that's all I need. We both have baggage, Max, but I'm done letting it control me. You said you came here for closure, and I think that's what we both need. We've had too much death and disappointment, so we don't know how to accept the good things when they happen to us. I'm done with that. I'm done with letting people go."

I was happy that he was battling his demons, but I'd been fighting mine all day, and I wasn't sure I could face another. I said, "You don't understand. Yes, I have feelings for you." His lips spread into a smile, and it almost derailed my thoughts. I pulled my face away from his and continued, "It was one of the hardest things I have ever done, leaving you. But I know myself. I know how I work, and that's why I don't trust myself to be with you. My heart is fickle and inconstant, and I'm terrified I'll wake up one day and feel differently."

He smiled sadly and said, "I think you're terrified that you won't."

My mouth snapped shut. As was becoming a pattern . . . he was right.

He continued, "And if you *do* wake up one day and don't want to be with me, I will fight for you like I am now." His thumb brushed against my lip, and he pulled me into his chest. "I'll remind you every day how amazing it feels when your body touches mine. I'll remind you of the good times, and help you forget the bad. I'll remind you who you are when life has beaten you down and made you doubt it. I'll bust down your door in the middle of the night and kiss you until you remember that your fears are just that, and they can't control you. I'll take my chances against your fickle heart if it means it's mine."

I was beginning to realize that it already was. I looked at the top of the hill over Cade's shoulder. I'd always associated this place with endings, but maybe it was about beginnings, too. I took a deep breath and said, "I'm going to be a raging bitch most of the time."

He was so much more eloquent than me, but I had a feeling that was a yes enough for him. A wide smile formed on his lips, and my heart felt like it filled my entire chest.

"I thought you were working on that."

I smiled back and shrugged. "Horrible attention span."

We laughed, and it released some of the pressure in my chest.

He said, "I'm not asking you not to be afraid. In fact, the day that you aren't is when I'll start to worry. All I'm asking is for that date you promised the day we met."

"I can do that."

He closed the space between us, and his lips met mine. The empty spaces in me were filled to the brim, and for the first time in a long time, the world felt right side up again.

41

Cade

After she was in my arms again, I was reluctant to let her go long enough for us to get anywhere. We grabbed blankets from the trunk of her car and cocooned ourselves away in the backseat. We kissed and touched and talked like we had all the time in the world.

I hoped that we did.

We lay wrapped up together, trying to fit both of us on a too-small backseat.

I said, "I remember this being a lot more comfortable in high school."

She lifted her head and raised an eyebrow. "Spend a lot of time in backseats, did you, Golden Boy?"

I pressed my fingertips into her sides, and she squirmed against me, laughing.

"I thought we'd established that the past was the past?"

I let her wrestle my hands off of her, and she pressed both of them flat against my chest. "Of course it is, but just to make sure your mind is firmly in the present . . ."

She kissed me.

Each new kiss from her outdid the memory of the last. I broke my hands out of her grasp, and she pouted against my lips. Then I tangled my hands in her hair, and she stopped complaining. It was cold in the car, but there was nothing but heat between us. Unlike the last time we'd kissed, she was in no hurry now. We alternated between talking and kissing until the sun shined from the other side of the sky, at which point both of our backs were killing us.

She asked, "This is how it starts isn't it? We're getting old."

"Oh yeah, you're already past your prime. Life only goes downhill from here."

She swatted my chest, and then pressed a kiss to the place where she hit me.

"I'm glad you fought for me," she said.

"I'm glad you let me."

It was around sunset when we returned to her parents' house. I'd told her that we could get a hotel, maybe rent a car and go on to Texas, but she insisted that she could face her parents again. When we pulled into the driveway, her mother was out the door and sobbing into Max's hair before we even closed the car doors.

"Your father tried to follow you, but he lost you in the

subdivisions. We tried calling you, but you left your phone here. Don't you ever scare us like that again."

Max's expression looked like she was being hugged by one of the Four Horsemen of the Apocalypse, but she was hugging her mother back.

"Your father has been torn to pieces. He's out there looking for you now."

"I'm okay, Mom. I just needed to deal with some things."

Her mother pulled back and held Max's face in her hands. She brushed her hair back tenderly from her forehead.

"I'm sorry about the things I said . . . Max." Max did the constant swallowing thing, which I knew meant she was about to cry. "Your father and I are just scared. We lost your sister, and now everything terrifies us." Max made a noise halfway between a sob and a laugh. "If it had been up to me, you never would have driven a car or left the house or done anything that took you out of my sight. We just want you to have the best life possible, and we tend to forget that it's not our wants that matter. You're an adult now, and it's time for your father and I to stop trying to control your life."

Max hugged her mother, probably the first hug she'd initiated in a decade, and Mrs. Miller burst into a second round of sobs.

It wouldn't be easy. Max was too hurt and her parents too upset for a cry session to fix everything, but it was the beginning, and that's all we can ask for in life—for a beginning to follow every end.

Max's father came home, and after close to an hour of the three of them talking and crying, Max looked like she needed a break.

"Why don't we go get you a dress for that gala?" I asked. "It's tomorrow, right? I bet the mall is open for a couple more hours still."

Mrs. Miller looked distressed at the mention of something as mundane as the mall, but she said, "They're open late for last-minute holiday shopping, I think. But we don't have to go to the gala, dear."

"Of course we do," Max said. "You've put a lot of work into this."

Her mom smiled, and I could almost see the broken thread between them being repaired. A thread was a long way from a bridge, but it was something.

Her mother tried to give Max her credit card to pay for the clothing.

"No, Mom. It's okay, I'll find something."

"Don't be ridiculous. I know you hate these things and are only doing it for me. So, let me pay. And get Cade something, too. Bethany was talking about putting him in one of Michael's old suits that's still in his closet. I'm sure he'd rather not look like he's going to the junior prom."

Max took the credit card but made quite clear to everyone (especially Bethany, who was eavesdropping from the dining room) that she was buying something cheap. Nothing fancy.

As it turned out though, even Max couldn't stomach the dresses she found at the department store, and we wound up at a vintage shop a few blocks away. The owner was getting ready to close when we walked in, but she offered to stay open a little bit longer. Holiday spirit and all that. Max looked like she was in heaven.

I found a suit pretty quickly—gray with a really subtle red

plaid. It came with suspenders, which Max approved of. She hooked her hands around them, and used them to pull my mouth down to hers.

I decided I was going to have to kiss her every half hour just to continue reminding myself that it was real.

Max tried on a few things—like a yellow beaded number that ended in the middle of her thighs that made me want to follow her into the dressing room. She tried on another that was dark green and cut high on her neck, covering her tree tattoo.

"That's gorgeous," I said. "But don't you dare pick that one."

"You don't think I should cover them?"

I backed her into her dressing room and closed the door.

"I don't think you should ever cover yourself."

She smiled and laid a hand on my chest. "Thanks."

"I mean it, I think you should just be naked all the time."

She laughed. "Oh, is that what you think?"

"Yes, I've put a lot of thought into it."

"I bet you have."

She reached up and curved a hand around the back of my neck. I took that as permission enough and pressed her into the mirror.

Her nails bit into my neck, and I groaned.

"Shh! You're going to get us into trouble."

"The best kind of trouble."

I marked a path from her mouth, across her jaw, and down her neck. Her head tilted back against the mirror, and she whimpered. The sound shot straight through me, and I strangled a groan in response.

"Somehow, I don't think this is what the owner had in mind when she offered to stay open a little longer for us."

I found a spot at the base of her neck just above her collarbone that made her say, "Oh God." I concentrated my efforts there, and she wrapped both hands around my neck like she was going to fall. Her breath came in heavy pants, and mine wasn't much better. I'd not meant for it to go this far, but touching her had a way of derailing my best intentions. I started to kiss lower, but the high neckline of her dress limited my travels.

I groaned, "This dress is definitely not the one."

She gave a shaky breath, and pushed me away.

After that, I wasn't allowed in her dressing room. She didn't even let me see the final dress. She made me return to the car because she wanted it to be a surprise, and because she felt guilty about taking too long.

When I finally saw her in the dress the next day, a black velvet bodice hugged her chest and gave way to a full white skirt that started beneath her breasts and trailed all the way to the floor. The white material was sheer and so layered that it reminded me of a cloud. There were dozens of smaller straps that went over her shoulders and tied in the back. The branches of her tattoo blended in with those and looked like an extension of the bodice. It was the kind of dress I could see her getting married in.

She stood at my door, smiling in a way that was demure and unfamiliar and set my heart racing. I'd experienced a plethora of emotions in my life. I'd made it my career to explore and portray those emotions onstage. When I looked at her, the feeling in my chest eclipsed them all, and I knew that I loved her.

Epilogue

Max

THREE MONTHS LATER

I hadn't told him that I loved him yet, even though he said it to me a few weeks ago. We'd just passed the mark of my longest relationship, and even though I wouldn't admit it to him, I was still afraid that I was going to screw this up somehow. I kept waiting for the other shoe to drop. I'd almost told him a dozen times, but those three words are the kind of thing you can't take back. Once they're out there in the universe, everything changes.

So, I was waiting for the right moment to make that change. Cade called them "beats," an acting term he'd taught me when we'd been working on some of my music together.

I brushed more blush across my cheeks and smoothed on my signature red lipstick. Cade knocked on the bathroom door and said, "You ready, babe? We're up next."

Cade and I were singing at an opening mic tonight . . . together.

There was a song, the first song I ever wrote actually, that I was finally ready to sing, but I didn't think I could do it without him. He hadn't been comfortable singing at one of the band's gigs, and I wasn't sure this was a song I wanted associated with the band. This song wasn't about getting a break or making money.

This song was just for me.

He asked, "Are you nervous?"

I smiled and said, "Only enough to throw up."

He laughed and said, "You'll be fine then."

The bar was about half full as we took the stage. It was a big enough crowd that I didn't feel like our singing was pointless, but not so big that I was overwhelmed. Cade pressed a kiss to my hand, and then took up the bass guitar. In true Golden Boy fashion, he'd learned to play in about a month so that he could play with me while I was writing. I took my guitar up, too, and adjusted the microphone.

The lights were just bright enough to cast the bar in darkness. I leaned into the mic and said, "My name is Max, and this is Cade. Tonight we're singing an original song that I wrote a long time ago. I've never played it in public, and I finally decided it was time." I took a deep breath. "It's called 'Ten Years.'"

I started with the familiar opening cords, and immediately all the old emotions rushed up under my skin. I took a deep breath, and thought about why I was doing this. The song had haunted me since I wrote it, and it was time to move past it.

I took a deep breath and started to sing. Cade sang with me, low and solid. His voice was an anchor to the song and an anchor to me.

> "In one second, I see ten years
> I picture a future of all my fears
> One blink, and I think
> Losing you is like losing me."

I met Cade's eyes and thought that in a few ways this song spoke to our situation as well. It had been three months, and we'd insinuated ourselves into each other's lives so completely. Even associating him with a song about loss made me have to blink back tears. I was in danger of saying all the cheesy things about better halves and soul mates that I'd always laughed at in movies.

> "Lights flash, the car spins
> Every time I close my eyes I see
> Broken skin, my life stretched thin
> Every time I close my eyes I see
> Broken skin and broken kin
> The end of you feels like the end of me.
>
> "There's a scream in my soul
> 'Cause I'll never feel whole
> I'm stuck in the moment. My mind's on repeat
> Trapped in an instant I can't delete

"Time unravels, my life unspools
The future has made us all into fools
You're lying there, and I'm stuck in my chair
All I'm allowed to do is stare."

I got so choked up on the verse that my voice broke, and I had to take a break and repeat some of the guitar part before I was able to come in for the next verse. Cade was so in tune and perceptive that he followed me easily.

"We're all slaves to the grave
Helpless to save
So we close our eyes to shut it out
Instead it becomes what we're all about."

I closed my eyes, and I did see it all as I sang. I remembered the images that had flashed through my mind of a life without Alex. I'd thought of all the moments in my life that she would miss, and how nothing would ever be the same without her. I was at nine years now, and though nothing was the same without her, life also wasn't as bad as I had pictured it would be.

I glanced at Cade. Life wasn't bad at all.

"In one second, I see ten years
Can't hold it back any more than the tears
I see black dresses, life's stresses

Imagine the grief, loss of belief
My life unfolds as yours is untold

"Every time I close my eyes."

Cade repeated the last line alone, and when I heard his low and steady voice, I finally felt like my ghosts had been put to rest.

People started clapping, and I looked at him over the microphone and mouthed, "I love you."

I blinked, and just like that I saw ten more years unfold.

ACKNOWLEDGMENTS

Thank you to William Morrow and Amanda Bergeron for believing in my writing, and working so incredibly hard to get it out into the world so quickly. And Amanda, thank you for helping make Cade as awesome as he is. Thank you to Jessie Edwards for being made of awesome and believing in sunken ships with me. Thanks also to Molly Birckhead, Pam Jaffee, and all the rest of the HarperCollins team for doing such a fabulous job.

Thank you to the epic and amazing Suzie Townsend. I am eternally grateful to have a literary gladiator like you on my side. Thanks also to Kathleen, Pouya, Joanna, Danielle, and the rest of the New Leaf Team. You guys keep my world spinning.

Thanks to Kathleen Smith for the information. Thank you to Jennifer, Colleen, Wendy, Sophie, Kathleen, and Molly for reading this book in advance and loving it. I was kind of petrified, and you guys gave me so much confidence. Thank you to Ana for all the things you do and all the things you are, and for making me feel like I'm more awesome than I am. Thanks to Lindsay for being the person with whom I can share absolutely anything, and for always sharing back. Thank you also to Joey, Patrick, Bethany, Shelly, Zach, Kristin, Sam, Marylee, Kendall, Swinter, Louise, Tyler, Brittany, Michelle, Heather, Amber, DeAndre, Matt, Mark, Mere, Michael, Leesa, and so many other friends. I'm so thankful to have you all in my life. Thank you to my former students (even though you aren't old enough to read this; close this book right now). Thank you to Marisa, Stacey, Sarah, Michelle, Jamie, El, Molly, Aimee, Kim, Kathryn, Nichole, Julie, and Marice. I love you guys.

I wish I could list each and every blogger, Twitter follower, Facebook friend, and reader who has supported me and my writing. But there are so many of you (for which I'm extremely grateful) that it could fill a whole other book. Just know that I appreciate and love you all so much. All of this is for you!

Thank you to my family. I have the best family in the world, and not just because we rock freckles better than anyone else. This all still feels like a dream. And well, it is a dream . . . one I couldn't have achieved without your love and support.

And to that guy I threw an Easter egg at in Queens at two in the morning because I thought you were someone else . . . I'm sorry for being the most awkward person to ever walk on two legs.

Can't get enough Cora Carmack?
Turn the page for a sneak peek at

FINDING IT

Most girls would kill to spend months traveling around Europe after college graduation with no responsibility, no parents, and no-limit credit cards. Kelsey Summers is no exception. She's having the time of her life . . . or that's what she keeps telling herself.

It's a lonely business trying to find out who you are, especially when you're afraid you won't like the you that's found. No amount of drinking or dancing can chase away Kelsey's loneliness, but maybe Jackson Hunt can. After a few chance meetings, he convinces her to take a journey of adventure instead of alcohol. With each new city and experience, Kelsey's mind becomes a little clearer, and her heart a little less hers. Hunt helps her unravel her own dreams and desires, but the more she knows about herself, the more she realizes how little she knows about him.

Coming Soon from Ebury Press

1

couldn't keep their names straight, and I wasn't even drunk yet.

I kept calling Tamás István. Or was that András? Oh, well. What did it matter? They were all hot with dark hair and eyes, and they knew only four words in English as far as I could tell.

American. Beautiful. Drink. And *dance.*

As far as I was concerned, those were the only words they needed to know. At least I remembered Katalin's name. I'd met her a few days ago, and we'd hung out almost every night since. It was a mutually beneficial arrangement. She showed me around Budapest, and I got generous with Daddy's credit card on occasion. Not like he would notice or care. And if he did, he'd always said that if money didn't buy happiness, then people were spending it wrong.

"Kelsey," Katalin said, her accent thick and exotic. "Welcome to the ruin bars."

I paused in ruffling István's hair (or the one I called István, anyway). We stood on an empty street filled with dilapidated buildings. I knew the whole don't-judge-a-book-by-its-cover thing, but this place was straight out of a zombie apocalypse. I wondered how to say "brains" in Hungarian.

The old Jewish quarter—that's where Katalin said we were going.

Oy vey.

It sure as hell didn't look to me like there were any bars around here. I looked at the abandoned neighborhood, and thought, *At least I got laid last night. If I was going to get chopped into tiny pieces, at least I went out with a bang. Literally.*

I laughed, and almost recounted my thoughts to my companions, but I was pretty sure it would get lost in translation. Especially because I was starting to question even Katalin's grip on the English language, if this was what "bar" meant to her. I pointed a crumbling stone building and said, "Drink?" Then mimed the action, just to be safe.

One of the guys said, "Igen. Drink." The word sounded like *ee-gan*, and I'd picked up just enough to know it mean, "yes."

I was practically fluent already.

I cautiously followed Katalin toward one of the derelict buildings. She stepped into a darkened doorway that gave me the heebiest of jeebies. The tallest of my Hungarian hotties slipped an arm around my shoulder. I took a guess and said, "Tamás?" His teeth were pearly white when he smiled. I would take that as a yes. Tamás equaled tall. And drop-dead sexy.

One of his hands came up and brushed back the blond hair from my face. I tilted my head back to look at him, and excitement sparked in my belly. What did language matter when dark eyes locked on mine, strong hands pressed into my skin, and heat filled the space between us?

Not a whole hell of a lot.

We followed the rest of the group into the building, and I felt the low thrum of techno music vibrating the floor beneath my feet.

Interesting.

We travelled deeper into the building and came out into a large room. Walls had been knocked down, and no one had bothered to move the pieces of concrete. Christmas lights and lanterns lighted the building. Mismatched furniture was scattered around the space. There was even an old car that had been repurposed into a dining booth. It was easily the weirdest, most confusing place I'd ever been in.

"You like?" Katalin asked.

I pressed myself closer to Tamás and said, "I love."

Tamás led me into the bar, where drinks were amazingly cheap. Maybe I should stay in Eastern Europe forever. I pulled out a two thousand forint note. For less than the equivalent of ten U.S. dollars I bought all five of us shots.

Amazing.

The downside to Europe? For some reason this made no sense to me—they gave lemon slices with tequila instead of lime. The bartenders always looked at me like I'd just ordered elephant sweat in a glass.

They just didn't understand the magical properties of my favorite drink. If my accent didn't give me away as American, my drink of choice always did.

Next, Tamás bought me a gin bitter lemon, a drink I'd been introduced to a few weeks earlier. It almost made the absence of margaritas in this part of the world bearable. I downed it like it was lemonade on a blistering Texas day. His eyes went wide, and I licked my lips. István bought me another, and the acidity and sweetness rolled across my tongue.

Tamás gestured for me to down it again, so I did, to a round of applause.

God, I love when people love me.

I took hold of Tamás's and István's arms and pulled them away from the bar. There was a room that had one wall knocked out in lieu of a door, and it overflowed with dancing bodies.

That was where I wanted to be.

I tugged my boys in that direction, and Katalin and András followed close behind. We had to step over a pile of concrete if we wanted to get into the room. I took one look at my turquoise heels, and knew there was no way in hell I was managing that with my sex appeal intact. I turned to István and Tamás—sizing them up. István was the beefier of the two, so I put an arm around his neck. We didn't need to speak the same language for him to understand what I wanted. He swept an arm underneath my legs, and pulled me up to his chest. It was a good thing I had worn skinny jeans instead of a skirt.

"Köszönöm," I said, even though he should have been the one thanking me, based on the way he was openly ogling my chest.

Ah, well. I didn't mind ogling. I was still pleasantly warm from the alcohol, and the music drowned out the world. And all my problems were thousands of miles away across an ocean. They might as well have been drowning at the bottom of said ocean for how much they mattered to me in that moment.

The only expectations here were ones that I had encouraged and was all too willing to follow through on. So maybe my new "friends" only wanted me for money and sex. It was better than not being wanted at all.

István's arms flexed around me, and I melted into him. My father liked to talk, or yell, rather, about how I didn't appreciate anything. But the male body was one thing I had no issue appreciating. István was all hard muscles and angles beneath my hands, and those girls were definitely a-wandering.

By the time he'd set my feet on the dance floor, my hands had found those delicious muscles that angled down from his hips. I bit my lip and met his gaze from beneath lowered lashes. If his expression was any indication, I had found Boardwalk and had the all clear to proceed to Go and collect my two hundred dollars.

Or forint. Whatever.

Tamás pressed his chest against my back, and I gave myself up to the alcohol and the music and the sensation of being stuck between two delicious specimens of man.

Time started to disappear between frenzied hands and drips of sweat. There were more drinks and more dances.

Each song faded into the next. Colors danced behind my closed eyes. And it was almost enough. For a while, I forgot the emptiness that lay beneath the excitement and desire and intoxication. And every time the void began to creep in, when the black behind my closed eyes felt suffocating, there was another drink in my hand to chase the dark away.

That was me. One drink away from the cliff's edge. I didn't mind so much, though. Life was more exciting on the edge, if a little lonelier.

I shook my head to clear my thoughts. There was no room for loneliness when squeezed between two sets of washboard abs.

New life motto, right there.

I gave István a couple of notes and sent him to get more drinks. In the meantime, I turned to face Tamás. He'd been pressed against my back for God knows how long, and I'd forgotten how tall he was. I leaned back to meet his gaze, and his hands smoothed down my back to my ass.

I smirked and said, "Someone is happy to have me all to himself."

He pulled my hips into his and said, "Beautiful American."

Right. No point expending energy on cheeky banter that he couldn't even understand. I had a pretty good idea how to better use my energy. I slipped my arms around his neck and tilted my head in the universal sign of "kiss me."

Tamás didn't waste any time. Like really . . . no time. The dude went zero to sixty in seconds. His tongue was so far down my throat it was like being kissed by the lovechild of a lizard and Gene Simmons.

We were both pretty drunk. Maybe he didn't realize that he was in danger of engaging my gag reflex with his Guinness-record-worthy tongue. I eased back and his tongue assault ended, only for his teeth to clamp down on my bottom lip.

I was all for a little biting, but he pulled my lip out until I had one half of a fish mouth. And he stood there sucking on my bottom lip for so long that I actually started counting to see how long it would last.

When I got to fifteen (*fifteen!*) seconds, my eyes settled on a guy across the bar watching my dilemma with a huge grin. Was shit-eating grin in the dictionary? If not, I should snap a picture for Merriam-Webster.

I braced myself and pulled my poor abused lip from Tamás's teeth. My mouth felt like it had been stuck in a vacuum cleaner. While I pressed my fingers to my numb lip, Tamás started placing sloppy kissing from the corner of my lips across my cheek to my jaw.

His tongue slithered over my skin like a snail, and all the blissful alcohol-induced haze that I'd worked so hard for disappeared.

I was painfully aware that I was standing in an abandoned building turned bar with a trail of drool across my cheek, and the guy across the room was now openly laughing at me.

And he was fucking gorgeous, which made it so much worse.

Can't get enough Cora Carmack?
Turn the page to see where it all began

LOSING IT

Love. Romance. Sex. There's a first time for everything...

As far as Bliss Edwards can tell, she's the last virgin standing, certainly amongst her friends. And she's determined to deal with the 'problem' as quickly and simply as possible.

But her plan for a no-strings one night stand turns out to be anything but simple. Especially when she arrives for her first class and recognises her hot new British professor.

She'd left him naked in her bed just 8 hours earlier...

Available from Ebury Press

1

I took a deep breath.

You are awesome. I didn't quite believe it, so I thought it again.

Awesome. You are so awesome. If my mother heard my thoughts, she'd tell me that I needed to be humble, but humility had gotten me nowhere.

Bliss Edwards, you are a freaking catch.

So then how did I end up twenty-two years old and the only person I knew who had never had sex? Somewhere between *Saved by the Bell* and *Gossip Girl*, it became unheard of for a girl to graduate college with her V-card still in hand. And now I was standing in my room, regretting that I'd gathered the courage to admit it to my friend Kelsey. She reacted like I'd just told her I was hiding a tail underneath my A-line skirt. And I knew before her jaw even finished dropping that this was a terrible idea.

"*Seriously?* Is it because of Jesus? Are you, like, saving yourself for him?" Sex seemed simpler for Kelsey. She had the body of a Barbie and the sexually charged brain of a teenage boy.

"No, Kelsey," I said. "It would be a little difficult to save myself for someone who died over two thousand years ago."

Kelsey whipped off her shirt and threw it on the floor. I must have made a face because she looked at me and laughed.

"Relax, Princess Purity, I'm just changing shirts." She stepped into my closet and started flipping through my clothes.

"Why?"

"Because, Bliss, we're going out to get you laid." She said the word "laid" with a curl of her tongue that reminded me of those late-night commercials for those adult phone lines.

"Jesus, Kelsey."

She pulled out a shirt that was snug on me and would be downright scandalous on her curvy frame.

"What? You said it wasn't about him."

I resisted the urge to slam my palm into my forehead.

"It's not, I don't think . . . I mean, I go to church and all, well, sometimes. I just . . . I don't know. I've never been that interested."

She paused with her new shirt halfway over her head.

"Never interested? In guys? Are you gay?"

I once overheard my mother, who can't understand why

I'm about to graduate college without a ring on my finger, ask my father the same question.

"No, Kelsey, I'm not gay, so keep putting your shirt on. No need to fall on your sexual sword for me."

"If you're not gay and it's not about Jesus, then it's just a matter of finding the right guy, or should I say . . . the right sexual sword."

I rolled my eyes. "Gee? Is that all? Find the right guy? Why didn't someone tell me sooner?"

She pulled her blond hair back into a high ponytail, which somehow drew even more attention to her chest. "I don't mean the right guy to marry, honey. I mean the right guy to get your blood pumping. To make you turn off your analytical, judgmental, hyperactive brain and think with your body instead."

"Bodies can't think."

"*See!*" she said. "Analytical. Judgmental."

"Fine! Fine. Which bar tonight?"

"Stumble Inn, of course."

I groaned. "Classy."

"What?" Kelsey looked at me like I was missing the answer to a really obvious question. "It's a good bar. More importantly, it's a bar that guys like. And since we *do* like guys, it's a bar *we* like."

It could be worse. She could be taking me to a club.

"Fine. Let's go." I stood and headed for the curtain that separated my bedroom from the rest of my loft apartment.

"*Whoa!* Whoa." She grabbed my elbow and pulled me so hard that I fell back on my bed. "You can't go like that."

I looked down at my outfit—a flowery A-line skirt and

simple tank that showed a decent amount of cleavage. I looked cute. I could totally pick up a guy in this . . . maybe.

"I don't see the problem," I said.

She rolled her eyes, and I felt like a child. I hated feeling like a child, and I pretty much always did when talk turned to sex.

Kelsey said, "Honey, right now you look like someone's adorable little sister. No guy wants to screw his little sister. And if he does, you don't want to be near him."

Yep, definitely felt like a child. "Point taken."

"Hmm . . . sounds like you're practicing turning off that overactive brain of yours. Good job. Now stand there and let me work my magic."

And by magic, she meant torture.

After vetoing three shirts that made me feel like a prostitute, some pants that were more like leggings, and a skirt so short it threatened to show the world my hoo-hoo in the event of a mild breeze, we settled on some tight low-rise denim capris and a lacy black tank that stood out in contrast to my pale white skin.

"Legs shaved?"

I nodded.

"Other . . . things . . . shaved?"

"As much as they are ever going to be, yes, now move on." That was where I drew the line of this conversation.

She grinned, but didn't argue. "Fine. Fine. Condoms?"

"In my purse."

"Brain?"

"Turned off. Or well . . . dialed down anyway."

"Excellent. I think we're ready."

I wasn't ready. Not at all.

There was a reason I hadn't had sex yet, and now I knew it. I was a control freak. It was why I had done so well in school my entire life. It made me a great stage manager—no one could run a theater rehearsal like I could. And when I did get up the nerve to act, I was always more prepared than any other actor in class. But sex . . . that was the opposite of control. There were emotions, and attraction, and that pesky other person that just *had* to be involved. Not my idea of fun.

"You're thinking too much," Kelsey said.

"Better than not thinking enough."

"Not tonight it's not," she said.

I turned up the volume of Kelsey's iPod as soon as we got in the car so that I could think in peace.

I could do this. It was just a problem that needed to be solved, an item that needed to be checked off my to-do list.

It was that simple.

Simple.

Keep it simple.

We pulled up outside the bar several minutes later, and the night felt anything but simple. My pants felt too tight, my shirt too low-cut, and my brain too clouded. I wanted to throw up.

I didn't want to be a virgin. That much I knew. I didn't want to feel like the immature prude who knew nothing about sex. I hated not knowing things. The trouble was . . . as much as I didn't want to be a virgin, I also didn't want to have sex.

The conundrum of all conundrums. Why couldn't this be one of those square-is-a-rectangle-but-rectangle-is-not-always-a-square kind of things?

Kelsey was standing outside my door, her high-heeled shoes snapping in time with her fingers as she roused me out of the car. I squared my shoulders, tossed my hair (half-heartedly), and followed Kelsey into the bar.

I made a beeline straight to the bar, wiggled myself onto a stool, and waved down the bartender.

He was a possibility. Blond hair, average build, nice face. Nothing special, but certainly not out of the question. He could be good for simple.

"What can I get for y'all, ladies?"

Southern accent. Definitely a homegrown kind of boy.

Kelsey butted in, "We need two shots of tequila to start."

"Make it four," I croaked.

He whistled, and his eyes met mine. "That kinda night, huh?"

I wasn't ready to put into words what kind of night this was. So I just said, "I'm looking for some liquid courage."

"And I'd be glad to help." He winked at me, and he was barely out of earshot before Kelsey bounced in her seat, saying, "He's the one! He's the one!"

Her words made me feel like I was on a roller coaster, like the world had just dropped and all my organs were playing catch-up. I just needed more time to adjust. That's it. I grabbed Kelsey's shoulder and forced her to stay still. "Chill, Kels. You're like a freaking Chihuahua."

"What? He's a good choice. Cute. Nice. And I totally saw him glance at your cleavage . . . *twice*."

She wasn't wrong. But I still wasn't all that interested in sleeping with him, which I suppose didn't have to rule him out, but this sure would be a hell of a lot easier if I was actually *interested* in the guy. I said, "I'm not sure . . . there's just no spark." I could see an eye roll coming, so I tagged on a quick "Yet!"

When Bartender Boy returned with our drinks, Kelsey paid and I took my two shots before she even handed over her card. He stayed for a moment, smiling at me, before moving on to another customer. I stole one of Kelsey's remaining shots.

"You're lucky this is a big night for you, Bliss. Normally, nobody gets between me and my tequila."

I held my hand out and said, "Well, nobody will get between these legs unless I'm good and drunk, so hand me the last one."

Kelsey shook her head, but she was smiling. After a few seconds, she gave in, and with four shots of tequila in my system the prospect of sex seemed a little less scary.

Another bartender came by, this one a girl, and I ordered a Jack and Coke to sip on while I puzzled through this whole mess.

There was Bartender Boy, but he wouldn't get off until well after 2:00 A.M. I was a nervous wreck already, so if this dragged on till the wee hours of the morning, I'd be completely psychotic. I could just imagine it . . . straitjacketed due to sex.

There was a guy standing next to me who seemed to move several inches closer with every drink I took, but he had to be at least forty. No thank you.

I gulped down more of my drink, thankful the bartender had gone heavy on the Jack, and scanned the bar.

"What about him?" Kelsey asked, pointing to a guy at a nearby table.

"Too preppy."

"Him?"

"Too hipster."

"Over there?"

"Ew. Too hairy."

The list continued until I was pretty sure this night was a bust. Kelsey suggested we hit another bar, which was the last thing I wanted to do. I told her I had to go to the bathroom, hoping someone would catch her eye while I was gone so that I could slip away with no drama. The bathroom was at the back, past the pool and darts area, behind a section with some small round tables.

That was when I noticed him.

Well, technically, I noticed the book first.

And I just couldn't keep my mouth closed. "If that's supposed to be a way to pick up girls, I would suggest moving to an area with a little more traffic."

He looked up from his reading, and suddenly I found it hard to swallow. He was easily the most attractive guy I'd seen tonight—blond hair falling into crystal blue eyes, just enough scruff on his jaw to give him a masculine look without making him too hairy, and a face that could have made angels sing. It wasn't making me sing. It was making me gawk. Why did I stop? Why did I always have to make an idiot of myself?

"Excuse me?"

My mind was still processing his perfect hair and bright blue eyes, so it took me a second to say, "Shakespeare. No one reads Shakespeare in a bar unless it's a ploy to pick up girls. All I'm saying is, you might have better luck up front."

He didn't say anything for a long beat, but then his mouth split in a grin revealing, what do you know, perfect teeth!

"It's not a ploy, but if it were, it seems to me that I'm having great luck right here."

An accent. *He has a British accent.* Dear God, I'm dying.

Breathe. I needed to breathe.

Don't lose it, Bliss.

He put his book down, but not before marking his place. My God, he was really reading Shakespeare in a bar.

"You're not trying to pick up a girl?"

"I wasn't."

My analytical brain did not miss his use of the past tense. As in . . . he hadn't been trying to seduce anyone before, but perhaps he was now.

I took another look at him. He was grinning now—white teeth, jaw stubble that made him look downright delectable. Yep, I was definitely seducible. And that thought alone was enough to send me into shock.

"What's your name, beautiful?"

Beautiful? *Beautiful!* Still dying here.

"Bliss."

"Is that a line?"

I blushed crimson. "No, it's my name."

"Lovely name for a lovely girl." The timbre of his voice went into that low register that made my insides curl in on themselves—it was like my uterus was tapping out a happy dance on the rest of my organs. God, I was dying the longest, most torturous, most arousing death in the history of the world. Was this what it always felt like to be turned on? No wonder sex made people do crazy things.

"Well, Bliss, I'm new in town, and I've already locked myself out of my apartment. I'm waiting on a locksmith actually, and I figured I'd put this spare time to good use."

"By brushing up on your Shakespeare?"

"Trying to anyway. Honestly, I've never liked the bloke all that much, but let's keep that a secret between us, yeah?"

I'm pretty sure my cheeks were still stained red, if the heat coming off of them was any indication. In fact, my whole body felt like it was on fire. I'm not sure whether it was mortification or his accent that had me about to spontaneously combust in front of him.

"You look disappointed, Bliss. Are you a Shakespeare fan?"

I nodded, because my throat might have been closing up.

He wrinkled his nose in response, and my hands itched to follow the line of his nose down to his lips.

I was going crazy. Actually, certifiably insane.

"Don't tell me you're a *Romeo and Juliet* fan?"

Now this. *This* was something I could discuss.

"*Othello* actually. That's my favorite."

"Ah. Fair Desdemona. Loyal and pure."

My heart stuttered at the word "pure."

"I, um . . ." I struggled to piece together my thoughts. "I like the juxtaposition of reason and passion."

"I'm a fan of passion myself." His eyes dipped down then and ran the length of my form. My spine tingled until it felt like it might burst out of my skin.

"You haven't asked me my name," he said.

I cleared my throat. This couldn't be attractive. I was about as sociable as a caveman. I asked, "What's your name?"

He tilted his head, and his hair almost covered his eyes. "Join me, and I'll tell you."

I didn't think about anything other than the fact that my legs were like Jell-O and sitting down would prevent me from doing something embarrassing, like passing out from the influx of hormones that were quite clearly having a free-for-all in my brain. I sank into the chair, but instead of feeling relieved, the tension ratcheted up another notch.

He spoke, and my eyes snagged on his lips. "My name is Garrick."

Who knew names could be hot too?

"It's nice to meet you, Garrick."

He leaned forward on his elbows, and I noticed his broad shoulders and the way his muscles moved beneath the fabric of his shirt. Then our eyes connected, and the bar around us went from dim to dark, while I was ensnared by those baby blues.

"I'm going to buy you a drink." It wasn't meant to be a question. In fact, when he looked at me, there was nothing questioning in him at all, only confidence. "Then we can chat some more about reason and . . . passion."

About the Author

Cora Carmack is a twentysomething writer who likes to write about twentysomething characters. She's done a multitude of things in her life—retail, theatre, teaching, and writing. She loves theatre, travel, and anything that makes her laugh. She enjoys placing her characters in the most awkward situations possible and then trying to help them get a boyfriend out of it. Awkward people need love too.

Follow her on twitter @CoraCarmack

Visit her blog at http://coracarmack.blogspot.com for updates about future awkward romances!